Girls From Da Hood 11

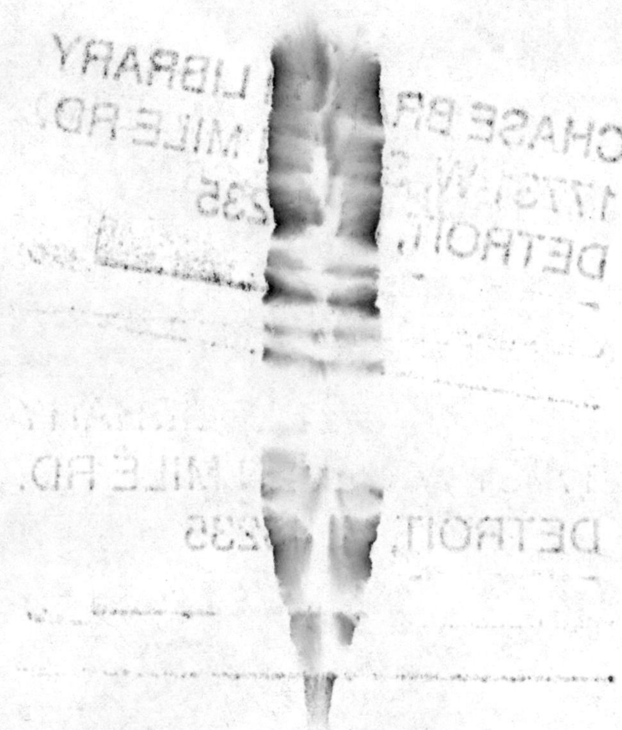

Girls From Da Hood 11

Nikki Turner, Katt, and Teeny

www.urbanbooks.net

Urban Books, LLC
97 N18th Street
Wyandanch, NY 11798

ISBN 13: 978-1-62286-764-6
ISBN 10: 1-62286-764-5

First Trade Paperback Printing September 2016
Printed in the United States of America

10 9 8 7 6 5 4 3 2 1

This is a work of fiction. Any references or similarities to actual events, real people, living or dead, or to real locales are intended to give the novel a sense of reality. Any similarity in other names, characters, places, and incidents is entirely coincidental.

Distributed by Kensington Publishing Corp.
Submit orders to:
Customer Service
400 Hahn Road
Westminster, MD 21157-4627
Phone: 1-800-733-3000
Fax: 1-800-659-2436

Girls From Da Hood 11

by

Nikki Turner, Katt, and Teeny

Trust Issues

by

Nikki Turner

Chapter 1

Rose M. Singer Center, Riker's Island, NY.

Kima's heart hammered as she looked in the rearview mirror and noticed the flashing red and blue lights getting closer and closer. When she heard the sirens, she just knew she would die of a heart attack. Kima knew the whooping sound meant she needed to pull the car over. She knew she hadn't done anything wrong. She drove just like she had been told to do. She signaled with every lane change. This wasn't good; she hadn't even made it out of New York yet. There would be hell to pay. Kima felt vomit creeping up her throat. She took a deep breath and thought about the instructions she had been given. A tall white cop approached the car from the left and one stood off to the right.

"Get out of the car, ma'am. You're under arrest," the cop said immediately.

"What did I do wrong?" Kima asked as the cop yanked the door open and pulled her out of the car. "I'm pregnant!" she cried. But it was too late. She had hit the ground. Luckily she landed on her knees and not her stomach. "Help!" she screamed.

Kima jumped, her body shuddering, as she was jolted by the nightmare. The loud sound of clanging metal had startled her out of her sleep, out of reliving the ordeal she had endured. She had been dreaming about her last day on the street. The first thing she felt when she opened her eyes was a sharp kick under her rib cage from her unborn baby. There were more clanging sounds and the lights over her head seemed brighter than they were the night before.

"Meal time! Let's rock and roll, ladies!" the fat female correctional officer screamed out as she passed Kima's cell.

Kima closed her eyes tightly and prayed that she was dreaming. When she opened them again, she realized it was real. She was definitely locked up. The smell of disinfectant from the little silver sink and toilet combo seemed to be more noticeable to her nostrils than before. Kima sat up even though her head was spinning. Then, another kick from the baby almost made her scream out. There was no denying it now, she wasn't dreaming at all. The pain in her back from the hard metal bed with the thin, worthless mattress told her it was very real. Kima put her face in her hands and started crying. Her almost thirty-five-week pregnant belly prevented her from leaning all the way over like people usually did when they cried from feeling sorry for themselves. The reality was that Kima was an inmate on Riker's Island. Not just any inmate either, but a pregnant inmate that was facing a lot of time.

"McCallister! Time to lock out! You're on the prenatal and court list for today! So get ya breakfast and let's go!" the same short, fat, female C.O. yelled at Kima through her cell bars.

Kima looked up from her wet hands and sucked her teeth. The hunger pangs and the hungry and angry kicks from her baby were the only things that motivated her into action. Kima did as she was told. Another kick from the baby sent a sharp stabbing pain to her heart. She rubbed her belly, trying to soothe her baby. *Maybe the baby can sense that shit is not right,* she thought to herself. This was not what Kima had planned for her own life. It was history repeating itself again. Kima too had been born in jail. She didn't have many memories of her mother, but her grandmother never let her forget that she had been born while her mother was locked up after being charged with accessory to murder. Kima had spent the first nine months of life as an inmate, and then she was separated from her mother and handed over to her grandmother. That is how the system worked with pregnant inmates. Kima thought it was almost better for the system to take the babies at birth, at least then, they could bond with whoever took them. That was the thought that had kept Kima up almost the entire night. She wondered how fucked up she would feel not only giving birth in jail, but to have the system take the baby away after she and the baby formed a bond. Kima wasn't sure what would happen to her baby. A boy she had planned to name Kori, after his father. She didn't deal with anyone in her family anymore except for the occasional hi and bye with one of her cousins. Kima hadn't heard from her so-called boyfriend, Kori, since she had gotten locked up. This wasn't how things were supposed to work out. Kori had promised her so many things, one of which was to always be there for her if anything ever happened. She had done so much and given up even more to be a rider for him. Kima was done being hurt over Kori's apparent abandonment, she was downright angry now. She was sure that Kori had probably figured out that she had gotten knocked. If he had answered his phone when she was given her phone call, he would have known exactly what happened to her. Kima couldn't even leave him a voice mail message because his mailbox was full. She was so mad she had even pondered whether she should cooperate with the police against Kori and get herself out of this mess that he had gotten her into. The day she got arrested, the police had badgered her for over ten hours trying to get her to flip on Kori. Kima wasn't having it. She had endured the verbal abuse from the cops, who had called her a piece of shit and worthless mother. No matter what they said to her, Kima held her ground. She wasn't snitching, especially not on the man she loved. Now, Kima was depending on Kori to get her out of this mess.

Kima washed her face and brushed her teeth inside her cell at the little sink, but she had to go to the communal shower to bathe, which she hated. Kima gathered the horrible smelling soap, shampoo, and lotion she had been given at intake and headed to the showers. She looked down at herself and just wished he could change her damn clothes. The pregnant inmates got to wear their own clothes, so Kima had the same outfit on that she had gotten arrested in four days earlier. Getting arrested on a Friday was the worst because she had had to wait the entire weekend for the chance to finally see a judge. All of her calls to Kori had been unsuccessful. As far as Kima knew, Kori had not even bothered to send someone down there to check up on her. For all Kori knew, Kima could've be being charged with all sorts of crimes and facing serious time.

Kima entered the shower stall, and there were three other pregnant women inside already. They obviously knew each other because they were talking and laughing. Kima couldn't figure out what could be so funny when they were in jail and pregnant. Didn't they know they would be giving their children the worst start in life, having them be born as inmates? She shook her head in disgust. Kima wasn't trying to make friends, so she had made up her mind she wasn't going to speak to them or join in their girlish banter. She didn't plan to be locked up that long. In Kima's mind, whether Kori bailed her out or she snitched to get herself out, she wasn't trying to have her baby behind bars.

When the women noticed that Kima had come into the shower room, they stopped talking and eyed her up and down. "That's her," one of the women whispered, turning from Kima back to her little group of friends. Kima heard her, but she ignored the woman's rude ass. Kima knew they knew who she was. Everybody in New York probably knew of her now, especially since her arrest had made the headlines in the *New York Daily News*. It had read PREGNANT WOMAN BUBBED DRUG QUEENPIN. Kima knew that was all bullshit. She was far from any drug queenpin. She was simply a chick that had gotten caught up and wouldn't roll on her man—a ride or die bitch. Kima didn't know if was worth it all now though.

The women continued to snicker and whisper about her as Kima took off her clothes and got into the shower. Fuck them bitches. Kima was thinking those chicks were all probably locked up for boosting or some other dumb hustle just to pay their rent and buy sneakers and clothes. She considered herself different. This incident was a fluke. A onetime thing that just went wrong. Kima had been living in a lavish brownstone in Bed-Stuy with her man before all of this bad luck happened. She had been able to rock the finest clothes and jewelry too. Yes, Kima considered herself different from the bitches she was locked up with, in her mind, she was above them. Although right then, just like them, she was behind bars with nothing and no one.

The giggling tramps finally left the shower area, leaving Kima relieved to be alone. She got finished and prepared to go back to her cell so she could attend her jailhouse prenatal visit and hopefully see her lawyer before she was dragged to court. Kima was waiting to go to court to be arraigned, something she wasn't looking forward to. The thought made her anxious, as she knew that was where she would find out just what the district attorney planned to charge her with. Kima was sure they were going to throw the book at her given what they had found on her. She could only hope that she would hear from Kori soon and he would replace her public defender with his own defense attorney, the one that had helped him beat two cases since Kima had been with him.

Kima dried her body and then wrapped her towel around her long, dark brown hair, and slipped back into her clothes. There were no mirrors and Kima was glad. She was sure that she probably looked tired in the face and her hair was certainly not the usual perfectly coiffed locks she was used to wearing. Her clothes felt grimy against her skin, but she had no choice but to wear them for yet another day. Just as she prepared to leave the showers, three women were walking in fast. It wasn't the same ones that had been in there earlier whispering about her. Kima got a good look at all of their faces this time. She rolled her eyes and stopped to let them go past her before she tried to walk out. Kima just let them come in to avoid any problems. She wasn't trying to bump anyone and get into any altercations. The safety and health of her baby meant more to her than that. Besides, she counted herself as lucky after the dust up with the police had almost caused harm to her unborn baby. All of the women were pregnant and none of them could afford to get into any bullshit or so Kima thought. The women had other plans. One of them, a tall, dark-skinned, skinny girl with old, ratty braids who looked like she had swallowed a basketball stopped in front of Kima. *Here the fuck we go,* Kima thought to herself as she stood holding her ground.

"Yo! Your name Kima, right?" the tall chick asked looking down her nose at Kima.

She was so skinny everywhere else on her body that her pregnant belly looked fake protruding grotesquely from her skeletal frame. The other two women, one that didn't look pregnant at all because she was so fat and one that was obviously not as pregnant as the tall one, were standing with the tall woman moving in closer and glaring at Kima.

Kima crinkled her face into a scowl. "Yeah, I'm Kima. Who wants to know?" she snapped, dropping her stuff and balling up her fists. Her street smarts told her to be ready for anything.

"I got a message for you from Kori," the dark-skinned chick said calmly.

Kima felt a sense of relief wash over her and her heart started to pump with excitement. She softened her face and unfurled her fists, letting her guard down when she heard her man's name. She immediately thought the girl would tell her that Kori said things would be okay, not to worry that he was going to bail her out or something good like that.

"What did he—" Kima started.

Bam!

"Ahh!," Kima stumbled backward as she was caught off guard by a punch landing directly in the center of her face. The bridge of her nose cracked and immediately began throbbing. "Oww!" she wailed. Her nose sprayed blood all over the front of her shirt.

Whap!

"Ahhh!" she screamed again, holding her face as the blood leaked through her fingers. "You bitch!" Kima screamed, gurgling blood. Her screams were short lived.

Crack!

Another close-fisted blow to the top of her head made Kima see stars. She felt herself being dragged down by her long hair. Kima's defenses were up, but she had no wins over the three females who were now on her like a pride of lionesses on a small animal. Kima's belly was big, which made her off balance. She was concentrating on protecting her baby now. She knew she didn't have any chance to win a fight with the three women. Kima fell to the floor and immediately curled up into a fetal position so she could protect her unborn son. Kicks, slaps, and punches rained down on her like a hailstorm. The three women were hitting and kicking her without mercy. She was bleeding from the side of her head now too. Kima kept her legs curled in and her arms over her belly in an attempt to keep them from hitting her in the stomach.

"That nigga said if you snitch, next time he gonna pay us to kill your ass!" the ringleader of the pregnant assailants spat.

"Yeah, and he said to tell you that that fuckin' bastard baby you carrying ain't his fuckin' baby either!" the fat chick snarled. With that, she lifted her foot and kicked Kima with all her might, right in her stomach. The pain rocked through Kima's abdomen like a volcano erupting.

"Agh!" she let out a bloodcurdling scream that felt like fire searing the back of her throat.

She immediately felt something warm leaking from between her legs and then her world went black from the shock.

Chapter 2

Kima's eyes fluttered open as the sound of voices around her filtered through her ears. She attempted to lift her left arm but something prevented it. Kima moved her eyes and noticed silver handcuffs glaring back at her. She looked around to see where the voices were coming from. There was a group of doctors standing at the foot of her bed. There was a C.O. posted up, sleeping in a chair near the window in the corner of her room. She looked up to her left and saw a monitor with numbers flashing. She also became aware of the oxygen mask covering her nose and mouth. Kima lifted up her free hand and saw the IV stuck in the top of her hand. The doctors were still talking, but none of them noticed that she was awake. Trembling and feeling weak, Kima slowly moved her free hand and touched her stomach. It was soft and mushy. It was also painful. Kima pushed on the flesh of her stomach again, this time with more force. She noticed her belly wasn't hard anymore. She couldn't feel her baby moving around like she usually did when she woke up. Kima's entire head was banging as she tried to see herself, but she couldn't look down because there was a bandage across her nose and the mask on top of that. Kima was thinking about her baby. Panic quickly set in and her heart started racing fast. The machine she was hooked to begin to beep loudly. One of the doctors whirled around. His eyes grew wide.

"Ms. McCallister, you're awake," he said, sounding a bit surprised.

"Where's my baby?" Kima rasped, her throat dry as dust. She used her free hand to pull the oxygen mask from her face.

"We are so glad to see you awake. You suffered some pretty serious injuries, especially to your head," another doctor continued, stepping closer to Kima's bedside.

"Where is my son?" she raised her voice as much as she could, given her condition.

She began coughing which sent a series of hot, stabbing pains through her lower stomach. The doctors all looked at one another. Kima eyed each one of them. Her voice had stirred the C.O. from his sleep and he stood up with a look of horror on his face.

"You should rest, Ms. McCallister. Really," a female doctor said, trying to push Kima's shoulder back down onto her pillow.

"I want my fuckin' son! Where is my baby?" Kima strained to scream.

The veins in her neck and at her temple were raised and pulsing against her skin. The heart monitors were screeching with rapid beeps. A piece of gauze on Kima's head began to get soaked with blood, as it was apparent she had busted a stitch.

"Y'all gonna have to tell her. This shit ain't good for her and I ain't trying' to do the paperwork on a dead inmate," the C.O. said moving closer.

The doctors looked at each other as if they were trying to figure out who would be charged with giving Kima the information she was requesting. Kima was thrashing now and kicking her legs. Her movement caused the metal from the handcuffs to dig into her wrists, but she couldn't even feel it. Kima didn't even feel the pain of the C-section incision burning through her abdomen as she bucked and screamed. Finally, the petite, female doctor stepped closer to Kima's bedside. The doctor was clearly nervous.

"Ms. McCallister, the injuries you suffered during the assault were pretty serious. The blow you took to the belly ruptured the placenta, which caused hemorrhaging inside the womb. When there is a disconnect of the placenta from the uterus, the baby can no longer get oxygen from you, which means you can no longer breathe for him. I'm so sorry, your son died in utero. When they got you here, he had already expired. We performed an emergency C-section to remove him. You were unconscious. I am so sorry for your loss," the doctor said regretfully lowering her eyes to the floor.

Kima flopped back onto the pillow. The words took a minute to sink into her head.

"No! You bastards killed my son! No! Agh!" Kima screamed at the top of her lungs.

Her voice was cracking and rasping. Blood soaked the head gauze now. The screams hurt her throat but she couldn't stop screaming.

"Get something to sedate her!" one of the doctors yelled to a nurse who had come busting into the room to see what was going on. The nurse turned on her heels and raced out of the room for something to get Kima under control.

"Get the fuck away from me!" Kima growled.

Her face was beet red and the heart monitors were going berserk. The doctors all looked horrified. Finally, the nurse skid back into the room and handed a syringe to one of the doctors. Kima was kicking so hard, it took all of them to hold her legs still enough to be injected. Thc doctor was finally able to plunge the needle into Kima's left thigh muscle.

"Owww!" she wailed. "Fuck off me!" Those were her final words as the medicine in the needle immediately took hold of her. Kima's body went slack, her head lulled to the side. Her hand relaxed so much the handcuffs scraped against the metal railing on the side of the bed. The doctors all looked at each other in relief.

"That was the saddest thing I've ever had to do," the female doctor said to her colleagues. She swiped at a tear from her eye.

"How does a girl so young, unmarried, and pregnant get herself into so much trouble?" one of the male doctors asked out loud to no one in particular.

"I see it every day. A lot of young women are doing hard time behind the choices they made in men," the C.O. answered as he made sure Kima was really knocked out again. He shook his head in disgust, turned and headed back to his seat next to the window. "I just often wonder what makes them stupid enough to do it," he said, folding his arms across his chest trying to get comfortable.

Chapter 3

One Week Earlier in Bed-Stuy, Brooklyn

Kima was roused from a deep sleep by Kori's deep voice coming from the first floor of their two-story home. She listened for a few minutes and could immediately tell he was stressed. He was cursing about something. Kima sighed. She hated when Kori was upset. He didn't like to talk about things and he would go into a shell, which made her miserable. Keeping Kori happy was paramount on her daily to do list because if not, there was always hell to pay for everyone around them. Kima got out of the bed and stood at the doorway of their bedroom to listen. She winced as her baby moved inside of her. Then she smiled a little bit. She had just found out she was carrying a baby boy. A son was always what Kori wanted. He already had three daughters from two other chicks. Kima felt proud to be the one to finally deliver him a son. It was clear that the baby was running out of room inside of her too, the thought of her baby growing bigger also made Kima smile. But more raucous cursing coming from downstairs interrupted her nice thoughts about the baby.

"Fuck you, the bitch disappeared? Fuck you mean, you can't find nobody to replace her?" Kori boomed. "You know how much money I'm losing while y'all niggas playing the fuck around! You tellin' me not one old bitch up in the hood wanna make some trap?"

Kima crinkled her eyebrows and listened. This didn't sound good at all. Anything that had to do with his money being funny would surely come with a hell to pay from Kori for everybody around him, especially her.

"This shit could cost me big paper! Find somebody by tomorrow or else niggas gonna be sorry!" Kori barked.

Kima jumped as she heard a loud crash. He had thrown his pre-paid cell phone against a wall. Kima couldn't decide whether to rush to his side and try to comfort him or go back to bed and act like she hadn't heard him. After a few minutes of contemplating, she made up her mind.

Kima put on her soft terry cloth robe, swallowed hard and waddled down the stairs. Kori was slumped in front of the TV, wearing just a wife beater and his jeans. His ACG boots were kicked off in front of the couch. His face was screwed up into an evil scowl as he mindlessly flicked the channels with the remote. Kima padded over to him, her belly leading the way. Kori kept staring at the TV, acting like he didn't even see her.

"Hey," Kima said softly as she sat down close to him, almost on top of him. He didn't return her greeting. She touched his leg gently and smiled.

"C'mon man, I'm not in the mood for no lovey dovey shit right now," Kori said, irritated.

Kima felt a flutter of hurt, but she was used to Kori's mood swings by now. She moved her hand from his leg and rubbed his arm anyway. Kori sucked his teeth. He yanked his arm away from her roughly, almost hitting her in the face with his elbow. She ducked back just in time. She exhaled loudly. It took a lot of patience to deal with him sometimes.

"What's the matter baby?" Kima asked persistently, her tone soft. "Is there anything I can do to make it better?" she soothed, being mindful to keep her hands off of him now.

"Psss. You can't do shit to help me right now. Fuck out of here. All y'all niggas is useless to me. You especially right now. Just a mouth to feed. Shit, you can't even give me no pussy to get my mind off shit with that fat-ass gut in the way," he snapped, his words cruel.

Kima felt a sharp pain behind her eyes as she fought back tears. Kori always said the meanest shit to her when he was in a bad mood. Still, she put her own feelings aside. Kima was so used to being there for him, she couldn't even help herself.

"Please let me help. Did something happen?" she pressed.

Kori just ignored her and got up from the couch. He walked toward his fully stocked bar and started mixing himself a drink. Kima sighed as she followed his every move with her eyes. She knew when he started drinking that it would be a long-ass night. Sometimes, she wondered what the hell she had gotten herself into falling in love with Kori.

When Kima met Kori, she was only eighteen, and he was twenty-six. The first time she ever laid eyes on him, was one night when she had gone to a basement party in Flatbush with some of her cousins. Kori was outside leaning up against his Benz, profiling. Kima had locked eyes with him that night but hadn't spoken to him. Because she noticed that he was there with another chick. She was a beautiful girl that had made Kima feel like a bum with what she had on. Kima never thought about Kori in the days after the party, that is, until fate made their paths cross again. Kima had run into Kori more than two months after their first encounter. She was coming out of her high school as he drove past it with his windows down, blasting his music. Kima didn't know it was him at first, she had just watched the noisy car ride by. Obviously, he had noticed her though. Kori had passed her, but appeared again after he had driven all the way back around the block, just to talk to her. Kori had taken notice of how pretty Kima was, not to mention her Coca-Cola bottle shape. In his assessment, Kima wasn't much of a dresser, but she was really pretty. She had bright, unblemished caramel skin, big round eyes, and full heart-shaped lips. Her eyelashes were long and thick and so was her hair. She stood about five feet, six inches with a tiny waist and her hips and ass were thick and round. Those were the assets that had definitely caught Kori's eye. He loved a nice ass on a woman. When Kori stopped at the corner as Kima tried to walk across the street, she took notice of him right away. He looked familiar to her, but at first she couldn't place his face. Kori looked like he had a lot of money and Kima looked like just the opposite. Kori turned his music down and leaned down so he could see her out of the passenger's side window from his side of the car.

"W'assup shorty? You got a minute?" Kori had called out to her.

Kima smiled at him. She was blushing like crazy, still in disbelief that he had stopped for someone like her. Kima was impressed with Kori's car, clothes, and the huge diamond pendant dangling from his chain. It had been her life dream to get a man like Kori. Just like her older cousin, Lawanda, had done. Lawanda had escaped their crowded project apartment thanks to her man and was living well now. Kima knew it was all due to Lawanda's boyfriend, Cess. Every time Kima saw Lawanda come around with new sneakers, jeans, and coats, Kima would say a silent prayer for a man just like Cess.

***

Kima's life wasn't easy. She was living with her grandmother while her mother served a long prison sentence for taking the fall for the murder of a well-known pastor. While her mother did time, Kima lived in a small cramped, two-bedroom apartment in the Kingsborough housing projects along with her grandmother, two uncles, and ten of her cousins. Her grandmother would often yell and threaten to send Kima to foster care if she did anything wrong. Kima and her cousins were constantly reminded that they weren't on her grandmother's lease and one phone call to housing would have them all living in group homes. They all believed her too. Kima slept on the bottom bunk of one of the many sets of bunk beds that were set up on walls throughout the apartment. The living conditions were not the greatest. They had a lot of roaches, hardly ever had toilet paper or soap, and there was a long clothesline that ran the length of the apartment where they hung their clothes after they washed them in the bathtub. Food was a luxury in their house. Kima's grandmother and her two uncles were the only two allowed to go into the refrigerator or cabinets without express permission. There was hardly ever anything to drink in the house and when her grandmother made Kool-Aid, if Kima wasn't the first to get one of the few glasses or cups in the house, she would miss out. Kima often woke up extra early on weekends, just to be the first one to use the three cereal bowls and to make sure she got milk for her cereal so she didn't have to use water. Kima hardly ever got anything new. She wore hand-me-down clothes, shoes, and coats from her cousin Cynthia, who was a year older than her. Not that Cynthia got anything new that often either, but when she was done wearing her stuff to death, it was passed on to Kima. Kima only owned five pairs of underwear that she washed over and over again. The summer she turned fourteen, she worked a summer youth job. Her grandmother took all of her money, with the promise that Kima would be able to buy school clothes. That never happened, so the next year Kima refused to work if she wasn't going to benefit from it. Kima was embarrassed, but she had no choice but to get to school early for free breakfast and to eat the free lunch. If she didn't, sometimes she would be hungry all day because at home, dinner was handed out in very small portions with no chance of seconds.

That day outside of her school, Kori and Kima spoke for at least an hour. He then offered her a ride home. When she sat down in his big body Benz, Kima knew right then that she would do anything to get with Kori. She did exactly that. Kima dealt with Kori's other chicks and she held on. He would leave Kima for weeks at a time with no calls or visits, but when he showed back up, she would accept him with open arms. Kima never questioned him about his business or about whom else he was seeing. Kori liked that about her because the other two chicks he was dealing with would stress him out. They would fight each other in the street, call him all times of the night, interrupt him when he was conducting business, and beg him for money. Kima did none of the above. She stayed calm all of the time. When he was with her, she made Kori feel like a king. If he wanted a massage she would do it. If he wanted her to cook she would do it. Kori could've gotten anything out of Kima; she gave new meaning to the term, cater to you. Kima never asked Kori for money, which made him want to give it to her. Kori really liked Kima's style. He also liked the compliments he got from his boys when he had her around. Kori could buy Kima the cheapest low end, name brand clothes and she would be head over heels happy. That made him feel good, so he stayed motivated to give her things. Kima carried herself with class and never put any pressure on him. Kori found himself spending more and more time with her. He started growing real fond of her and when he found out that none of the dudes in Bed-Stuy could say that they had run up in her he was really all in. Kori considered Kima wifey material. After a year of seeing her on his terms, he picked her up from her grandmother's house one day and told her he was moving her out of the projects. Kima was nineteen, but she was still scared of what her grandmother and her uncles would say. But the day she left home, nobody even cared. They didn't miss her when she was gone. In fact, she ran into Cynthia one day and Cynthia told Kima that their grandmother was happy to have one less mouth to feed. Kima never looked back after that. Her life became all about Kori. Although she started community college that year, she didn't continue. Kori wanted her where he could put his finger on her at all times. At home. He would shower her with gifts, clothes, jewelry, and he even got her a car. Kima couldn't ask for anything more. The one thing Kori didn't do, was put money in her pocket. Although she carried designer bags, there was never any cash inside of them. Kori told her to ask for what she wanted and he would give her what she needed, but he was not putting any money in her hands. Kima was fine with that, she wasn't planning on going anywhere anyway, she reasoned.

Kima endured many lonely nights when Kori didn't come home. She also suffered through the many calls and texts from other women to his cell phone. Kima had weathered the storm of Kori's baby mothers coming to his house acting out. In a way, she felt superior to them because she was the one inside while they banged and kicked on the door for him. Kima never made a fuss.

Kori would explain things away by telling her he had to conduct business so he that was why he hadn't come home. He would tell her the girls calling didn't mean shit and that she was the one that he was coming home to. He would tell her the crazy chicks were just his baby mothers, but she was wifey. Kima was fine with all of that. She considered herself, *numero uno,* and she played her position. Kori picked and chose when he took her out. He selected and purchased her outfits too. Kima was a kept woman. Coming from where she had come from, it was all she could expect out of life in her eyes.

The one thing Kima couldn't stand was Kori's temper. After she had been living with him for two years and the novelty of having material things had worn off, Kima noticed how everything set Kori off. If shit with his hustle didn't go right, he'd take it out on her. If he didn't cum hard enough during their sex sessions, he'd take it out on her. When one of his workers had gotten killed, Kori took it out on Kima. It had gotten to a point where she began to find ways to keep him happy so that she wouldn't catch the wrath. It had gotten so bad that Kima would do anything to keep Kori happy so she didn't have to endure what would come if he was not content.

Kima stayed up fighting her sleep as Kori drank himself into a rage and practically destroyed their home again. They had just replaced two mirrors, had a wall fixed, and purchased a new dinette set that Kori had destroyed during one of his fits of rage. Tonight, Kima was thanking God for her big belly because that was the one thing that had kept Kori from his usual with her. But nothing would keep him from screaming and saying mean things to her. Kima expected him to blame her for his problems at some point too. It was a routine occurrence, but something about this time just seemed to give her a deeper feeling of dread than the other times. Especially now that he had polished off almost an entire bottle of coconut Cîroc.

"I do everything for you! I do everything for my dudes! I do everything for everybody else! But what the fuck do y'all muthafuckas do for me? Right now, I don't have nobody to fuckin' get my trap down south! These worthless niggas I fuck with got warrants so they can't go. Sending them would be like taking them to a judge's doorstep and saying sentence this nigga to life," Kori slurred.

He stomped back and forth in front of the couch in front of Kima. She just listened. Her eyes were burning because she was so exhausted, but she had to make Kori believe she was on his side. She nodded as he ranted.

"How you gon' feed that baby? Huh? How we gon' eat? That North Carolina flow is my bread maker. You think a nigga eatin' off of these li'l Brooklyn street sales?" he screamed.

Kima's head dipped. She was so tired. Kori's booming voice snapped her right out of her nod. "Ride a Greyhound? That shit won't work. They're checking those shits with dogs these days! Take a plane? With all the, Bin Laden bullshit, that won't fuckin' fly no more either! Times are changing! This bitch, Junie done got her ass locked up! Fifty years old, and she gets locked up for stealing sheets and towels out of Macy's! Stupid-ass bitch! I was paying this bitch a stack for each of those trips! She been running my shit for years! Her old ass never got stopped, she don't draw no suspicion on the highway. But they said this bitch was greedy so she went and got herself, locked the fuck up!" Kori continued.

He was pissy drunk. This was the first time Kima was hearing anything about his business. He never told her shit. That's how she knew this situation was pretty damn bad. Kori confiding in her was like a Blood doing the Crip Walk—unheard of.

"A woman ain't gonna draw no suspicion out there. Jake ain't watchin' no bitch. But these dudes, nah, they can't ride dirty. Them niggas as hot as the fuckin' Sahara Desert. That's all I need for one of these scared-to-death-ass niggas to get knocked. They would be singing like Billie Holiday to the fuckin' cops. My probation officer would love nothin' more than to violate me and send my ass to Attica! Is that what niggas want? Huh? My ass being sent back to the pen? Then how y'all gon' eat? I'm feeding all y'all niggas off my plate! How y'all gon' eat if I get locked the fuck up?" Kori boomed.

His voice was rising and falling like hard waves crashing against rocks. He finally got tired of pacing and flopped down next to Kima. She jumped. She didn't like when he was this riled up. He could be unpredictable. Kori sat quietly for a few seconds, his chest heaving up and down. Kima could tell his mind was racing too. The alcohol had a grip on him for sure.

"What the fuck I'ma do now?" Kori asked softly, putting his head in his hands.

Kori made Kima's heart break. She wanted to take all of his problems away. She touched the back of his head gently. She rubbed him, comforting him. Kima didn't have an answer for him. She closed her eyes, wishing that she did. Nothing came to mind right away. Sleep was setting in on her now, her mind was fuzzy and her back and legs ached. Kima was silently wishing for a solution. Her eyes closed involuntarily.

"What the fuck I'ma do?" Kori exploded.

Kima jumped so hard she almost died from being so scared. She jumped back and pulled her hand away from his head. Kori turned toward her angrily and grabbed her face roughly. He put his scowling face close to hers, she could smell the alcohol on his breath so prominently, she felt like she could taste it.

"Tell me what to do," he snarled, pressing his fingers into her face.

Kima's eyes were wide and fear danced in them. Her cheeks burned under his rough touch.

"How the fuck I'ma feed your freeloading ass now?" he hissed.

His eyes looked like fire. Kima didn't want to look at him anymore. She closed her eyes tightly. Tears were running out of the corners of Kima's eyes as she squeezed them shut. Her mind raced with options. She remembered him saying women don't get looked at on the highway. She wanted to come up with a solution. She wanted him to stop making her hurt every time shit didn't go his way. She wanted Kori to feel about her now, like he did in the beginning—like she was the solution and not the problem. Without thinking clearly, sleep deprived and in pain, Kima opened her lips and struggled to speak through Kori's tight grasp.

"I . . . I . . . can take it down there," she stuttered. "You sa. . . said women don't draw no suspicion. I'm pregnant, so they really won't suspect me, right?" she offered, her voice wavering with uncertainty.

Kori's face softened a little bit and he let her face go with a shove. Kima rubbed her sore cheeks and continued to cry. He put his head back into his hands. Kima was wondering if he was going to say he was sorry. She just knew he would say hell no to her offer. Kima thought there was no way a man would let his woman, pregnant with his child, risk herself just for money. Kori was quiet. He looked like he was deep in thought as he ran his hands over his low-cut hair. Kima remained quiet as well, instantly regretting what she had just thrown out there.

"You would really do that for me?" Kori finally asked, lifting his head and turning toward her.

Kima felt a hot flash in her chest. This wasn't how this shit was supposed to go, but she knew she couldn't turn back now. The baby moved inside of her. She wondered if her unborn son was telling her this was a bad idea.

"I would do anything for you Kori, anything for us," Kima replied touching her stomach.

Chapter 4

Dame, Smoke, Rusty, and Chucky all stood around with their hands shoved in their pockets and their heads down. They felt fucked up that they couldn't take Kima's place on this run. Kima noticed their doomsday looks, but she didn't comment or let it sway her decision. The guys' ominous reactions to the news of her trip, left an empty feeling in the pit of Kima's stomach. She didn't know they had had a conversation on the way to the spot about how grimy Kori was for having his pregnant shorty running weight down I-95. Kori's dudes were saying they never seen a nigga that desperate or that low. Smoke had even proclaimed that if he was Kori, whether he was on parole or not, he would've taken the chance himself before he risked his shorty riding dirty. Especially, a shorty pregnant with his son. Behind Kima's back, Rusty had even stepped up and volunteered to do the run in place of Kima, even though Rusty knew he had a bench warrant out for him. Kori had told them all hell no. His decision was final. Kima would be making the quick trip there and back. To the guys, Kori was acting like this shit was legal and there was nothing to it. They all knew better. Not only would Kima have to watch for cops, there was also the very real possibility of niggas trying to stick her up once she got down there. Either way, his boys all agreed that Kori was a grimy-ass muthafucka for sending a pregnant chick. His pregnant chick at that.

Kori walked in to the room wearing a mean mug as usual. He slammed the bricks down on the table, shaking everybody in their boots. Kima had a poker face on. Nobody could tell what she was thinking. But Kima knew how she was feeling inside. The feeling was definitely familiar. It was the same way she felt when she was eight years old, the first time her grandmother had taken her to see her mother in prison.

The Family and Children visiting area at the Bedford Hills Correctional Facility for women had been crowded with people that day. Kima noticed a lot of kids there, all ages. Kima sat up straight in the chair and her grandmother sat to her left. When her mother was brought out, Kima didn't move. Partly because she didn't know who the woman walking toward their table was until her grandmother stood up to give her mother a hug. Kima suddenly felt lonely in that room full of people. Her mother grabbed her and held her tight for a long time. Her mother was sobbing, but the feelings of sorrow escaped Kima. She felt sick to her stomach. She had never met her mother that she could remember. Kima had felt like strangers surrounded her; even her grandmother seemed like someone she didn't know. Kima hadn't said much during the visit as she listened to her grandmother fill her mother in about her growing up. Kima felt like she was having an out-of-body experience, but somewhere deep inside she wanted the strange woman sitting across from her in the orange jumpsuit to love and accept her. Kima had felt empty and alone, but she remembered thinking that if she could just make the woman she was told was her mother love her, everything would be better in her world.

It was exactly how she was feeling now. Kori's love and acceptance was all Kima had in the world. Although his agreeing to let her traffic drugs across state lines left her feeling hollow inside, somehow Kima believed that if she did this for him, it would make things perfect.

"I want this shit hidden good. Make them niggas have to take the bumpers off to find shit," Kori instructed, like he was saying something that could protect Kima.

His cronies moved in to the table and began picking up the bricks of cocaine. They all filed out of the room to go stash the drugs in the hidden compartments of the car like they usually did when Junie was driving it. Once they were alone, Kori walked over to Kima and grabbed her in an embrace. Her heart was hammering but she didn't say anything. She just lifted her arms and half-heartedly hugged him back. It was time for the mental warfare game he liked to play and she knew it all too well.

"You don't have to do this if you don't want to," he said stroking her hair. She was expecting this mind game. Kima remained quiet. "I mean, I need this really bad right now. We need it, but if you're not comfortable with doing this shit, let me know now before it's too late," he said, full of game and manipulation.

Kima pulled away from him. She knew better. She knew that if she said no now, there would be a price to pay. Besides, he had drilled it in her head that the cops don't really fuck with female drivers unless they do something dumb. Kori had convinced Kima that if she played by the rules of the road, this plan was fool proof and he would even give her some money of her own for a change. None of that mattered to her more than making that man happy.

"No, I'm ready. I can do this one time, no big deal," Kima replied.

"You a rider baby girl," Kori said smiling. "Remember everything we went over. All you gotta do is make it to Richmond and those dudes will take the car from you from there. They're gon' put you on the Amtrak right back to me. I will be at the Amtrak station waiting for you and my boy," Kori said, reaching out and touching Kima's swollen stomach.

His touch sent a chill down her spine, but not in a good way. She shrank back from him like he had just touched her with something hot. It was the first time he had ever touched her belly or really acknowledged the baby inside her in a positive way. “Everything gon’ be all right. Drive the speed limit, use your signals, just be normal. Ain’t nobody watching no female, you can trust that,” Kori assured her again. Kima just nodded her head and began to walk toward the exit.

“Yo, after this, we gettin’ married. As soon as you drop little man, I’m wifing you officially. You hear me?”

Kima didn’t smile, she didn’t agree, she didn’t even turn around to let him know she’d heard him. She just remained quiet and kept on walking.

Smoke came back inside. “It’s all done.”

He looked at Kima like he felt sorry for her. Kima rolled her eyes and walked out of the door. Kori started after her. Smoke grabbed Kori’s arm, halting him. “Yo, my nigga. You sure you wanna send Shorty in her condition?” Smoke whispered, concern lacing his words.

Kori’s eyebrows dipped in the middle and he bit down into his jaw. “C’mon nigga stop all that before you put the blight on her. Let me find out my bitch is more gangsta than your soft ass,” Kori retorted, pulling his arm away from Smoke.

“A real leader will never send his people to hell purposely. This operation needs a new nigga in charge,” Smoke mumbled to himself, as he watched Kori with disdain. Smoke thought there was nothing worse than a selfish leader.

Kima slid behind the wheel of the rental. Before she could close the door, Kori grabbed it. “What, I don’t get a kiss n’ shit?” Kori asked, leaning down into the car. Kima looked up at him with sad eyes. She let him kiss her on the lips. She barely returned it.

"Remember what I said. Everything gon' be good with this. Ain't shit gonna go wrong," Kori said, closing the door.

Kima started the car, looked at Kori one last time from the window and then she pulled out. She looked up into the rearview mirror. Smoke and Rusty were watching the car leave the block. Kori wasn't even standing there watching to make sure she even got off the block. All she could see was the back of his head as he walked away. It stood out in her mind, that he had already turned his back on her.

"That's the car, right there," Junie said nervously as she slumped down in the back of the unmarked police car. They all watched the rental make a right at the corner.

"You sure?" one of the narcs asked. "That's a female driving that car."

"I'm sure. He probably got another female to do it after he heard I got locked up. Just like he would get me to run his shit. He thinks cops don't fuck with females when they drive," Junie replied. She had found out before she got knocked that Chucky was going to get a chick name Alicia to get him a Budget rental car. Junie knew that Alicia always got midsized cars. Junie had called Alicia to ask what kind she had gotten this time so she would know when she went to pick it up. Alicia had fallen for it and told Junie the make, model, and color of the car.

"You better be right about the car because if this doesn't pan out, your ass is going to jail for a long, long time," the other narcotic detective snapped.

Junie sucked the four or five teeth she had left in her mouth. She hadn't even been able to put her dentures in for the ride over there. "My intel is on point. Just hurry the fuck up and get from around here before I be dead fuckin' with y'all," Junie shot back. She slid further down into the seat. The narco driving pulled out from their spot and began following the rental car.

"Why is she driving all the way to the belt and not going through the city?" he asked Junie.

"Because Kori says so. He is paranoid about the tunnels in the city. I'm telling you, he's been doing this shit for a minute. Even though you might get the car and whoever is driving it, ain't no guarantee they're gonna snitch. Everybody is scared of Kori and without his hands being dirty, y'all might just be ass out. I did my part," Junie replied.

"I guess it's a chance we will have to take," the narco driving retorted. He was secretly hoping that Junie's ass was wrong. The other cop picked up his radio.

"Orange cat to blue mouse," he said into the radio in code.

A voice filtered through in response. "The C.I. says the route is Belt Parkway to Verrazano toward Jersey to pick up I-95. We want this arrest, so don't let her leave Brooklyn. The New Jersey plate is as follows: Edward, Oscar, Charlie, one five one . . . Stop the car as soon as you have a clear one. We can't afford to let this one out of our jurisdiction," the officer said.

Junie put her head down on her lap when she heard herself being referred to as a confidential informant. Her stomach rolled with nervous cramps. If Kori ever found out that she pulled the plug on his operation, she would be pushing up daisies. Junie felt kind of sorry for the poor bitch driving the car. She knew firsthand how much coke Kori was moving down that highway.

***

It seemed like Kima had been driving for hours and she hadn't even gotten out of Brooklyn yet. The baby leaning on her bladder didn't help any, even though she used the bathroom right before she left. Kima was finally in Canarsie, but she had to pee really badly. She pulled onto Rockaway Parkway and parked the car on a little side street away from all of the stores. She didn't care what Kori said about not stopping until the first rest stop in Jersey, she had to piss and there was no way her bladder would hold through the traffic in Staten Island with a big-ass baby pressing down on it. Kima locked up the car and then raced inside the McDonalds to use the bathroom. Her bladder was so full the stream of urine seemed to take forever to get finished. Her nerves being on edge probably didn't help either. When she exited the bathroom, she noticed a white man ordering food and a bum sitting in a corner talking to himself; nothing to be suspicious about. Kima wanted to order something but she couldn't risk being in that McDonalds another minute. Kima was relieved to see that the rental car hadn't been touched while she was gone. She climbed back in and headed for the Belt Parkway.

Kima eased the car past the Canarsie Pier, and a quick memory of Kori bringing her there in the beginning of their relationship crossed her mind. She smiled a little bit. The longer she drove alone, the more she forgave him for putting her out there. Kima was starting to believe everything would be fine and in a minute, she would be back in her bed with Kori holding her and rubbing her belly. Not to mention, her son would be entering the world in a few short months.

Kima merged into traffic on the Belt and signaled her way into the middle lane. She planned to ride that lane until she got to the exit for the Verrazano. Kima saw a cop car appear out of nowhere and her heartbeat sped up.

"Stay calm. They ain't after your ass," Kima chanted out loud a few times to herself.

She started thinking maybe she was wrong when it seemed like the cop car wouldn't move from behind her. "What the fuck!" she cursed loudly, peeking at all of her mirrors. She suddenly had to pee again.

Kima's heart hammered as she looked in the rearview mirror again and noticed that the cop car had thrown on its lights. She watched as the flashing lights drew closer and closer. "God, please let them pass me," she prayed out loud.

It was like God didn't hear her or maybe He wasn't listening. When Kima heard the scream of the sirens directly behind her, she just knew she would die of a heart attack. She knew she needed to pull the car over.

"What the fuck?" she cursed as she eased the car toward the shoulder of the road.

She knew she hadn't done anything wrong. She couldn't figure out why they were signaling her to pull over. Kima started playing shit over in her mind. She drove just like she had been told to do. She signaled with every lane change and did the speed limit. Kima started to regret that she had stopped at that McDonald's. *Maybe it was that.* All kinds of thoughts ran through her mind as she waited for the police officers to approach the car. Kima's hands trembled as she fumbled for her license and the paperwork for the rental car. *This isn't good. I haven't even made it out of New York yet.*

Kima was praying they would just give her a ticket for whatever they had stopped her for and let her go about her business. Anything other than that, and there would be hell to pay from Kori. Kima felt vomit creeping up her throat. She took a deep breath and thought about the instructions she had been given—*Stay calm, be nice, make sure they see that you're pregnant.* She went over Kori's words in her mind. A tall white cop approached the car from the left and one stood off to the right. Kima rolled down the driver's side window prepared to hand him her license and paperwork on the car. She noticed right away that the cop on the left of the car had his gun out. Kima crinkled her face in confusion. It wasn't that serious. Kima put her hands up in defense. She wasn't trying to be the victim of NYPD's next, *accidental,* shooting.

"Get out of the car with your hands up ma'am!" the cop screamed at her. His gun was still pointing in her direction.

"What did I do wrong?" Kima asked, still holding her hands up high so he could see she didn't have a weapon.

"Get out of the fuckin' car now!" he barked.

Kima's stomach was in knots. She felt a serious wave of nausea come over her. All Kima could think about was Kori. He would whip her ass if this didn't go the way it was supposed to. The cop holstered his gun as the other cop came around with his gun drawn on her now. The white cop yanked the door open and pulled Kima out of the car roughly.

"I'm pregnant! Please don't hurt my baby!" she cried out.

It was too late. From the force of his pull, she hit the ground. Luckily, she landed on her knees and not her stomach.

"Help!" she screamed.

"Nobody can help you right now," the cop said as he roughly placed the handcuffs on her.

"Call for the dogs and a female officer to search her. I'm sure we will find plenty of drugs in this car," the officer said.

Kima hung her head and the tears came in a flood. Her life was over either way she looked at it. Not only that, Kori was going to be fucking pissed.

Chapter 5

Six Months Later. Protective Custody Unit. Riker's Island, NY

Dear Kima,

I hope you are okay. I got your letter. I read about the baby and I am so sorry. I wanted to come to your court dates, but Cess has been having some of his own troubles out here and I've just been caught up. Anyway, I know you asked for some money on your books and I'm going to try to do that as soon as possible.

About that other thing you asked me about. I finally caught up with Kori. I had to search for his ass because he moved. Of course when I finally found him, he was with another woman already. I guess it didn't take him long to figure out that you were not coming home so he moved right on to the next one. Sorry for telling you this, I just want to be honest with you, like I promised I always would.

Anyway, Kori made it clear that he wants no parts of you or the case. He said hiring his lawyer to defend you would be like admitting he was guilty. He didn't seem remorseful about the baby either. He handed me two hundred dollars and told me to take care of your commissary. Yes, two hundred dollars for your life. Can you believe that bullshit? I know you must be getting angrier and angrier as you read this shit. I couldn't believe the audacity of that motherfucker so I threw the money right back at him. He was looking really well- dressed to death in his usual name brand shit. He was rocking some big, gaudy diamond watch and a different chain from the last time I saw him with you. Oh, yeah, and he got a new car. I think it's a Bentley, but I can't be sure. I guess he found a way to make some money after all.

I also saw Smoke. He wanted to come and see you, but I told him I didn't know how you would feel about that. I am going to try to visit you before they send you upstate. I know you told me that you already got sentenced and that Riker's was only the holding jail, so I'm gonna try to hurry up and come. I can't believe they gave you that much time for just driving a car with drugs in it. They know you didn't get the drugs yourself. Seems to me, women get harsher sentences and are doing hard time for being drug mules, while the real drug dealers and so-called kingpins get away with a slap on the wrist. Shit, I thought when they tried to revise those fucking Rockefeller drug laws it would've made shit better for girls like you. I guess not. I am going to reach out to that organization you told me about, the one that advocates for women like you caught in these situations with severe sentences and doing hard time behind a man.

I'm so glad you thought to write me, because I would've never known what was going on with you. Grandmother didn't have anything positive to say about your situation, so I won't bother repeating it. I promise to be there for you as much as I can.

Please stay strong. As for Kori, we will figure something out. If not, God will deliver justice to his ass. Please stay strong and I will see you soon.

Love Always,

Your best cousin Lawanda.

Kima could not control the tears streaming down her face as she folded her letter and placed it back in the envelope. Reading about Kori doing so well and that he had already moved on with his life was enough to send Kima into a yearlong depression.

The worst of it though, was picturing some other chick sleeping next to him in her bed. That shit made Kima boil inside with anger. Kima had regretted that she didn't snitch on Kori and tell the cops where she had gotten the drugs. She was still kicking the shit out of herself for that move. Kima didn't know if it was out of love or fear that she decided not to tell. She had taken the full fall for the drugs and on the urging of her public defender Kima had pled guilty to two counts criminal possession of cocaine. The prosecutor had agreed to drop the other ten possession counts, the charge of intent to distribute, and the criminal enterprise charges as part of the plea agreement. Kima had been offered a lesser sentence if she would cooperate with the narcotics officers, but she had refused. Even when they had yelled in her face and threatened to take her baby away as soon as he was born, Kima still stayed loyal to Kori. Even after her baby died and he had left her for dead, Kima didn't tell. Somewhere deep down inside, she held out hope that he would come around and get her the assistance she needed. It never happened. All of those sacrifices she made for him, just for him to turn around and betray her.

***

Kima lay down on her bunk and just cried. The unit she was on housed women at high risk of being injured in general population so it was an open dorm style area. It was part of the infirmary unit inside the women's jail. Most of the general population inmates said the letters PC, in protective custody, really stood for pussy city. Kima didn't care. She knew that once she got upstate, life in prison would take on a whole different dimension. She just hoped that she wasn't placed in the same house as her mother. That would just be too much for her to handle. Kima was facing ten to fifteen years and that was a reduced sentence because she had 'pled guilty and taken full responsibility for the crime.' The judge also acknowledged that Kima had lost her child in jail. He called it a tragic waste of life for selfish reasons. Those words made Kima's legs buckle. She had always felt solely responsible for her son's death, no matter who had commissioned the beating that killed him.

"Kay Kay . . . w'assup?"

Kima's thoughts were interrupted when she heard the familiar squeaky voice approaching from her side. She turned and saw her jailhouse friend, Allison. Kima wasn't in the mood for Allison's bubbly personality. As she got closer, Allison could tell Kima had been crying.

"What's the matter chica?" Allison asked, sitting down on the end of Kima's bed.

Kima tossed the letter in her direction, she didn't really feel like talking, besides the letter would explain it better anyway. Allison picked it up and looked at Kima strangely.

"Just read it," Kima said in an almost inaudible whisper. Allison read the letter at a feverish pace, her head moving side to side as she scanned the loose leaf. Allison's eyes turned dark and her face hardened as she read each line.

"That *puta*! Fucking *maricón*!" Allison spat in her Puerto Rican dialect. "You know what? When I get the fuck out of here, I'm going to see his ass," Allison threatened.

Kima had forgotten that Allison only had another two weeks on Riker's. The thought of Allison leaving her made Kima feel even worse.

"I'm never gonna forget about you Kay Kay so don't be sad. Look, whatever you want me to do for you when I get back in the world you know I got you," Allison said, rubbing Kima's knee. "Here, read this shit right here. Take your rec time and go to the law library. This shit right here helped me and a few bitches upstate get an early release," Allison said, tossing a thick packet of papers at Kima.

She picked them up and could tell they were legal briefs. *Here we go again*, Kima was thinking.

Allison was like the jail lawyer, always spitting about getting cases over turned on shit like illegal searches and lack of rights. Kima just figured Allison was talking shit.

"Don't just hide that shit under your bunk. When I leave out of here, you better read that shit. I'm telling you, there might be something between them pages that's gonna save your ass, chica," Allison said seriously.

"You know what? There is something you can do for me when you get out. I want to know it's done before I get transferred upstate. Promise?" Kima asked seriously, ignoring what Allison was saying about the legal briefs.

"I got you. Just say the word and it's a done deal. Shit, especially if it's something to get back at that no good nigga of yours I'm down for sure. You know I'm Puerto Rican, we love revenge," Allison replied. She looked at Kima and they both started laughing.

"You know you just made that shit up just now," Kima laughed.

"But it got a bitch feelin' better and shit, right? A'ight then. My work is done here," Allison chuckled.

Little did she know, Kima had a bigger job for her than she thought. Revenge was an understatement.

Chapter 6

Allison and Kima held each other in a long embrace. Kima was sniffling back the snot that threatened to escape her nose, but Allison's face was dry. She would miss Kima, but she couldn't bring herself to cry. Allison was happy as hell.

"C'mon chica, don't be crying and shit. You're making me sad on my release day, when a bitch like me is supposed to be jumping for joy. I told you, you gon' be a'ight in here. If you would just listen to me and read that shit I gave you, you'll be joining me soon," Allison said.

They let each other go and Kima swiped at the tears on her face. "This is a happy day, you're right. I'm sorry if I'm gonna miss a crazy Puerto Rican chica that made my days doing this time easier," Kima said, smiling at her friend. "Just be good out there," Kima told her.

"C'mon, I know you didn't mean nothing. I'm a real lovable bitch so I know you gon' miss my ass," Allison said trying to put Kima at ease. "You know the first thing I'm going to do when I hit the world. I'm not going to let you down Kay Kay. For real, I'ma tell you somethin', I never had a female friend before I met you. I never got along with chicks, but you were different from day one. I'm your true friend," Allison told her.

That had touched Kima's heart. She had never had a female friend either. Kima never trusted anyone like she trusted Allison. Kima guessed doing time together could make the most unlikely of people formulate a bond.

"Diaz, let's go! Unless you plan on staying with us another year or something," a male C.O. called out. Allison smiled at Kima one last time. "I'm coming, fat ass!" Allison snapped at the C.O. She and Kima laughed.

"Doing hard time ain't nothing for ride or die bitches like us. It's those bitch-ass niggas that can't make it inside the walls. That's why they send us to do their fuckin' dirty work like pussies," Allison called over her shoulder.

Kima nodded in agreement. Although she felt sad, Kima was excited about the possibilities of what Allison could do for her from the outside. Kima walked back over to her bunk and picked up the paperwork Allison had given her. Kima finally took Allison's advice and began to read the thick stack of legal size papers. After the first couple of lines, and before long, Kima was enthralled with what was contained in those documents.

Smoke shifted his weight from one foot to the other as he waited outside of the BBQ's in downtown Brooklyn just like Kima had asked him to do in the letter her cousin had passed on to him. He scanned every chick that passed by the restaurant, wondering which one was going to be this girl named Allison. Smoke looked at his watch for what must have been the twentieth time.

"Ssss," he hissed out a long breath of air.

He hated when people didn't keep their appointment times, but more than that, he hated to be stood up. After forty-five minutes of waiting, Smoke shoved his hands down into his pockets and got ready to walk away. He jumped when he felt a hand on his arm from behind.

"You're Smoke, right?" a real cute, light-skinned, thick female asked, smiling. Smoke took immediate notice of how attractive she was with her seductive cat-like eyes.

"You Allison?" he asked, eyeing her up and down.

"That's me. Sorry I'm late. I'm from the Bronx. That train shit had me all fucked up," she laughed.

Smoke could hear her accent. "Damn, I would've came and got you. That's a long-ass ride," he said, pulling open the door for her.

"It's all good. I would take that long-ass ride for my girl Kay Kay," Allison replied. She noticed the look on Smoke's face. "Oh, I mean Kima. I called her Kay Kay while we were locked up together," Allison explained.

"Oh, a'ight. I gotchu," he said.

They were seated and the conversation immediately shifted to business. Smoke laid out his idea for the plan and Allison shared Kima's side of it. Over their Texas-sized drinks and sticky wings, Allison and Smoke devised the perfect layout of how shit was going to go down.

Smoke was happy with the plan too. The one thing he felt the best about, was the fact that doing business with women didn't draw any suspicion. If any niggas from Kori's hood had seen Smoke and Allison together, they would've just assumed they were out on a date. That's exactly what he wanted too.

Allison checked herself in the mirror one more time. The form fitting dress Smoke bought her was perfect on her body. It looked like someone had poured her into it. Allison had butterflies in her stomach, but she couldn't wait to meet the infamous Kori. After what she learned about him and knowing what he had done to Kima, Allison told herself she would even do another bid behind getting revenge on his ass. The money Kima had arranged for her to get as a result wasn't bad either. Allison took a cab to the party in the city at a place called Nobu. It was swanky just like she suspected. All she had to do was get Kori's attention, from what Smoke had told her, Kori had a serious addiction to pretty women with fat asses, so she didn't think she would have a problem.

Once she was inside of Nobu, Allison didn't see Kori or Smoke right away. She climbed up on one of the beautiful, shiny metal, ultra-modern bar stools and ordered a Coco-Loso. Allison nursed her drink and took in the atmosphere. After being locked up for more than three years, the club scene was all new to her. The music wasn't, since inmates watched all of the new videos and heard all of the new songs just like people in the world did.

Allison's heart jerked in her chest when she noticed Smoke walk into the club. He was surrounded by dudes and from what Kima and Smoke had described, the nigga in the middle, with the huge cross, blinging on the center of his chest, was Kori.

Kori and his crew quickly grabbed a spot on one of the leather lounge chairs that extended from the far back wall of the place.

"Perfect! Right near the bathroom so all I have to do is get his fuckin' attention," Allison mumbled to herself.

It was on and popping now. She caught eye contact with Smoke as he approached the bar and ordered a bottle. Allison winked at him and jumped down from her seat. The plan was in motion and there was no turning back now.

Allison swayed her hips and sauntered past Kori and his boys. Just like they all predicted, Kori took the bait. *My girl is locked up behind your no-good ass, and you out here in the world chasing pussy. It's gonna be so good turning the tables on your ass,* Allison thought as she smiled at Kori. "I'm Allison, and you are?" she asked using the most seductive voice she could conjure.

"I'm that nigga that can change your life forever," Kori said smoothly.

Wrong nigga! I'm that bitch that's gonna change your life forever, Allison screamed silently. "Where can we go to talk in private? It's too busy in here. A girl like me wants all of the attention," she said to him batting her long false eyelashes.

"Say no more," Kori replied excitedly standing up. He just didn't know that would be his last stand as a free man.

Chapter 7

Crash! Bang! Bang!

"What the fuck!" Kori belted out as he jumped up and whirled his head around in response to the loud noises coming from downstairs in his house.

Kori's heart began thumping painfully in his chest. It could only be one of two things going on—niggas were coming to get his ass or the police was raiding his shit. Kori finally got enough of the cobwebs of sleep and liquor from his mind and bent down at his bedside in an attempt to reach for his ratchet, but it was not between the bed and his nightstand where he always left it.

"Fuck!" Kori cursed.

The sounds seemed like they were getting closer to him. It sounded like a herd of wildebeests trampling through his house. He looked over at the side of the bed where the girl he had picked up last night was supposed to be, but the spot was empty.

"Where did this bitch go?" Kori mumbled looking for anything he could use as a weapon.

It had only been a few seconds after the banging noises started that Kori finally heard the words he always dreaded hearing ever again in life.

"Police! Don't fucking move!" Kori was staring down the barrel of a huge semiautomatic weapon.

Kori threw his hands up in surrender. "What the fuck is going on here?" he asked as the police officers moved in on him. He was forcefully yanked from his bed and thrown to the floor in a prone position on his stomach.

"It's a visit from the Easter bunny. What the fuck you think is going on?" said one of the many cops that were now pillaging through is place.

"Y'all better have a fuckin' warrant to be here. My lawyer is gonna have a field day with this shit," Kori snarled, chuckling confidently afterward.

He never brought anything home with him so he was far from worried. He was placed on the floor on his stomach and his arms were pulled behind his back as they placed the handcuffs on him.

"I wanna see your fuckin' search warrant!" Kori screamed.

One of the cops got down on one knee near Kori and got close to Kori's ear. "I'll do you one better. I'll show you our evidence and our search warrant," the cop hissed, dropping the search warrant and a gallon-sized freezer bag full of white powder next to Kori's head.

"That's some bullshit! Y'all muthafuckas planted that shit! This is some fuckin' bullshit!" Kori screamed as he thrashed against the handcuffs.

"You should probably watch who you bring home from the club," the same cop said, then he busted out laughing.

"You won't get away with this shit! I got long paper and a good lawyer! When I finish with you, your ass gonna be mopping up French fry grease at McDonald's, you fuckin' pig!" Kori spat.

The rest of the officers continued to tear the house up. They found another bag full of pure, uncut cocaine in a canister in the kitchen. Kori was a parolee, one strike away from his third strike. He knew he was going to be facing down a life sentence this time. As he was carted out of the house and loaded into the back of a paddy wagon, Kori could only wonder if his predicament was a karmic consequence of how he had treated Kima.

***

"Jacobs! You got a visit!" the C.O. called out. Kori sat up in his cell and looked at the C.O. strangely. "You gon' move or what? I said you got a visit," the C.O. said again.

Kori just wanted to make sure he had heard him correctly. Kori hadn't had a visitor since he had been sent upstate. He got up and prepared for the tier walk to the visit house. Kori's mind raced with a million different possibilities of who could be visiting him. It couldn't be any of his boys; none of them would dare put their names down on a prison visit form for fear of immediate arrest. Kori didn't fuck with his parents, although he was sure his trifling-ass family had read about him in the papers and knew about him blowing trial. Kori had put it all on the line and lost.

Kori was escorted into the visit house, where he was searched again for the third time since he had left the tier. When the door to the visit room opened and the C.O. pointed out the visitor, Kori's jaws went slack and his mouth hung open. His legs felt weak and he couldn't move. Kori was in disbelief.

"You gonna go visit with that fine-ass thing, or you gonna stand here stuck on stupid, Jacobs?" the C.O. urged, giving Kori a small shove on the shoulder to move him along.

Kori blinked back tears. For the first time he thought he was feeling what true love felt like. After everything he had done, after all of his betrayal, lies, and leaving her for dead, Kori was staring at his visitor—Kima.

Kori moved slowly to the table and he stood there for a few seconds. Kima had a smirk on her face. Kori couldn't really say it was a smile. She didn't stand up to greet him either. Kori was at a loss for words. He had a simple looking smile on his face.

"W'assup, Kima? I sure didn't expect to see you visiting a nigga like me," Kori said, breaking the awkward silence between them.

Kima nodded. She too was fighting back tears that burned in the back of her eye sockets. Kima told herself she wasn't shedding another fucking tear over Kori's ass and she meant it. She looked down at her hands to get her focus back.

"Don't you want to know how I got out?" she asked dryly.

"Um, I mean, I'm just glad that you did. It doesn't really matter, right? I told you things would be a'ight for you," Kori replied.

His words came across the table like a forceful open-handed slap to Kima's face. She squinted her eyes into little dashes and leaned into the table.

"Don't you fuckin' dare take credit for me getting out of prison. Because of you, I lost my son. I was facing fifteen fucking years and you never once even checked on me. But you know what? I got out because I'm smart, because someone told me to do my homework," Kima gritted through clenched teeth.

"I'm sorry for everything. I was just dumb. I was scared of the cops n' shit, and the baby—" Kori started.

"You better not even mention my baby. You have no right, the baby you had murdered," Kima spat. Kori hung his head in shame.

"Kori, I only came here for one thing. I came to tell you that when you do dirt, dirt is all you can expect in return. See, you thought I was going to be the one doing hard time. But somebody in the cards had other plans. I guess you can say the tables have turned and only one of us will really be doing hard time," Kima said angrily as she stood up. Kori looked up at her like he just wanted to fade away. "Oh, yeah, about all that you didn't do for me when I was locked up, well I guess I got my revenge for all of the suffering. I'm sure you remember her, don't you?" Kima said calmly placing a picture of Allison down on the small metal table that separated her from Kori. He looked down at the picture and then looked up at Kima.

"What the fuck?" Kori said, his eyebrows furrowed in confusion.

"You should watch who you bring home from the club to our . . . Oops, I mean your house," Kima said, letting out a wicked laugh. Before Kori could say another word, Kima sauntered away.

"C.O., I'm ready to be let out," she called out as she kept walking. "I hate being behind bars for anything, especially visiting a nigga doing hard time," she said laughing again. Kori looked on in shock. He was left speechless.

When Kima exited the prison she saw her ride waiting for her. She rushed over to the car and slid into the front passenger's seat.

"You a'ight, baby girl?" Smoke asked her.

Kima looked over at him and smiled. "I am just fine. I don't think your boy could believe how the cards played out though," Kima replied.

"Fuck him! He probably almost died when he saw that you were out!" Allison screamed from the back seat. Kima turned around in her seat with a big smile on her face.

"Girl, he looked like he had seen a ghost," Kima told her. They started laughing.

"Did you tell him it was on a technicality like how I got out?" Allison asked.

"Hell no! I wasn't telling that nigga shit. I wasn't giving his ass no ideas to be up in the fuckin' law library researching," Kima answered.

The three of them drove for a while laughing and talking. Smoke and Kima dropped Allison off at her place near Gunhill Road in the Bronx. But not before Smoke handed her a small duffle bag with cash. Allison thanked him and told Kima she would see her in a few days for their girl's night out.

When Smoke and Kima were alone, he leaned over in her direction and grabbed her head. He pulled her close to him and kissed her deeply.

"Thank you for agreeing to my plan. I knew it would all go smoothly. Nobody knows that nigga Kori better than me, not even him," Smoke told her.

"It was my pleasure. Thank you for coming through for me when I was on lock down. If it wasn't for you, not only would I still be doing hard time, but that nigga would still be walking around in the world while I served his bid. I am grateful," Kima said solemnly.

Smoke drove her to the gravesite her cousin Lawanda had bought for her son. Kima took a deep breath before she got out of the car. Smoke held her hand as they walked together to the site. Kima broke down when she looked down at the slate headstone. Smoke hugged her tightly while she cried into his chest. Kima and Smoke stayed at the cemetery until she was all cried out. Then, they drove back to his place.

"You can stay here if you want to, baby girl. I'm sayin', I'm feeling you. I always have been," he said to her as they sat in his living room.

"I just came by to get the money. I am going to go off and start my own life. I want to live for me for a change. I hope you can understand that," Kima said softly.

Smoke nodded his agreement. He handed her the money as promised. Kima stood up and before she left his house she turned to him. "When we are made, we don't ask to be born into this hard knock life. Life and death in the hood simply put is hard, whether you doing the hard time inside or outside," she said with finality.

Smoke understood just what she was talking about. Shit was hard where they came from, and probably in every hood in America was just as hard.

Twisted Triangles

by

Katt

Chapter One

The sound of the ringing Bluetooth in his ear broke thirty-one-year-old Mike B's sleep, causing his body to jerk. He realized he had dozed off with the ear bud in his ear watching *Straight Outta Compton* on bootleg. It had been a long day for him. He had been grinding and pushing himself for the past few days, tying up all loose ends so he could prepare to get on the road and go handle some important business in the south for the weekend. Apparently, sleep had finally caught up to him. He wiped the cold out of his eyes and looked over at his iPhone, laying onto one of the many pillows on his bed and looking at the screen. His spider senses went off when he saw the name that appeared across his screen. It was a number he was only used to seeing if it was something of importance or an emergency. It was one of the only few clean numbers he would talk on. At three a.m., he was sure it was one of the two.

"What's wrong?" he wasted no time asking, hitting the ANSWER button on his Bluetooth.

"Did I wake you?" his girlfriend, Lenore, asked.

Her voice was raspy and her tone was low like his. Without even knowing what was wrong, he knew something was amiss. They had been dealing with each other long enough to know the only time her voice sounded like this was when she was tired and couldn't sleep.

"You know I never sleep," he replied.

A light chuckle could be heard on the other end of the line. "Yeah, that's what I was just thinking." He could tell she was now smiling through the phone. "Besides, even if I was, you know I'd answer for you. W'assup tho'? What's wrong?"

There was dead silence for a moment. He could tell she was trying to conjure up whatever made her call him. An eerie feeling overcame him. He knew whatever it was had to be bad. Her next words confirmed it.

"Something happened to your cousin."

"Twan?"

He was now wide awake. He knew that was the only cousin she could be referring to. He never introduced her to anybody else in his family besides him.

"What happened?"

"Not sure, but I hear somebody was shooting up at the diner," Lenore offered. "Denise and I were just getting back in town from New York and stopped to get something to eat. By the time we got there, we saw the ambulance pulling off. We overheard your cousin was in it."

"Are you fuckin' serious?"

The words tore into Mike B's chest like hot slugs.

"I wish I wasn't, babe. I saw Jeff up there. Have you spoken to him?"

The mentioning of his right hand man made him lean over and retrieve his other phone from the night stand. He noticed he had a few missed calls from his partner and a few numbers not locked in his phone. An eerie feeling swept through him for a split second. He didn't believe in coincidences.

"Not yet. About to hit him up now. He's been trying to reach me. I fucking dozed off."

"Okay, I just got to Denise's house. I'm dropping her off then coming to you."

"See you when you get here."

Mike B discontinued the call and wasted no time calling Jeff on his other phone.

Jeff picked up on the first ring.

"Nigga!" he boomed into the phone.

"I just heard."

Mike B could tell by the sound of Jeff's expression, what his girl had just told him was what it was.

"Meet me at the spot in the a.m.," he then said.

"Say no more."

Mike B hung up the phone and laid back on his king size bed. All he could think about was how he was going to look his aunt in the face after he had promised her he would protect his younger cousin in the streets with his own life.

Later that morning . . .

Mike B slipped from up under a lightly snoring Lenore, and climbed out of bed. She had managed to take his mind off of the present situation with some bomb head that knocked him out quicker than Mike Tyson in his prime. But he was wide awake now, and the situation was back fresh on his mental. The time on the digital alarm clock displayed a little after seven as the time. Mike B exited his bedroom. Moments later, he was opening the front door of his east end home to find, the *Courier News* newspaper at his feet. He pulled the plastic off the newspaper as he made his way to his vehicle. There was no doubt in his mind that whatever happened last night would be in today's paper. When he slipped it off of it and opened it up, the front page and headlines caused a sharp pain to jolt through it. The words SHOOTING AT PLAINFIELD DINER LEAVES ONE DEAD illuminated off the page. Mike B scanned the article.

Union County

A local Plainfield resident was reportedly shot and killed at Kennedy Fried Chicken Diner on Park Avenue. The victim has been identified as 25-year-old Antwan Roberts. Our sources say that police found Robert's body riddled with bullets. No weapon was recovered and police are ruling Robert's death as a homicide.

No one has been arrested or charged on the matter, but sources also tell us that Roberts, who went by the street monniker "Twan" had an extensive criminal record, and although it has not been confirmed, police believe that this may be a drug-related incident. If you have any information concerning the death of Antwan Roberts, please contact the Plainfield Police Department or 1-800-CrimeStoppers.

Fighting back tears, Mike B flung the newspaper off to the right of him. All types of thoughts flowed through his mind. Despite the fact that someone close to him in blood and on his team was murdered, Mike B still had to keep a level head if he wanted to get to the bottom of things. He was already weighing up potential and possible explanations and scenarios as to how his little cousin had been killed and by who. But first, he needed to talk to Jeff to see what he knew. With that in mind, Mike B whipped his SUV from alongside of the curb headed to what he and Jeff called their Think Tank.

Chapter Two

"Hello?" an out of breath Lenore answered the phone just in time.

"Damn, what were you were doing? Playing with yourself?" Denise chuckled.

"No bitch." Lenore spat. "I was in the shower," she retorted as she unraveled the towel wrapped around her body and began to dry off.

"Whatever," Denise dismissed her response. "Anyway, how did Mike B take it?" she asked instead.

Lenore sighed. "I told you, for as long as I've been dealing with him, he's been hard to read. We didn't talk when I got in."

"Oh, well Jeff left up out of here early to meet up with him."

"I know. M left early too. When I woke up around eight, he was already gone." Lenore offered.

"Jeff said he's positive Mike B is going to wig the fuck out and go ham though," Denise rebutted. "I think so too. He loved that nigga Twan like a brother."

Lenore grimaced as she continued drying off. She knew how Mike B felt about his younger deceased cousin. Although they did a lot together and he did a lot for her, at times, she felt he had showed his cousin more love and attention than he did her. She knew up-close and personal they were. Still, he was not a man that wore his emotions on his sleeve.

They had been together for two years, after Jeff and Denise introduced the two. They had hit it off the first day they had met. Lenore was fresh out of the hood of Englewood, California but looked and carried herself like she belonged in Hollywood. Her tall model's frame and shea butter complexion was right up Mike B's alley, which is why he wasted no time locking her down. It was then she got to know the man that everybody looked at as "the man" in the small East Coast city. The first year the two had been together, she learned that he was not only a private person, but very secretive and more of a homebody. He stayed out of the limelight and played it very low key. He concealed both the way he moved in the streets, as well as his feelings and thoughts, but spoke with his actions. By the way he lived, she could tell he had major paper, but he had never brought drugs around her or handled any business with her present. Had it not been for the gun he always toted when he stepped outside of his crib, a big time dope boy and gangster would not be what came to Lenore's mind when she thought about what he did for a living or who he was. When it came to how he felt about her, he had never really expressed his love to her verbally, but he showed it every chance he got through gifts and quality time. Outside of her, she knew there were only two other people Mike B loved and cared about: Jeff and Twan.

"Yeah, he did," she replied to Denise's statement.

"Well, time will tell just how much he loved him." Denise concluded.

"I'm going to handle what I need to handle this morning. I just wanted to check in and get an update from you."

"Everything's good over here. I'll keep you posted," answered Lenore.

"Okay, baby girl. I'll talk to you later. Love you," Denise ended.

"Love you too. Talk to you later."

Lenore scrolled through her phone until she found the song she was looking for in her playlist then tossed her phone onto the bed and snatched up her lotion. Nikki Minaj's voice blared through her S7 as she stood in front of the full-length mirror lotioning and massaging her breasts. Her hands slithered down past her midsection onto her inner thighs and hips. She couldn't help but admire her flawless body as she bent over to lotion her legs. At twenty-seven years old, she believed she could stand next to the best of them. She was used to turning heads of both men and women wherever she and Denise went from the malls to the gym.

As she bent over, her legs buckled as a sharp pain jolted through her left side. She grabbed hold of her side as she dropped to her knees. The excruciating pain lasted a few more seconds before it abruptly stopped. Lenore exhaled. This was the second time the pain had hit her out of nowhere, but this was the worst out of the two. The pain was enough to convince her it was time to look into what was causing it. With that in mind, Lenore decided to change her plans for the day.

Chapter Three

"How you not gonna know nothing? You be out there damn there every day." Mike B chimed in response to Jeff telling him he had no leads or information about who murdered his cousin.

His tone was too aggressive for Jeff's taste, but he understood his friend was hurting. So, he stood there and took the venom that Mike B spat.

"Bruh, I don't give a fuck right now!" Mike B continued. "Somebody is gonna be held accountable for this shit, dead ass. I need you to go out there and press mutha-fuckas and find out who pushed Twan."

Jeff nodded. He had already expected that that's what Mike B would want him to do. The two had been making moves together long enough for him to know how he wanted certain things to be handled. He practically knew him like a book.

Mike B lit up a Dutch Master filled with a gram of loud exotic weed. "Let's count this paper and inventory this product," he said in between pulls.

"That shit stink, yo," Jeff complained, followed by a futile attempt to fan the smoke out of his face before continuing. "Put ya li'l mans shit on. I'm tired of that shit they listening to upstairs." Jeff screwed up his face, showing his displeasure.

Mike B chuckled and pulled up the Sound Cloud of a young artist, who was the son of one of his mans, Base. It was from an Atlanta group called, Flyght Gang Campaign. He then pulled out a half of a pint of Hennessey.

Meanwhile, Jeff retrieved the scale and some cut for the cocaine and heroin they just smuggled from upstairs. Since the tender ages of twelve, they learned how to cut coke, dope, play poker, shoot dice, sex girls, and a lot more boys their age should not have to know.

People rarely saw one without the other. Chicks they met and dudes they did business out of town thought they were brothers because of how close they were and how much they resembled each other. Not to mention, their birthdays were only eleven days apart and their parents grew up together the same way they had. Mike B and Jeff had all of the little girls turned out off of their swagger, and most of the boys despised them.

The sounds of the track "My Plug" had both Mike B and Jeff head nodding while they rotated the blunt back and forth, counted and rubber banned money, and weighed up product on the triple beam scale.

"Let's hurry up and get this done so we can bag it up."

"This some good shit," Jeff said, wiping the mixture of cocaine and heroin off of his nose.

"Nigga, you sniffin' that shit? You crazy," Mike B warned.

"Fuck that. This shit got me feelin' real mellow, like I ain't got a worry in the world."

Mike B paused, glared at his partner through glossy eyes, and continued.

Mike B had never seen Jeff indulge in anything other than weed and alcohol. It caught him by surprise to see him messing with something much stronger. He was not in the mood to have a conversation about it though. His focus was on moving the rest of the work he had in the street and avenging his cousin's death. He made a mental note to question Jeff on his new extra activity. An hour later, their task was complete.

"We got two hundred and fifty bricks of dope, and sixty bands worth of coke packaged up. Cash wise, we got the one-fifty for re-up money and thirty-three for the kitty, plus whatever we got left," Jeff concluded.

"Not bad for a couple of hood niggas," Mike B informed. He scooped up the thirty-three and tossed ten of it back to Jeff.

"Good looks." Jeff thanked. "Oh, and that ain't including our weed flow and the dough we're already stackin'," Jeff added.

"That's w'assup, but now that we got this out the way, I wanna take it to this joker out here. Like I said, every nigga we ever had problems with, I want you to—" He paused. "Matter fact, we pulling up on muthafuckas, you feel me?"

Jeff gave an agreeing head nod.

"So later, we ridin', my nigga," Mike B announced.

"Say less."

"A'ight after we clean this shit up I'm going to transform and chill with baby girl for the time being."

"Yeah, I gotta put time in with Denise my damn self."

"Y'all stay beef, my gee." Mike B shook his head. "How sis doing anyway?"

"She good. And we not beefin'," Jeff corrected. "Like you said, I just been out in these streets, for us, my nigga. A lot of the time, I know my ass should be in the house."

Mike B looked at him oddly. "Bruh, I thought you was out there like that 'cause you wanted to be, not because you thought or feel you gotta be. Nigga, you after this shit right here, you can chill back any time for however long you want. You still gonna eat."

It was now Jeff's turn to have a distorted look on his face.

"Good lookin' for that, bruh. I really didn't know it was like that. But now I do."

"Come on, my dude, you my bruh. We fam."

They gave each other a pound and hug.

"Let's knock this shit out so we can get up outta here." Mike B was the first to break the bear hug.

"Facts."

They rapidly cleaned up and stashed their material. Ten minutes later, they were out the door, pulling off in different directions.

Chapter Four

Mike B and Lenore laid snuggled up under each other like Siamese twins after a hearty meal and great, yet exhausting sex. Occasionally, the sharp pain she had felt previously would resurface causing a little discomfort, but nothing major to complain about. She was actually a freak for pain. When she went to the emergency room, they refused to see her because she had no medical insurance or New Jersey I.D. After going ham on them, she abandoned the idea of spending the day in a doctor's office and put it off. She chalked it up as a sign not to delay what she had initially set out to do. The quality time felt good to her. It almost made her forget about the tough choices she had to make earlier that day. She nestled up under Mike B as he pushed play on the next episode of *The Walking Dead*. Just as the show was about to start, the sound of Kendrick Lamar echoed from below the bed. The sucking of Lenore's teeth illuminated in Mike B's ear.

"Come on with that" babe. You already knew ahead of time I was going to have to leave back out.

"I know," she replied dryly.

Mike B shook his head as he raised up and leaned over. He scooped up his jeans. When he pulled his phone out of the clip, he saw Jeff's name plastered across it. He replied to the text and then flung the covers off of himself.

"Babe, I gotta go."

He had already slipped his right leg into his jeans.

Lenore stared at him with wide eyes. "Be careful."

"Thanks, baby. But it's them niggas that should've been careful," he snarled.

Lenore didn't respond. She could see in his eyes, he meant business. It was times like this that made her realize who her man really was in the streets. She climbed out of bed and walked over toward him. She pressed her body up against his and looped her arms up under his.

"Just be safe."

Mike B spun around. He loved the way she concerned herself about his well-being. He didn't trust many, but she was on that small list.

"I will." He kissed her on the forehead and then wrapped his arms around her waist. "I promise," he added, and then he was out the door.

Chapter Five

Mike B cruised down West Fourth Street until he reached Plainfield Avenue. He waited for the red light to turn green, then made a right headed toward West Front Street. He felt invisible as he and Jeff cruised through the town like two Grim Reapers, in his black on black Range. Mike B leisurely blazed up a blunt as he cruised up the block.

He glanced at his watch. It was just thirty minutes shy of being the evening. The sun would be going down soon and Mike B wondered if he would still be alive by then. At the rate he and Jeff were going, he knew it was a possibility that they could get caught slipping, but he wasn't thinking straight, so he didn't care.

He stopped at the red light on Front and Madison, better known as the, Spanish Harlem, of Plainfield. Passing Jeff the blunt, he scanned the flow of bodies through the limo tint. Papis and Mamis dominated the hood, holding down their territory with fierce pride, controlling all of the drug traffic within a five block radius.

Mike B watched as several Spanish men openly made drug transactions in front of McDonald's and pushed up on nearly every attractive female that passed by. They laughed and joked as if they didn't have a care in the world.

"Look at these bean eatin' muthafuckas!" Jeff cursed. "They think shit sweet."

He continued. "I been trying to tell you that nigga Juan was the nigga behind that shit!" he spat, referring to Twan's death.

Mike B shook his head. He was not as sure as Jeff was. He wasn't even sure that anybody they ran down on had anything to do with Twan's murder. The only reason he was riding on Juan and his squad was because of the information they came across about him pulling out a gun on his cousin in the Mickey D's parking lot.

It surprised Mike B that people were even outside, with all the chaos and bloodshed that was happening. Since the death of Twan, he and Jeff had been on a rampage in the city. Since the streets weren't talking, they decided to force them to. Any block they had beef or a problem with, they ran down on. After being called every name in the book by his younger cousin's mother, right before she fainted, Mike B was out for blood. It was surprising that the police hadn't linked the random shooting to them, with all of the snitching going on in the city.

Mike B bent the corner as the light turned green.

A thick Spanish chick came strolling by in skin tight jeans, switching the fat ass that God had blessed her with. As she crossed the street, she and Mike B's eyes met and locked onto each other. Jeff blew her a kiss. She put her open palm up, then closed it into a fist as if she caught his kiss, then seductively flipped him the bird.

Jeff was just about to tell her where she could put her finger, when a bullet tore through the windshield, slamming into Mike B's stereo system in his Range Rover. Not even a second later another bullet struck his driver's side head rest just as he managed to duck. Both he and Jeff spilled out of the SUV at the same time, with guns blazing. They had heard that the Papis were on point when it came to strange vehicles patrolling their area and heard stories how they popped off at the drop of a dime, but they didn't expect that.

Within minutes, Madison Avenue turned into the Wild Wild West. Seeing the Spanish shooters running for cover built Mike B and Jeff's confidence up. Jeff took it to them like he was returning a football punt while Mike B scurried over to the Range and followed.

From afar, Juan sat in his six-four, sipping on lean, while looking on as his plan began to unfold. In a matter of minutes, his block erupted into gun battle. He had spotted the black Range Rover the first time it came through the area. This is why he sent the pretty Spanish girl to squat on its return and walk past it when she saw it. Juan hadn't met a man yet that could resist the side of Camillah's natural, perfect, heart-shaped ass. He had a feeling Mike B and Jeff would be coming his way, once the word got out about Twan's death. It was no secret that there was bad blood between him and Twan, so it was only right the finger be pointed at him and his team, since whoever was responsible for Twan's death was a mystery. Although he was from El Salvador, his roots were in Plainfield. So he knew enough about dudes in the streets to know that they suited up for war when one of theirs fell, and if they didn't know who did it, they would go off halfcocked, accusing any and everybody.

Juan reached for his .45 automatic from up under the seat and made an attempt to cock his gun and exit his candy coated six-four. Unsuccessful at cocking his weapon back the first go around, Juan realized the Sprite and cough syrup had begun to take an effect on him. The shattering of the glass of his driver's window made him realize just how zoomed he was. He ducked for cover and mashed down onto the gas pedal. The tires spun out for a full three seconds before they gripped the pavement and the six-four shot forward.

Juan ducked down low as Jeff continued to unload on the fleeing car. Within seconds, he was through the red light and nearly four blocks up the street on Madison.

"Yo, let's get the fuck outta here," Mike B yelled as he pulled up on Jeff.

Jeff hopped in the SUV with his smoking gun, and moments later, they too had vanished into thin air. Sirens could be heard wailing in the air as they escaped. As they neared the light, two more Papis appeared out of nowhere and began unloading in their direction. Mike B slammed on the brakes, grabbed his other piece and began returning fire out of the half cracked window, making them dive for cover. The 59 bus had stopped in the middle of the intersection, blocking Mike B's way. He knew staying put would be the death of him and the SUV would soon become his coffin. So he whipped in front of the bus and shot wildly down the narrow street of Madison Avenue.

After dropping Jeff off for the night, Mike B cruised down Seventh Street, observing his surroundings. He hooked a left on Berkman and took the back route to his crib. Nothing out of the ordinary today, but then why should there be. Mike B calculated each step down to a flawless precision. Especially when it came to being around Lenore. He knew his only vulnerable weakness, was her. If he was to be defeated, it was through her, but he was convinced that she was a true rider so that was the least of his worries.

He stopped four houses short of his and checked the leaves behind the gate. Everything was in place, no trespassers.

Mike B, with the help of Jeff, had been putting in work around their city like a thief in the night. Mike B strategically came up with ways of running down on potential guilty parties, but still they were no closer to getting any answers about the murder of his cousin. By now, with

she felt Mike B's boy turn solid and shift to a grinding movement once again. The heat of Mike B's cum filling her melted every muscle and nerve in her body. They stood motionless in the same position for a few seconds, speaking through kisses and showing the pleasure of their orgasm in their posture.

Mike B put her down and switched the water from the shower to the faucet. He stopped the drain and sat against the wall as the tub filled. After getting done in the shower and drying off, Mike B opened the door for Lenore. The direct sight of the bed made her all mushy on the inside again. The room was pitch black except for the candles illuminating the bed and the light for the stereo playing Sade. The closer she got to the bed, she saw the oils, lotions and incense for Mike B's set up. He hugged her from behind and kissed her on the neck. He unwrapped the towel and laid her down on her back, he fluffed up the pillow and placed it behind her head. After lighting the incense, he filled his hand with oil and rubbed her whole body down. He watched the flickers of the candle flames reflect off the shine of her body. He started out rubbing her temples and jaw bones before moving down to her neck and shoulders. He paid special attention to each bicep, forearm, and hand, then reapplied some lotion to her chest and stomach. He gently caressed it into her skin and worked his way down to her legs. He kissed the little hairy patch between her legs and got an inviting thrust from her hips. He smiled as he descended and concentrated on her thighs, rubbing the knots and tension out of them before going down to her shins and feet. He passed up and down her legs in a chopping motion before flipping her over to concentrate on her back and enjoy the sight of her voluptuous ass. He made sure he took his time on the back of her neck, back arms, and back. He was anxious to rub on her ass and didn't want to speed past any muscle. When he got to her ass he applied extra amounts of lotion and oil all up and down her calves. He'd bunch up her ass cheeks in his hand and keep mushing it around and continued that process all the way down to the bottom of her calve and up to her ass cheeks again. Then he'd smooth her ass cheeks out with open palms and squeeze her thigh while splitting the muscle with his thumbs pressed together applying pressure. Again passing the back of her knees to her calves and back up again. Each time his hand brushed past her inner thigh and her wet pussy, he came away with her juices on his hand.

Lenore couldn't contain herself it was all too perfect, What she needed was Mike B to fill her up to make it complete. She was too relaxed to move, so she just parted her legs and remained on her stomach. Mike B filled her up with long slow strokes, massaging her pussy with his dick. He came around with his hand and rubbed her clit at the same time, kissing and sucking on her neck and back. Lenore's body was asking for this for so long that it wasn't long before she was feeling her nerves go numb and if it was possible, her body reaching a level of relaxation that made her feel like she was melting. Mike B wasn't selfish. He eased back and let Lenore dictate the rhythm she preferred, letting her get the full pleasure out of her orgasm.

They continued at it for the next few hours. Kissing, sucking, scratching, and most of all cumming. They resembled a couple trying to squeeze into each other and become one. In Mike B's mind, that was the overall goal. He wished he could've been attached to Lenore forever.

Mike B lay in bed watching the rhythm of Lenore's breathing rise and fall. She was wrapped all over him so he couldn't sneak out like he had been doing nearly every night.

She was the only thing that reminded him that he was not the monster he was acting like out in the streets. He looked down at her. At that moment, he felt like the luckiest man alive. He threw his free hand behind his head and stared up at the ceiling. An image of his cousin appeared on the off white ceiling. Mike B closed and opened his eyes. When he did, the image still rested over top of him. He slammed his lids shut for a second time. He could hear his cousin Twan's voice in his head. *Get them muthafuckas for me, cuz,* echoed in his mind. Mike B's eyes shot back open. He looked down at Lenore for a second time.

Moving snail like, he eased his arm from up under Lenore's head and literally fell out of the bed and onto the floor, careful not to wake her. In five minutes flat, he was dressed. He didn't feel right laying up or around doing nothing, while his cousin's killer was still roaming and running around in the town. But on the other hand, he was tired. He tried to fight it, but his eyes began to feel heavy. He knew his body needed to recuperate. He'd been up for seventy-two hours now. *A couple hours of sleep won't hurt*, he thought as he drifted off to the sounds of Meek Mill.

The sunrise peeked through the blinds, resting on Mike B's face. He got up and went to freshen up and shower with Lenore right behind him. Twenty minutes later, he was showered and dressed. Lenore was in the kitchen setting the table and getting her cook on. The food smelled delicious and before Mike B knew it, he was at the table with the same look the puppies had in anticipation of eating.

"Why you looking like that?" Lenore asked with a smile on her face.

"Because a brother hungry." Mike B rubbed his belly.

"Who you rushing?" Lenore was pouring coffee and juice and also serving the food. "Don't think about touching that food until I'm at the table with you."

"Yeah, okay," Mike B said as Lenore put other last pan in the sink. "Come here. You're not going to torture me!" He pulled Lenore to his lap, as she giggled with little resistance.

"What you going to eat, me?" Lenore asked, kissing Mike B.

"Don't tempt me. You look just as delicious as this food."

Lenore casually strolled over to her chair, teasing Mike B by taking her time. As soon as she sat down, he started digging at the food like he was in a race.

"Slow down, negro. It ain't goin' nowhere." Lenore slyly remarked.

Coming up for air, Mike B peered up at her and smiled. "My bad, babe, but I gotta go. I told Jeff."

"I know." Lenore nodded and grimaced.

Mike B scarfed down the remainder of his food and stood. He walked over to Lenore.

"This shit will all be over soon enough," he expressed. "I can't let these jokers think they can violate out here in these streets, especially me and my squad, and think ain't nothing gonna happen," Mike B explained.

"I know, I get it," she solemnly replied.

"I know you do, babe. That's why I fucks with you." Mike B threw his arms around Lenore. "You my rider. I love you." He kissed her on the side of her face.

Lenore flashed a half of smile and puckered her lips. "I love you too."

Chapter Six

"Did you see that shit on the news?" Denise asked as she focused on folding her Victoria's Secret thongs and placing them in the top dresser draw of her dresser.

"Yeah, I saw it," Lenore confirmed.

"Jeff came home looking all spaced the hell out and hyped. I tried to ask him what happened, but he didn't want to talk about it. He just kept pacing back and forth saying, fuck them bean eatin' muthafuckas. I think he was high," Denise admitted.

"Yeah, Mike B just came in took a shower and went to sleep. I knew something happened, just didn't know what. This morning, he told me he had to get rid of the Range. I didn't even ask why, but I figured something happened." Lenore rebutted. "But, you think Jeff was high?"

"Come on now, you know I been around him and it enough to know when somebody fucking around," Denise reminded her. "Plus, lately this muthafucka be going for hours, when on his best, fifteen minutes and he's out like the bedroom lights," she chuckled. "At first I thought he was fuckin' with some other bitches, but it's definitely the drugs. Nigga be fucking the shit outta me with the dope dick."

"Girl, you shot out." Lenore joined her in a light chuckle.

"Well, outside of weed, I know Mike B not messing around like that. And like I told you time and time again, he a beast in the bed. Even last night, he did some fly romantic shit and we got it in for hours," Lenore bragged.

"Okay, bitch, you don't have throw it up in my face, unless you sharing. You already know I share." Denise laughed again, but was serious at the same time.

"Anyway, moving right along." Lenore side stepped and ignored her comment. "So, shit really started hitting the fan." She switched subjects, referring to what they believed to be Mike B and Jeff's handiwork on the news.

"Yup, I guess so. A few weeks from now, this shit will have come to a head. And when it does, we're not gonna be nowhere near it."

"I'm with you on that, girl," Lenore agreed.

"Yeah, but on another note, Jeff told me he came up with something. Said he'd fill me in on it later. I'll let you know when he lets me know," Denise added.

"Okay," was all Lenore answered. But in her mind, she had so much more she wanted to say.

The vibration of her phone caused Lenore to look at her screen. When she removed it from her ear, she instantly recognized the unsaved number.

"Hey, I gotta take this call, but I'll either see you or talk to you later."

"Okay, bitch, you better."

"Bitch, bye."

Lenore laughed and clicked over.

Chapter Seven

Denise knew that Jeff had been busy and why, but she had a serious problem with not being able to hide her feelings. A bit of a brat at times, she was stubborn and wanted what she wanted, when she wanted it. The frustration of not being able to have him around when she wanted him was really starting to get on her nerves. Although he had constantly reminded her of the bigger picture, still she didn't like how things were going lately. She blamed it on a lack of satisfaction. Jeff was handling his business in the streets but not in their bedroom, since he and Mike B had gone on a rampage. She smashed the speakerphone button to hang up, turned around with a visible attitude plastered on her face. She stomped over to the island picking up the bottle of water, took a drink, and then headed up the back stairs. She went down a long hallway lined with art, then through French doors and into her bedroom.

Their master bedroom was huge, at least 1,000 square feet, mostly decorated in white, much like the suite she and Jeff stayed in at the Caesar's Palace out in Las Vegas, which was Denise's favorite getaway spot being as though she was a West Coast chick. There was a flat screen above the fireplace that was double sided so it could be watched while in the bathroom as well. She grabbed the remote control and turned on the fireplace and the music. Denise entered the bathroom and started running water for a bath.

"I need to take a bath to calm myself down," she said to herself.

The marble tub was oversized and could easily seat four. There were beautiful bottles of bath extras all around the tub along with candles, white towels and washcloths, and a flat screen TV on the wall, above the tub. From the ceiling hung a Swarovski crystal chandelier, which looked like a smaller version of the one hanging in the entryway.

Denise reached across the tub for a crystal bottle marked Jasmine and poured two capfuls into the bath water, then grabbed a washcloth and threw it into the running water. While the bath was running, she entered an oversized, walk-in closet where everything was categorized by color and season. One wall from top to bottom was nothing but shoes. This closet looked like it came straight out of *MTV Cribs*, just as the house did.

Forgetting the fact that she was running a bath, she rushed back into the bathroom just in time to turn off the water. She undressed and climbed into her perfect bath.

"Oooooooooohhhh," Denise moaned as she entered the water.

She laid back and closed her eyes. There was no better feeling to her than lying in the hot tub with the music on. She remembered as a child, watching old movies and seeing beautiful women of all shapes, sizes, and colors in their luxurious bathtubs. She would tell herself repeatedly that one day, that would be her. Looking at what the characters on television had was one of the only reason Denise watched movies, other than wanting to be an actress herself. Each show or movie that she watched gave her the inspiration that she needed to imagine achieving the lifestyle she dreamed of living. School was not her thing, so she needed to choose a career that did not require a degree. Now, she was so thankful that she accomplished everything she always said she would, including what she had been dreaming about since she was fifteen years old.

Denise was in her place of meditation; the warm bath was caressing her body in all the right places. Suddenly, she felt cold water hit her breasts. She shot straight up and opened her eyes. It was Jeff, standing over her laughing.

But Denise was not laughing. "Are you stupid?" she screamed at him. "Do you think that's funny?" Jeff put his head and his cup down.

"Bae, I'm sorry, I was just playing."

"You need to think of a better thing to do next time. Playing was fun, and that was not fun or funny to me." Denise grabbed her towel and got out of the bathtub. She walked into the glass shower screaming. "What are you doing here anyway? I thought you had somewhere to be. Aren't you working again today?" she asked sarcastically.

Jeff shook his head and smirked. "Yeah, I'm working today. But I'm taking my lunch break early." A grin appeared across his face.

He stepped into the shower and moved in close to Denise. She stood on her tippy toes to wrap her arms around his neck. He pulled her in tighter. Her breasts pressed against his chest and her nipples hardened as she began kissing him passionately.

The shower was oversized with two shower heads. There was more than enough room for the both of them. The showerhead behind Jeff was spraying water all over him causing his dark skin to glisten. Denise was trying her best to avoid the spray, not wanting to get her hair wet.

Even though Jeff pissed her off at times, that was part of what she liked about him. She never knew what to expect. She could feel his long hard rod pressing up against her pelvic bone while they kissed. The longer his length grew, the more her secretions ran between her inner thighs. She felt butterflies in her stomach from the anticipation.

Before she knew it, he was lifting her up and guiding himself inside of her. The penetration of his length made Denise gasp for air, arch her back, and lean her head back just a little too far. The second shower head installed directly behind her rained down on the freshly pressed hair she was trying so hard to save. Denise let out a sigh when the water ran down her face realizing that her hair had to have gotten wet. But she didn't care anymore. Jeff had her moaning loud, as if this sex was fifty times better than the bath, she was just taking. It had been a while since he had sexed her with such authority and conviction. *He gotta be high,* she thought. But at that moment she didn't care. He left no inch of her body untouched; always starting with her ear then working his way to the nape of her neck, and then onto her Hershey's Kiss shaped nipples. Jeff knew her nipples were her erogenous zones so he paid extra special attention to them. From the time they first began having sex, she always had multiple orgasms and then it fizzled out. But whenever he was high, he sexed her like he used to. Subconsciously, she told herself the reason she probably stayed with him was that she loved the feeling and got off watching the fluid explode from her body. Jeff wasn't the best lover she had ever had, but when he was on, his lovemaking session was on point.

After Denise had reached her third explosion, Jeff let her down, spun her around, spread her ass cheeks, and began to thrust himself deeply into her, with long rough strokes. Denise was holding onto the shower wall trying to run from him but to no avail. Jeff was in a zone now and nothing could break his focus. His mouth was open, his moans were hard and his pumps were rabbit like as he gripped Denise's petite waist. Denise could feel his legs shaking and the pattern change in his strokes she knew he had hit his peak. Jeff began to kiss up and down her back as he caressed her outer thighs. Denise held on to the shower walls as she tried to match his rhythm. When she felt his juices spraying her inner walls and him collapse onto her back a smile came over her face as she looked over her shoulder at him. Jeff noticed her movement and looked up at her. They both broke out into laughter from the intense sex scene. He glanced over at the digital clock.

"Just in time. Mike B should be here any minute."

Denise rolled her eyes.

"Come on baby, don't start. I just gave you a stress reliever." He joked but was serious.

"Whatever," she dismissed him with the wave of a hand.

"No, it's not whatever," Jeff corrected. The irritation could be heard in his tone. "We've gone over this already," he reminded her. "You know what I'm trying do. And this is the only way it can be done. Once I let Mike B know I got info on the nigga responsible for Twan's murder, this shit is gonna come to an end."

Denise shook her head in agreement.

The sound of the ringing doorbell caught both of their attention.

Jeff leaned over and kissed her. "Trust me, I got this." he flashed her all thirty-two of his God given teeth.

"Make it happen baby," she smiled.

Jeff returned her smile and made his way into the living room.

"Who is it?" he called out of force of habit.

He already knew who it was, which is why he was already making his way to the door.

"It's me."

“What’s good, my boy?” Jeff met Mike B with a hug.

Mike B immediately caught the stern facial expression Jeff bore.

“What it do, my nigga?” Mike B returned the hug.

Jeff stepped to the side and let his partner enter. He waited for Mike B to make his way to the couch before he went into why they needed to meet this morning.

Mike B watched as Jeff plopped down in his recliner. He could tell his friend was itching to say something. He knew him like a book. Rather than ask, he waited until Jeff decided to tell him.

Jeff began nodding, he clapped his hands together.

“I know who the bitch-ass nigga was that violated, bruh,” Jeff spat abruptly.

Mike B eyes widened as if he had just seen a ghost. “Who?”

He badly wanted to know. His adrenaline had gone from zero to one hundred in a matter of a millisecond. He could feel his jaws tightening as he waited for Jeff to announce the name of the person he would soon be responsible for putting in the dirt.

“First, let me tell you how I found out it was this nigga,” Jeff stated.

Mike B nodded, although he felt the name was more important than how he came across it.

“So check, Denise and Lenore were out at Hugo’s at Karaoke last Tuesday.”

The mentioning of his girlfriend caused Mike B to raise an eyebrow. At that moment, he became more interested in the story than the name. He was eager to know how his girl’s name was tied in to the person responsible for killing Twan.

Jeff could see the puzzled look on Mike B’s face.

“Relax, nigga. Baby girl ain’t got nothing to do with this shit.” He let out a light chuckle. “But they’re the ones who found out who was behind it.”

Mike B was more confused than ever. “Bruh, stop beating around the bush and talkin’ in riddles. What’s good?” Mike B was not in the mood for charades.

Jeff shook his head. “You right, my bad big bruh. Bottom line is this, some li’l chick from the east end that get her hair done where Denise and Lenore go was up in Hugo’s. According to them, this chick comes over to where they sittin’ with their bottle and invites herself to a seat. You know Denise, she ready to pop off on the li’l chick. But the bitch start complimenting the both of them on how pretty they are, so on and so forth and says it’s her birthday. They offer her a drink, one turns into two and the next thing you know, she copping another bottle. Denise said she peeps the broads clutch and she was loaded, so she wound up asking her what she did for a living. This bitch start running her mouth. Talking about, she doesn’t do shit but stay fly and fuck with niggas that can appreciate her fly. She said she just start going in, bringing up the last nigga that she used to be fucking with on the low in the city, until he started beating her ass. Denise said, then out of the blue, she started pillow talkin’ about what a muthafucka supposed to been bragging about over the phone to somebody. Apparently, he was poppin’ off at the gums about a young boy he had to lay down from Third last week.”

Mike B listened attentively. He had already begun to start following Jeff’s point.

“We been in these streets, my nigga. The only young nigga from Third that got pushed is Twan.”

Mike B grimaced as he nodded and rocked on the couch. He had been siting erect the whole time Jeff was telling the story.

“So, who’s the nigga?” Mike B asked for a second time.

Jeff stared at him for a moment. Then out of nowhere, a snarl appeared across his face.

“My archenemy.”

Chapter Eight

Mike B's mind was flooded with all types of thoughts the whole ride home. He played back the story Jeff had run down to him about who was behind the murder of his younger cousin. The name resonated in his mind. He knew the name all too well, just as he was all too familiar with the bad blood. He knew how much Jeff despised the owner of the name he had been given. As he listened, he weighed up the validity of the source and the story. Realizing that they had been running down on the wrong people and still got nowhere, Mike B was growing tiresome of it all. They had been shooting dudes in the legs and asses, looking for answers, but this was a different story. Mike B's agenda was to kill the person responsible for his cousin Twan's death. He knew there were casualties in war, but he just wanted to be sure he was killing the right person. Although Jeff was considered to be his right hand, after seeing him sniffing the drug that day, he felt he had to double check everything that Jeff brought his way. But the fact that Jeff mentioned his ride or die chick was present when the information was obtained, he felt Jeff's story was solid. Mike B made a mental note to ask Lenore why she hadn't come to him with the info herself, the way Denise had with Jeff. But now that he had a name and a face, Mike B was already contemplating when and where he intended to get justice for his cousin.

Chapter Nine

Three days later. Early Friday morning.

"Wake up, muthafucka!" a voiced boomed and echoed throughout the secluded area of Greenbrook Park.

A forceful slap accompanied the words. The blow delivered across the face of the man who laid sprawled out in the knee deep bloodstained snow brought him back to consciousness.

The man's eyes shot open. He gasped for air. After taking a deep and long breath, the bleeding man tried to regain his vision. Blood shot out of his mouth as he let out a painful sounding cough. Although he couldn't see it, he could taste the salty, thick liquid fighting its way back down his throat passage. He could feel the blood that managed to escape his mouth freezing up on his face from the winter chill. Trying to lift himself up with his elbows, he still fought to clear his blurry eyes as he attempted to focus on the two images that stood over him. He was stopped by a pressing foot in his chest.

"What the fuck you think you doing? Lay your bitch ass still," a voice and the owner of black Gortex boot planted in his chest growled.

The sound of a cocking gun followed the threat.

A chill ran through the man's body as snow from the boot managed to find its way in the unzipped top part of his jacket. His teeth began to chatter from the coldness as the snow dissolved into liquid. It melted, seeping through his Polo sweater, tee, and wife beater, until it reached his bare chest. His heart rate quickened from the cold snow turned water, as it trickled downward.

The owner of the boot raised his foot from off of the chest of the man he and his partner had abducted. Gaining better balance, he plunged his boot back into the man's chest again, only this time, he put more of his weight behind it. The impact nearly caved the man's chest in.

The bleeding man's body was already stiff and sore. Still, he managed to tense up in an attempt to minimize the pain he believed it would cause. The assault had only added to the pain he had already felt. He was torn between that, and the cold running through his entire body from laying in the snow for God only knows how long. He was still somewhat in a daze from the previous blows he had received that had knocked him unconscious. The cold made it difficult for him to think straight. He wasn't sure whether he was freezing due to the snow he felt underneath him or because he was simply bleeding to death. His senses were now on high alert. For the life of him, he couldn't figure out why he was in the predicament he was in, nor could he narrow down who was behind it. He recalled having a few run-ins and minor altercations with a few dudes in recent months, but nothing so major that it would warrant someone wanting to kidnap him or possibly want him dead, he believed.

Had it not been for the black, North Face jacket and the insulated socks he wore under his beef and broccoli, Timberland boots, he was sure he may have frozen to death. He remembered seeing on the news before he had stepped outside that the temperature was in the low thirties. As cold as it was that early morning, he had doubled back inside the building and retrieved his gloves. But none of that mattered now. The only thing that mattered was that when he opened his eyes, he saw silhouettes of the barrels of two guns pointed at him by two blurred images. They stood to the left and right of him. He knew that death could very well be his final fate. Especially, since he noticed neither of the two men wore masks.

At first Greg Livingston, known as Gee-Live to everyone in the street, couldn't make out the images of the two faces that stood before him. He was still somewhat distorted from the blow he had taken to the back of the head. The last thing he remembered was coming out of building 540 where he could often be found around his housing projects. He was heading toward the back where he had parked his Suburban. His intentions were to head out to New York for the day. The twenty stacks that lined his pockets was strictly for shopping, balling out in one of the city's known strip clubs and whatever else the night had instore for him. He had packed an overnight bag and had no intentions on returning back to New Jersey that night. But his plans were changed, rather interrupted when he grabbed the driver's door handle after hitting the alarm and power locks on his key chain.

From there, everything else was a blur. Gee-Live had blacked out. Judging by the throbbing pain on the left side of his head and the two gun men who stood over him, it was self-explanatory what had taken place.

Gee-Live could feel himself choking on his own blood. He made a second attempt to try to sit up by using what little strength he possessed as he tried to collect both his vision and thoughts, only to be knocked back down by the foot of one of his assailants.

"Nigga, don't make me blow your fuckin' face off. I told you before to lay your bitch ass down!" spat Jeff.

Ever since they had gotten the word that Gee-Live from the projects was who they were looking for, Jeff had been itching to slump the kid he hated with a passion. It took a whole lot of reasoning and sternness for Mike B to prevent him from killing Gee-Live when they first rolled down on him. Jeff was assured that he would get his wish when the time was right. Mike B knew how much Jeff disliked Gee-Live. The animosity and tension between the two stemmed back to their childhood before Mike B and Jeff were even a team. Jeff was originally from the New Projects, the same projects as Gee-Live. They had practically grown up together. From what Jeff had told Mike B, for as long as he could remember, Gee-Live was very competitive in any and everything he got involved in. Whether in school or in the neighborhood, from sports to girls. Jeff was the total opposite. He was more of a get by type of dude, like an average Joe, but he didn't mind how Gee-Live was because that was his boy, his friend and ace-boon-coon, up until the time they both decided to experiment in the drug game, for similar but different reasons. Gee-Live's was because his mother couldn't afford to keep buying him all the latest fashion which he had become accustomed to. Jeff's reason was because his mother simply couldn't afford to buy him anything, at all. So, they decided to get down together. To get on, they stole a couple stashes from some of the careless hustlers around their projects, who made the mistake of stashing the packages and taking their eyes off of them one minute too long. That's when the problems started to occur. Initially, the two of them had jumped into the game head first as partners, fifty/fifty. But as time progressed and money started rolling in, Gee-Live, being the competitive individual that he was, sometimes spent more than his share of their weekly take. That bothered Jeff. He confronted Gee-Live about his spending habits. Gee-Live assured him that he'd slow down and make it up to him. Jeff was cool with it and everything was back to business as usual. That is, until the next problem arose.

Because Gee-Live liked to dress and party so much, Jeff felt it necessary to at least step his wardrobe up and start hitting the scene with him being as though they were a team. But unbeknownst to him, everyone was under the impression that he actually worked for Gee-Live. At least that's what one of the girls he took to the Loop Inn Motel one night after a party, told him. At first, it hadn't registered to him what the girl actually said until she was asked to repeat herself.

"I said, Gee-Live treat you better than a lot of other niggas treat their workers."

Jeff laughed hysterically and asked the girl what made her think that he worked for Gee-Live.

"That's what he tells everybody," she stated going on to say how Gee-Live always bragged about his boy Jeff being a go-getter and how he keeps his pockets laced.

Hearing the girl's words had Jeff fuming. For some reason, he believed the girl because she had no reason to fabricate such a story. Jeff felt like he had just been shot in the heart by his best friend. He had been nothing but a loyal friend and partner to Gee-Live, and in return his kindness had been taken for granted and as a weakness. For all Jeff knew, his reputation in the streets was nothing more than being Gee-Live's flunky, and the thought of his man playing him like that infuriated him more. Jeff cut his night short with the young, tender redbone that had given him information that was more valuable than she could ever imagine. Just before she got out of his rental car, he handed her three hundred dollars.

"What's this for?" the girl had asked, puzzled.

"You deserve that. Get yourself something nice," replied Jeff as he pulled off.

After making it to the projects in record time, Jeff had confronted Gee-Live about what was told to him by the girl. Needless to say Gee-Live took the nonchalant approach and laughed it off. Neither denying or admitting the allegations, his laughter was enough to convince Jeff of the evident. Jeff shot a quick, short but effective right hook to Gee-Live's jaw, knocking the smile clean off of his face. A fight erupted. Massive punches were thrown. Punches turned into grabbing as the two friends continued tearing up the little two-bedroom apartment. Gee-Live was very athletic and strong for his size, but he was no match for Jeff, who was naturally cock strong. As they tussled, somehow Jeff got up under Gee-Live gaining good position. All in one motion, he scooped him up off of his feet and dirt slammed him, while coming down on top of him.

"You fake-ass nigga!" barked Jeff.

He choked Gee-Live with both hands.

Gee-Live lay there helplessly.

"If I ever hear you breathe my name again or even look at me sideways, I'll kill your punk ass!" threatened Jeff.

What he wasn't aware of, was that he was already close to taking Gee-Live's life. The pressure he applied was cutting off his air passage. Had it not been for Gee-Live's mother coming in from her sunrise service at church, Jeff may have surely caught a body that day. Hearing his name caused him to release Gee-Live's throat and climb off of top of him.

He got up and walked out the door, leaving Gee-Live's mother standing there bewildered at him lying on the floor gasping for air. That was the last time the two had ever come in contact with one another.

It wasn't until three months later that he and Mike B linked up after Jeff's hooptie had stalled on him in New York. He had just purchased an eighth of a kilo of crack and couldn't afford to get caught out of pocket by NYPDs finest or risk taking the train back to Jersey, knowing police accompanied by K-9s would be floating through Newark Penn Station.

Mike B saw Jeff and offered to give him a jump, thinking that his battery had died out on him. Mike B knew who Jeff was because he made it his business to know all the people in his town that either got money or did stick-ups. His motto was, know your surroundings. From what he knew about Jeff, it was enough to decide to help him despite the fact that he himself was dirty, traveling with ten ounces of coke. Had it been the other way around, he would have wanted someone to shoot him some bail too, and based on the reputation that Jeff had in the streets of their hometown as being a good dude, there was no doubt in Mike B's mind that Jeff would have done the same for him.

Realizing that it wasn't the battery, Jeff left his hooptie and rode back to Jersey with Mike B. And just like that, the two hit it off. Merging Jeff's new spot with Mike B's old one, the two became a team along with Mike B's younger cousin, Twan. That was seven years ago.

Now, Jeff was faced with his archenemy, once again. Gee-Live had violated, according to the rules of the game.

Gee-Live fell back into the snow as his vision began to clear. The first voice he heard when he first regained consciousness was unfamiliar to him, but the second one who had just kicked him back down again was unmistakably familiar to him the second time he spoke.

"Jeff?" he asked surprised as he now gained his full eyesight back.

Without having to look over to his right, he knew the other party involved was Jeff's new right hand man, Mike B.

Disgusted by his name being said by Gee-Live, Jeff ran down on him and grabbed him by the throat. He forced the silencer of his 9 mm Beretta in Gee-Live's mouth. He shoved the gun so hard into Gee-Live's mouth that it knocked his two front teeth out. "Didn't I fuckin' tell you if I ever hear you spit my name again, fuckboy, I'd kill you!"

Gee-Live's eyes widened as blood leaked from his mouth. Seeing Jeff again put him in a state of panic, remembering Jeff's words clearly as if it were yesterday.

For years, Gee-Live had gone out his way to avoid Jeff, as the two came up in the game. He contemplated many of times about having Jeff killed, especially since he heard how Jeff's guns had been going off like crazy. He always believed that it was just a matter of time before Jeff's guns were directed at him. But still, he couldn't bring himself to go through with it. Truth be told, despite how he shitted on him back in the day, he still had love for Jeff. But for not going with his first instinct, he was now faced with his biggest nightmare coming back to haunt him. He knew the right thing to do was to swallow his pride, put his ego to the side, and apologize for disrespecting his former right hand man. Instead, he let them drift apart and never spoke Jeff's name again, good or bad. Since then, they had seen each other in passing and in local spots, but never said a word to the other.

His only question now was, why? For the life of him he couldn't think of anything he had done to Jeff, or Mike B for that matter, who he had figured had to be the other gunman, because the two had been inseparable for the past seven years. Why was he in the predicament he was in, he wanted to know. He knew Mike B was a money getter and had a reputation for being a force to be reckoned with. He had never done business with him personally, he was sure of and to his knowledge, he doubted if he had bumped heads with Mike B or Jeff when it came to females.

Gee-Live's eyes widened as Jeff squeezed the side of his face with his left hand and stuck the barrel of his gun deeper inside of his mouth.

"Yo, Jay, chill," said Mike B placing his hand on Jeff's shoulder.

Against his better judgment, Jeff let up off of Gee-Live who was grateful for Mike B intervening.

Gee-Live figured that he had a better shot at saving his life by trying to clear up what he had to be a case of mistaken identity or a misunderstanding, because he was now 100 percent positive that he had done no wrong or spoke no vain to or about Jeff or Mike B.

"Mike B—Mike B, what's good? What I do?" asked Gee-Live almost in a crying manner, referring to Mike B by his street name.

Despite that, an instant smirk came across Mike B's face. If looks could kill, Gee-Live would already be dead. The murderous look in Mike B's eyes was enough to make Gee-Live second guess his decision to choose dealing with Mike B over Jeff. Whatever he was being accused of, Gee-Live knew that it was some heavy shit, judging by the facial expressions both Mike B and Jeff wore.

Mike B expected Gee-Live to play stupid, thinking that to be his best bet. It didn't matter though because today, there was nothing he could do or say to convince Mike B to change what he had already decided to be the final outcome of their encounter.

"Yo, don't insult my intelligence nigga," Mike B advised. He erased the smirk off of his face. "You know what the fuck this is about."

Gee-Live gave Mike B a puzzling look. Had he known why he was laying in the snow, bleeding from the back of the head, with two guns pointed in his face, and his life in jeopardy, he probably wouldn't admit what he had done, but the fact of the matter was that he really had no clue as to what the ordeal was about, not even an inclination.

"Mike B, man that's my word, I don't know what the deal is. I'd never disrespect you kid, let alone cross you," cried out Gee-Live as sincerely as he could.

"Yes, you would, you cross-artist muthafucka!" stated Jeff with conviction. "That's why I don't fuck wit' your bitch ass now! Mike B, let me go 'head and slump this nigga, B," Jeff suggested.

"J, calm down, baby. I got dis," Mike B calmly said, trying to keep his friend at bay.

Jeff was making it real difficult for him.

"Yo! Fuck that! Why you keep babysitting this bitch-made nigga?It's been confirmed that he did it. Ain't nothin' else to talk about. Fuck all this rappin' shit. Body this nigga or let me do it so we can get the fuck up outta here," spat Jeff.

"Do what? What I do?" Gee-Live asked again, hearing Jeff say that it had been confirmed.

He did it, and it's been confirmed, played in Gee-Live's mind. Whatever "it" was he was determined to find out.

By now Mike B was beyond pissed off, both at Jeff's impatience and Gee-Live's dumb role he continued to play. He was tired of playing games with Gee-Live. His only thought and concern now was to get to the bottom of Gee-Live's actions and then make him pay for them with his life.

"Jeff, like I said, calm down, dawg. I got dis," repeated Mike B.

Jeff instantly calmed down. He wasn't afraid of Mike B or in the habit of listening to him, but he knew how emotional the situation was for his friend and he wanted to respect however Mike B chose to handle things.

"Yo, I'ma ask you one time and one time only," Mike B started out with, directing his words to Gee-Live. "What did my cousin do to you?"

The question caught Gee-Live by surprise. To his knowledge, he didn't even know any of Mike B's family, let alone his cousin. He pondered on the question. Gee-Live drew a blank. *Who the fuck is this nigga's cousin?* he asked himself. *And what the fuck he got to do with me?*

The few beefs and altercations he had pending had all been handled and wrapped up. Either they had been resolved, war or peace. No matter the case, Gee-Live was victorious or satisfied with the outcome. He quickly ran through his mental enemy file cabinets, opening up old files of his past and recent street beefs. One in particular stood out. He thought back to the *Courier News* article he had read a few mornings ago. *Oh, shit,* he thought. *That's who he gotta be talkin' about*, Gee-Live concluded. It dawned on him who Mike B was referring to, and a light went on inside his head.

"Who Twan?" he asked nervously, the obvious becoming apparent to him.

"Who else, muthafucka?" intervened Jeff, but Gee-Live ignored Jeff and kept his attention focused on Mike B.

"Come on, M. I know you don't think I had somethin' to do with that. What sense would that make, knowing that that was your peoples and how you get down? I ain't have no beef with Twan, kid," stated Gee-Live, hoping that he sounded convincing enough for Mike B to believe him.

Little did he know, Mike B was already convinced, just not of what Gee-Live would have wanted him to be convinced of.

"So you trying to tell me that you and my cousin ain't have no words a couple of weeks ago at the First Fridays at Venue and he ain't throw no drink in your face at Hugo's after that?" asked Mike B, seeing the surprised look on Gee-Live's face as he spoke the truth.

"Nah, I mean yeah, we had words," Gee-Live managed to get out, fumbling over his words. "But yo, we deaded that shit last week, before he got killed. That shit wasn't about nothin'. I swear to you, B, me and your fam peaced that up, and it wasn't no love lost. That drink shit, I ate that," ended Gee-Live.

Mike B studied Gee-Live as he spoke. Partially what he was saying made sense, but the other part he had never heard before. No one ever said that anything was squashed between Gee-Live and Twan, and both he and Jeff had many ears to the streets. Had it not been for a friend of Jeff's girlfriend that was sleeping with Gee-Live, Mike B and Jeff would have never made mention of it. The girl insisted on remaining anonymous that told Jeff's girl about how Gee-Live obsessed over seeking revenge on Twan. The news was relayed to Mike B's girl, who told him. Because of the valuable information and how he obtained it, Mike B respected the wishes of the anonymous girl and didn't press the issue with his or Jeff's girl to give him a name, especially since her initial stories about the two incidents at First Friday's and Hugo's checked out and were confirmed to have happened.

For his final performance, Gee-Live deserved an Oscar. Had it not been for what he found in Gee-Live's truck, Mike B may have believed him. However, there was no way in the world he would be able to explain how he possessed something that Mike B knew his cousin Twan treasured.

"You squashed the beef, huh?" Mike B asked dryly.

"No doubt! I don't have no reason to lie to you, M."

"You don't have no reason to lie to me, huh?" he repeated Gee-Live's words with that same sarcastic tone.

"Nah dawg, agh!"

Before he could get his words out Mike B shot him in the kneecap.

"So, what the fuck was you doin' with this in your truck? Huh, muthafucka?" he shouted, revealing his cousin's fourteen karat rose gold diamond clustered ring.

You never caught Twan without it on. It was the only piece of gold jewelry that he owned once everyone switched to Platinum. Only Mike B knew the significance behind the ring that everyone wondered why he constantly wore along with his Platinum iced out shines. It had been the last thing his Aunt Dean, who was Twan's mother, had bought Twan before she died and he swore to never take it off as long as he lived. To find it in Gee-Live's Navigator, only told Mike B one thing.

"Mike B—Mike B, please man don't kill me. I swear to God I didn't have nothing to do with Twan's death and I never seen that ring before in my li—"

The two shots ended his words in midsentence. "You don't have a life no more, muthafucka!" spit Mike B, finishing Gee-Live's last word for him as he pumped two in his head with his silenced. 40-caliber.

"Come on J, let's roll," he then turned around and said to Jeff.

"Hold up!"

Jeff stood over Gee-Live and dumped three more shots into his lifeless body then followed up by spitting on him before they fled the scene.

Lenore sat and waited anxiously around the corner in her charcoal grey, E350 Benz. It had been nearly a half an hour since she had arrived at the park and pulled behind her boyfriend's truck. For a minute, she began to worry because this was her first time ever being a part of Mike B's business affairs. When she was asked to play a part in some business he had to handle like the one she knew he was handling today, she was surprised. She was used to being in the house worrying. Now she sat not too far from where Mike B and Jeff were, worrying. Based on what she believed, they were behind schedule. She hoped that nothing had gone wrong. Just as her worry began to really set in, she saw two figures buck the corner, hiking their way toward her direction with snorkel jackets on. She was certain that the two individuals had to be Mike B and Jeff. She adjusted her seat, which was once reclined, and started up the car as they approached. Mike B jumped in the passenger's side of Lenore's Mercedes as Jeff went and hopped in Mike B's Audi.

"What took so long?" a concerned Lenore asked.

"Nothing," was the only response.

She knew that meant he didn't want to talk about it, so she left it at that.

"Here take these. I need you to do what I told you to do with them."

Mike B handed Lenore the two guns he and Jeff just used on Gee-Live. For the past year, Lenore had been Mike B's ride or die chick, and to him she was definitely a rider. He had met her through Jeff's girl, Denise, who Jeff had been with for the past few years. Jeff shared with Mike B how Denise was actually the female that unconsciously pulled his coat to how Gee-Live was telling everybody that he worked for him, which resulted in Jeff splitting with Gee-Live that night and getting down with Mike B months later. From the door, Mike B was feeling Lenore who at the time, had just moved out to Jersey from the West Coast. She possessed all of the qualities that he was attracted to in a woman, both inside and out. She was pretty, had a nice body, knew how to cook, was intelligent both school and street wise, and was a freak in the bed. What attracted Mike B to her the most, was her knowledge of the streets and guns. She was from the hood but wasn't hooded out and that's what he liked.

Lenore knew all there was to know about guns, from taking them apart to filing down serial numbers. She had shared with Mike B how her father was in the military and taught her all about weapons. Her reason for leaving L.A. was due to the fact that she had shot her abusive lover four times in the chest leaving him for dead. Mike B could tell by her eyes that she had seen a lot and been through a lot. It was then that he had vowed to be there for her and in return, she made that same vow, which was why when he got into an altercation at a club one night and a beef erupted, she was the one who shot the dude that Mike B couldn't see coming up on his blind side. When Mike B heard the shot behind him, he turned around and saw the wounded dude laying on the ground and finished him off. That night Lenore got rid of both the one she used and Mike B's gun. She had saved him from going to jail, but most importantly, she had saved his life. Earning a spot in his heart and gaining his trust. From that day forward, Mike B made sure she never wanted for nothing and that she never had to be in the streets again.

"I'll meet you back at the house after I drop Jeff off, a'ight," said Mike B.

He leaned over to give Lenore a kiss, with one hand on the door handle.

"Okay," replied Lenore as they broke their kiss.

Mike B exited the Benz and hopped in his Audi truck. Lenore gave him and Jeff a few minutes head start before she herself pulled off. Like normal, she unlocked her cell phone and called her best friend. *So far so good,* she thought as she scrolled down to Denise's number.

Chapter Ten

"Hello?" Denise answered, sounding cautious seeing the blocked number coming across her caller ID screen. Normally, she didn't answer block numbered calls, but today she made an exception. She figured it was the call she was expecting.

"What's up, ma?" Lenore's voice came through the receiver.

"Hey girl!" Denise replied ecstatic to be hearing Lenore's voice. "Where you at?"

"I'm in the area," responded Lenore, not wanting to give her specific location.

"How'd everything go?" Denise then asked concerned.

"According to plan."

"Where's Mike B and Jeff at?"

"Mike B went to drop Jeff off at his place."

"So how long before you get here?" asked Denise.

"Within the next hour or less, as soon as I take care of a few things I'll be there. Did you take care of what you were supposed to?" asked Lenore.

"Yeah, everything's good on my end. I got it," answered Denise.

"Okay, I'll see you when I get there."

"All right, and Lenore," Denise stopped her before she hung up.

"What's up?"

"I'm glad everything went all right," she said.

"Me too, ma. I'll see you soon."

Chapter Eleven

"Yo, Ja, I'll get at you next day kid. I'm takin' it down for the day, a'ight," said Mike B, parking his SUV in Jeff's, Bridgewater condominium parking lot.

"A'ight, no doubt I'm fallin' back for the day too. I'm probably going to call up Denise and have her come thru, so we can Netflix and chill and shit."

"I feel that. Tell her I said what's up."

Mike B's mind was elsewhere. He was still thinking about what he had just done. Normally he wouldn't even think twice when it came to putting in work. But something about Gee-Live and the way he was acting didn't sit right with him. He was expecting a different reaction than what Gee-Live had offered. True, he had killed the man he believed to be responsible for killing his little cousin, but Gee-Live's denying it was what had Mike B somewhat disturbed. From what all he knew about him, Mike B couldn't believe that Gee-Live had went out without a fight, or at least popping shit. He was known for boasting and bragging so his pleading, begging, and denial behavior didn't add up to Mike B. *Why the fuck would he not fess up if he knew I was gonna push him anyway?* Mike B pondered.

"Yo?" Jeff's voice snapped him out of his trance.

Mike B wiped his face with both his hands. "My bad, dawg. My mind just drifted."

"To what, nigga?"

He peered over at his friend oddly.

"Nothing. Shit ain't about nothin'." Mike B brushed the thought off.

Jeff shrugged. "Yeah, no question. Tell sis I said what up too, I'll holla back," said Jeff, hopping out of the Audi.

"Will do."

"Cool. One." The two men dapped each other.

"Catch you later." Mike B offered.

Jeff nodded. "Get you some rest, my dude. You seem out of it." Jeff suggested right before he reached for the passenger's door handle. Seconds later, he was out of the SUV, heading toward his condo.

Mike B backed out of the parking space and pulled off as the latest bass track knocked in his factory system. "I roll me a blunt then I sit and I meditate, so many snakes in the grass, I don't walk, I just levitate."

He sang along with the chorus as he navigated his way toward Route 22 East highway and headed back to Plainfield.

Chapter Twelve

Knock! Knock! Knock!

Her knuckles rattled on the door in rapid succession. She paused then knocked two more times. On the fifth knock, Lenore could hear the safety latch being taken off from the other side. It wasn't that Denise hadn't heard the first three, because she did. The knocks could have come from anyone she believed. But the second set of knocks was her way of knowing who was on the other side of the door. It was their own secret knock that only the two of them knew about. Had the second set of knocks been any different, Denise would have known that something was wrong and would have known what to do. The two of them had discussed and had their routine down pact.

Lenore waited patiently for Denise to open the door. When it finally opened, Denise stood there in a white wife beater and a pair of black boxer briefs that hugged her hips and rode up in between her inner vanilla thighs. Lenore stood there for a few seconds before she entered the apartment. Denise gave her a suspicious look, wondering why she was standing there the way she was. Neither of the two girls spoke a word. They just stared at one another. Then all of a sudden, a smile came across Lenore's face, breaking the ice.

"Come here," commanded Denise with open arms.

Lenore stepped inside the apartment and embraced Denise. She closed the door behind her with her foot, wrapping her arms around Denise's waist. Palming two hands full of her ass as the two of them passionately kissed.

Denise parted her lips and opened her mouth as Lenore's pierced tongue explored the inside. As their tongues intertwined, Lenore pulled Denise into her closer by the hips as if they were one, causing their breasts to touch, pressing up against one another as their pelvises touched as well. Feeling the heat coming off of Denise's body was driving Lenore crazy as she released one of Denise's ass cheeks with one hand and placing it inside of the boxer briefs Denise wore.

"Damn, you wet," whispered Lenore who had broken their lip lock and was now seductively kissing and sucking on Denise's left ear as she massaged Denise's pierced clitoris with two fingers.

"You got me like this baby," Denise moaned.

She knew how to turn Lenore on. The two of them had been lovers for the past six years off and on. Ever since Denise had moved out to L.A. where she met Lenore. At the time, Lenore was in a relationship with another female who was very possessive over her. After meeting Denise, she somehow managed to find time to spend with her and instantly fell in love with her. One particular night when Lenore thought that her lover would be gone for the evening, she snuck Denise over to her house. Unbeknownst to her, her lover suspected something and set Lenore up, catching them in the bed together. Lenore's lover pistol whipped Denise then threw her out of the house naked. She then beat Lenore half to death. It was because of that, Denise returned back to Jersey just as it was because of that, Lenore had worked up the nerve to shoot her lover after being severely beaten again when she stated that she wanted to be with Denise.

Lenore continued to kiss and suck on Denise's body, trailing her tongue and lips down from her ear, to her neck, then from her collarbone to the cleavage of her breast.

"Did you do what we said?" asked Lenore through the kisses that she planted between Denise's breasts.

"Yeah, it's all on the bed," Denise replied in a seductive manner.

With that, Lenore grabbed the bottom of Denise's wife beater and lifted it over her head, revealing her coconut shaped breasts. Denise raised her arms to assist, and then she too began undressing Lenore.

Within seconds, the two of them stood in the nude. Again Lenore kissed Denise, gently, letting her tongue roam the outer part of Denise's lips, as she scooped Denise's 115 pound. frame up by her thighs. Denise wrapped her legs around Lenore's waist as she was carried to the bedroom. When they reached the room, Lenore's inner thighs began to moisten at the sight of the bed. She carried Denise over and laid her on top of all the money scattered on the bed that Denise had taken from Gee-Live's house. Denise scooted up on the bed. Some of the hundred dollar bills began to cling to her skin. She parted her legs then grabbed two hands full of the money and poured it all over her breasts. That turned Lenore on. She climbed on the bed, slithering her way up to Denise, climbing on top of her. With Lenore's honey tone skin and Denise's milky cream tone, the two favored a caramel fudge sundae together. Now that Denise's breasts were fully exposed, Lenore began sucking on her nipples, letting her tongue ring roll around each nipple. Denise massaged Lenore's shoulders as her tongue continued to explore her body. With each kiss and touch, Lenore had Denise in a world of ecstasy, sending a million different sensations through her entire body. By the time Lenore's lips reached the final destination, Denise was soaking wet. She was so turned on behind fulfilling her fantasy of wanting to make love on riches, that she climaxed twice before Lenore's mouth even touched her clit. As soon as Lenore brushed her tongue across Denise's clit, Denise's body shuddered. Knowing that she had brought Denise to an instant orgasm, Lenore shifted her body. She climbed on top of Denise upside down, straddling her in a 69 position, giving Denise easy access to her love box. Without hesitation, Denise began to make love to Lenore's pussy with her mouth. For the next hour Denise and Lenore spent their time bringing each other oral pleasure. After multiple orgasms, the two of them stretched out on top of the money with one another's juices and perspiration all over their bodies, exhausted from their lovemaking.

Realizing that time was of the essence, Lenore began to get up off of the money filled bed.

"We have to get up," she stated. "We still got something's to take care of before our flight."

"I know," said Denise now raising up from off the bed. "I'm going to jump in the shower right quick, get all the money together and put it back in the suitcase."

"A'ight, I'll be in the shower as soon as I'm done."

"Okay," Lenore smiled, walking to the shower.

"How much is it anyway?" she stopped and asked.

"A little under a hundred bands," answered Denise.

"Not bad. Not bad at all," Lenore stated with a smile.

Denise returned the smile. "All in a day's work."

The two of them shared a laugh.

"All right, handle your business ma. Oh! I almost forgot, make that call."

"I'm on it." Denise wasted no time retrieving the burner phone she had on top of the nightstand.

Chapter Thirteen

Despite the fact that it was only a twenty minute drive from Jeff's crib to Mike B's, it was a long drive for him due to the slickness of the highway roads. Mike B's truck had top of the line tires, but they were no match for Mother Nature. The closer he got to his town, the nastier Route 22 seemed. Because of the city's negligence, ice blanketed the streets and piles of slush covered the side of the road. Along the way, Mike B by passed two accidents, thanking his lucky stars that he himself was able to merge on to the highway thus far, and at the same, time cursed the city for their laziness. As he continued to drive, a smile appeared on his face seeing the sign that read: ENTERING PLAINFIELD.

He was glad to be reaching his destination shortly. As he was coming up on the exit he passed a state police car that sat on the right shoulder. Paying the car no mind, knowing that he was riding legit, Mike B put on his right turn signal, bearing off to the right. As he turned on to the exit, he noticed the blue flashing lights glaring in his rearview mirror, and wondered why on the world was he being pulled over.

"Un—fuckin—believable," he cursed to himself, convinced that the police officer who had just pulled him over was either racial profiling because he was young and black with a truck that cost more than the cop made in two years, or he was just being a dick on a cold, wintry day.

Mike B pulled over alongside of the street and threw his truck in park as the police car pulled behind him. As the door of the police officer's car opened, Mike B cautiously watched through his rearview mirror as the tall white officer, who could have easily played the stunt double for Officer Poncherelli in the hit 80's TV show, *CHIPS*, stepped out the car. Mike B sat in the truck, impatiently waiting for the officer to approach. He was more than curious to find out the reason he had been pulled over, but the officer never approached his vehicle. Instead, he continued to stand behind his car door.

Seeing this alarmed Mike B. In his day, he had been pulled over for many routine stops and had never had any cop display the type of behavior he saw the officer displaying at that time. There was nothing routine about what he was witnessing so he grew suspicious.

"What the fuck?" Mike B said under his breath.

Taking a closer look into his rearview mirror, he now saw two more police cars behind the original officer's car that had pulled him over. He had been so focused on Poncherelli's twin, that he hadn't even noticed the additional cop cars, just as he didn't notice Poncherelli's twin with his weapon drawn, until the other two officers exited their vehicles with their weapons drawn also. Each man was pointing their gun in the direction of his truck.

By now, Mike B was in a state of confusion. He knew that there had to be some type of mistake that he was caught up in, but whatever that mistake was, he'd find out at a later date. The odds were not in his favor right now. Three possibly happy-go-lucky white cops with guns and one black male without one was not a good look in Mike B's eyes. He rationalized the predicament he was in. He had heard about many cases on the highway where dudes had been shot and sometimes killed for simple DWB; driving while black. *There is no way I'm going to become a statistic today,* he told himself.

"I said turn off the vehicle and throw the keys out of your driver's side window with your left hand. Now!" Poncherelli's twin repeated.

Mike B heard him the first time but had no intentions of complying with the orders. He knew that it was either now or never as he continued to study the three officers through all three of his mirrors now as they began to inch up slowly from both directions after Mike B refused Poncherelli's command.

Mike B put his hand on his stick shift, preparing to make his move. He eased his foot on the clutch of the Audi, while still carefully watching the three officers who hesitantly continued approaching the SUV. Once he had the clutch down, he was ready to make a run for it. When he was about to throw the Audi into first gear and accelerate on the gas pedal, the officer shouted.

"Don't even think about it!" he yelled, startling Mike B, causing him to release his foot from up off of the clutch.

Mike B was just at the stage where he had worked his nerve to throw the Audi into first gear and accelerate on the gas pedal. The driver's door of his SUV was yanked open by yet another officer, Mike B had no clue where he came from.

"Now slowly keep your right hand on the steering wheel and turn your vehicle off with your left hand," the new comer instructed.

This time, Mike B complied. By now the other three officers had swarmed the SUV, one of them snatching open the passenger's side door with his gun pointed at him.

"Do you have any weapons in the vehicle, sir?" the pale-faced officer questioned.

"No."

Judging by the look on the pale cop's face and ice blue eyes, Mike B was positive that he was one of the trigger happy cowboys who would have gunned him down. Had it not been for the fourth officer, whom Mike B felt to be level headed, he believed his blood would've been spilled where he sat.

"Ten forty-two, we have apprehended the suspect and are now taking him into custody," radioed the fourth officer.

Suspect? wondered Mike B. *Suspect to what?* he tried to ponder, as the officer on the passenger's side began to read him his Miranda Rights. The fourth officer ordered him out of his Audi.

"Hands on top of your head!" the officer ordered.

Mike B complied. He began roughly patting him down. Ending his search for weapons, the fourth officer grabbed hold of Mike B's hands.

"Put your hands behind your back," he chimed, despite the fact that he was already forcefully putting them behind him for Mike B. In one swift motion, he slapped the cuffs on Mike B.

"What I do?" Mike B exclaimed.

He conjured up the most innocent face he could, but they weren't buying it.

"You'll find out soon enough," the fourth officer offered.

"It was my stop. You want me to take him in Miller?" Asked Poncherelli's twin.

"It don't matter. I'll take 'im. You'll still get the credit for it, Steve," replied the fourth officer who was referred to as Miller.

"All right, I'll see you back at the station."

During that time, Mike B said nothing. He was still trying to make sense of the whole ordeal. It wasn't until he was in the back of the police car, that a slim possibility came to mind. He wondered if the officer named Miller would give him any answers, but knew the only way to answer that question was to ask, so he took a shot at it.

"Excuse me," he cleared his throat.

"What is it?" Officer Miller continued to write on his clipboard, never looking up or turning around to look back.

"Why was I pulled over and what am I being arrested for?" Mike B asked more direct questions.

Miller wondered if he should answer. It seemed to him, that someone of his caliber should have some idea why he had been stopped and arrested. Sooner or later, he would find out Officer Miller told himself.

"You were pulled over because there is a state wide APB out for your arrest."

"What? For what?" asked Mike B before Officer Miller could finish, knowing that APB stood for an All Post Bulletin.

"For murder," answered Miller, leaving out the part that said proceed with caution, suspect may be armed and dangerous.

"Murder?" Mike B tried to sound surprised. "That's crazy!" he said, but deep in the back of his mind he had already drawn up that conclusion but wondered how.

Miller studied his puzzled facial expression through his rearview mirror. For Officer Steve Miller, it was never anything personal, just a job, and his job was to uphold the law, to protect and serve. He was not a judge or a jury, so whether Mike B had been guilty or not was not his concern. Officer Miller's only concern was to deliver the detainee to the Plainfield Police Department, and that's what he intended to do, as he radioed in his destination to the dispatcher.

"Ten forty-two, I'm in route."

Chapter Fourteen

"You got everything?" Lenore directed her question to Denise as she zipped the duffle bag of money shut.

"Yeah, I think so. Let me check to be on the safe side." Denise began to backtrack her steps.

"All right, I'ma be in the car, don't take too long you know we got to make another stop and take care of that before we hit the airport," reminded Lenore.

"I know," replied Denise somewhat sadly, at the thought of remembering what it was they actually had to take care of. She had wished that Lenore had forgotten, though it was apparent that she hadn't and Denise knew that what she had agreed to, had to be done or else they would not be able to get away with their twisted scheme scot-free.

Reading the change in Denise's facial expression caused Lenore's alarm to go off inside of her head. Without having to ask, she knew what the new look was for because it was that same look she had given when Lenore first mentioned the initial plans that needed to be carried out in order for it to be successfully executed. Lenore had to spend hours convincing Denise of the importance of that particular part of their plan. Now here it was, months of planning, and Denise's old feelings about the situation decided to resurface. She couldn't believe that out of all the times in the world, Denise waited until the end of their plan to get on some self-righteous shit. The last thing either one of them needed right now was for one of them to become weak. Lenore knew that she stood strong in her spot. She had continuously showed that the only things she cared for was Denise and the money. Now she needed to know if Denise felt the same way.

"Why you lookin' like that?" Lenore started out asking. "I know you not getting soft on me now?"

Denise was caught by surprise by Lenore's questions. She had tried her best to conceal her personal feelings about their final plans, but it was obvious that she hadn't done a good job. Ever since Lenore had informed her of what she felt needed to be done, Denise played the plan over and over inside of her head in hopes of finding a flaw in it, but she never could. Still, she rather they quit while they were ahead and catch the flight to Florida where they intended to enjoy the rest of their lives together.

"No it ain't even like that, but—"

"There is no but," spit Lenore. "We've been plannin' this shit for the past nine months and now we're gonna see it all the way thru. You need to let me know how you carryin' it now before we leave this spot so I'll know how to carry it from here on out," stated Lenore with conviction. "You're either with me or you not!" she ended dryly.

This was not what Denise wanted. Her intentions were not to get Lenore upset with her and have to second guess her loyalty. Although it was not direct, Denise caught the threat that Lenore made toward her, and understood. If the shoe were on the other foot and she stood in Lenore's position, she too would have said the same because there was a lot at stake to be wanting to fold now when she had been in the game playing along all this time. The fact of the matter was that Denise loved Lenore and there was nothing that she wouldn't do for her or with her. This was one of those times where she knew she had to step up to the plate and prove that.

"You right, boo. My bad, I'm trippin'. You know I love you, and I'm wit' you," said Denise walking up on Lenore.

"I know ma," replied Lenore with a smile running her fingers through Denise's honey blonde hair.

The two of them shared a passionate kiss. "Come on, handle your business, we don't have time for this," said Lenore, breaking their tongue tie.

"Okay," Denise replied giving Lenore one last peck on the lips.

"I'll be in the car."

Chapter Fifteen

Mike B sat in the interrogation room handcuffed to the chair. He was no stranger to the little Plainfield Police Station office they used to question arrestees. He knew that the particular room they had him in was for those who were being questioned or charged for shootings or murders. On numerous occasions when he was on his grind and had to do what it took to come up in the game, he had frequented this same room, more so when he and Jeff got down together, but only to spend no more than a few hours of being badgered by the local authorities before he was released and free to leave due to lack of proof to form a solid case against him. Now here it was once again, and he was faced with a situation he knew would result in the same outcome, or so he thought.

He directed his attention to the entrance of the room as the door flung open. A grin formed across his face as the white, grey haired officer walked in. Just as he thought, they sent their number one top detective to interrogate him, or rather he volunteered for the job once he heard who they had in custody. Mike B was familiar with Detective Frank Wilson, head of the Plainfield's Homicide Division, and the best in his field.

Just as Mike B was familiar with Detective Wilson, Wilson was also equally familiar with him. The two of them had been playing cat and mouse for quite some time, since Detective Wilson was on the narcotics force and Mike B was a mere block hustler. The ending result always being Detective Wilson winding up an unsatisfied cat. Today, Detective Wilson was determined to catch a mouse. The two of them exchanged stares, having admiration for the other, each for their own reasons.

"Tsk! Tsk! Tsk!" Detective Wilson started out with.

Mike B was not only familiar with Wilson, he was also familiar with his tactics. Wilson always started his line of questing out with the irritating sounds of sucking his teeth for as long as Mike B could remember, since the first time nearly ten years ago. Mike B anticipated Detective Wilson's next move as if they were playing a game of chess.

"Money Mike B Carter," said Wilson adding Mike B's street name to his full name. "Today is not your lucky day," he said as he always did when he began his interrogation.

This time, his words were slightly different from the previous times he had opened up with in the past. Today he seemed more confident with his words, as if he was sure of what he had just said. Still, Mike B continued to sit there in silence. He anticipated Wilson's next words, as he knew what was to follow.

"Before I tell you what I got on you, is there anything you want to tell me that will help you in the long run, because right now it doesn't look good for you, kiddo. I mean, it really doesn't look good for you," said Detective Wilson putting emphasis on the word really.

Same ole Wilson, thought Mike B, but this was the first time he had ever heard him emphasize his ending words. Mike B smiled on the inside. He chalked Detective Wilson's last commitment up as being a new scare tactic incorporated into his stale curriculum to add a little spice to it. Detective Wilson's track record and his reputation of arrests and convictions on shootings and murders preceded him and spoke for itself, so Mike B was fully aware that he was no slouch. What worked on others could not budge him. Mike B felt that if Detective Wilson was going to come at him, he'd better come correct or don't come at all. The last thing he would do would be get all scared and nervous, causing him to tell on himself or another. Let Mike B tell it, he was as strong as they come. Pressure didn't bust pipes when it came to him. He was a diamond.

"Nah, I don't have nothing to say to you, Wilson," spoke Mike B. Cool, calm, and collected.

Now it was Wilson's turn to smile. If he had a dollar for every time he had heard Mike B say that to him over the years, he'd probably be a wealthy man. However, something in his gut told him that before he left that room, Mike B would in fact have something to say to him.

"So I guess you want to talk to your attorney now, huh?" asked Wilson, beating Mike B to the punch, knowing that those would be the next words he spoke.

"Do I need one?" Mike B asked nonchalantly.

That was the cue that Detective Wilson had been waiting for. "This time I think you do, kiddo," replied Detective Wilson, slapping the manila folder he held in his hand on the table.

This was also nothing new to Mike B either. He had gone through these procedures a thousand times, but this time, without even looking in that folder, he had a bad feeling about the contents. He began to reflect back on what Detective Wilson said about today, 'not being his lucky day.' As Detective Wilson's words circled in his head, Mike B slid the folder close to his person and opened its cover. As he looked at the black and white copied photos, he wondered no more because there, just as plain as day, laid Gee-Live's lifeless body in the blood stained snow where he and Jeff had left him.

Detective Wilson observed Mike B's reaction to the photos. He was a highly trained expert in reading body language, facial expressions, and the reading of the eyes, but as usual, when he presented Mike B with portfolios of what he believed to be his handy work, Mike B maintained his composure and remained motionless. But had he been an expert in internal body language, he would have known that Mike B felt like he had just been slapped in the face with a bag of bricks at the sight of the photos. Mike B knew that Detective Wilson was watching him closely with this hawk eyes, which made him extra careful not to break a sweat. He closed the folder and slid it back toward Wilson, then looked up at the detective who was already staring at him.

For a moment, there was a brief silence, with the exception of the wall clock hands ticking away at each second. "Why you showin' me this?" asked Mike B, breaking the silence, knowing that he had to ask that question like he always did or else Detective Wilson would suspect something.

Little did he know, no matter how much he tried to play the role, he could not convince Detective Wilson otherwise this time.

"You don't know why?" asked Detective Wilson, impressed by Mike B's coolness.

"Nah," replied Mike B plainly.

"So that's your story and you're sticking to it, huh?"

"You ain't got nothing on me man. This is some bullshit right here," answered Mike B, showing a little sign of emotions.

"Is that so," Detective Wilson shot back dryly, picking up on Mike B's mood change.

"Yeah, I know so, 'cause I got an alibi."

"An alibi? You don't say," Detective Wilson replied sarcastically. "Who is this alibi?"

"Jeffrey Smith. I was at his crib all night and this morning until I got arrested," said Mike B confidently, not aware of the fact that he had just made a fatal mistake with his choice of words. Instantly, Detective Wilson picked up on Mike B's error and intended to capitalize off of the situation.

"Why would you tell me of your specific whereabouts for yesterday evening and this morning Money? I never made mention of the time of Gee's death. You do know who Gee is, don't you?" asked Detective Wilson, ending his statement with an obvious question.

The fact that Mike B was so quick to give his specific whereabouts during the time of the victim's death convinced Wilson that he was on to something.

By now, little beads of sweat started to formulate and trickle down from underneath Mike B's arms onto his sides as the palms of his hands began to perspire as well. At the time, he hadn't realize what he said, or rather how it came out. He cursed himself for his carelessness, but it was too late, he couldn't take what he had said back, the damage had already been done. Now his only hope was to salvage what was left.

"Yo, Wilson, man, come on with the games, yo. You know I know who that cat is or was in them flicks, and you know I ain't have nothing to do with that dude's death either," stated Mike B boldly in an attempt to convince Detective Wilson that he had no involvement in what he was being accused of. Judging by the smirk on the detective's face, he was not doing a good job of it.

"How do I know that?" asked Detective Wilson, changing his smirk into a puzzling expression.

"'Cause you know."

"Excuse me, sir," a voice came from behind Detective Wilson causing Mike B's words to be interrupted.

Both Mike B and Detective Wilson turned their attention to the direction of the door, each recognizing the feminine voice that intervened in the cat and mouse game the two men were just playing. It was Detective Lisa Robinson, Detective Wilson's partner, and someone who Mike B was infatuated with. Despite the fact that she was an officer of the law, he knew that his infatuation for her was like playing with fire. Sooner or later, the ending result would be him getting burned being in the line of work that he was in and she was in.

"What is it, Lisa?" asked Wilson, already having an idea why she had come to the interrogation room.

Mike B too wanted to know what would cause Detective Robinson to interrupt the interrogation knowing that Wilson didn't like to be disturbed when he was working on a suspect. Normally when Mike B paid visits to the police station, which was not often, or whenever he saw Detective Robinson out on the streets, he would flirt with her or ask her out when he caught her by herself. After all, she was by far one of the prettiest light-skinned sisters he had ever come across, not only on the police force, but in the entire population. She had qualities that Mike B appreciated in a woman: Independence, intelligence, and class which only heightened his attraction to her. But today was not any normal day for him and he was not in the mood to be doing any flirting or anything for that matter with the female detective. His only concern as far as her was why was she there.

"Sir, we just received the results of the DNA back on that," was all she said.

"All right, I'll be right there," replied Detective Wilson.

"Okay," she replied back.

Just as she was about to close the door, she shot Mike B a blank stare and rolled her eyes at him, and then she was gone as the door closed. Mike B paid the look no mind. *Just like a chick,* he thought. His mind was more focused on her words. He had watched enough crime stories and cop shows to know what the letters, DNA, meant. The question was, DNA to what? Picking up on Mike B's curiosity, Detective Wilson decided to fish a little more before he concluded his questioning, by allowing Mike B one last courtesy chance to speak his mind, if he had something to say.

"So, Money, you say you have an alibi? You don't know nothing, and you don't have anything to say, right? Correct me if I'm wrong," stated the detective, requiting Mike B's words back to him.

"That's right, I don't know nothin' about nothin' so I can't have nothin' to say. I told you I was wit' my man all last night and this mornin', check it out. His number is two two—."

"Oh, we know his number and we're, 'checking it out,' as you say," said Wilson, mocking Mike B.

Detective Wilson had had enough of Mike B's theatrics. He had given him more than enough chances to make the situation light on himself, but Mike B chose to play the tough role, so because of that, he had blown his opportunity. In a way, he felt a little sorry for Mike B because he honestly believed that he, like so many other young African American males, was bred to be the way that he was. A mere product of his environment, but the fact of the matter was, he broke the law and there were penalties behind that. Detective Wilson reflected back on the many times he felt strongly that Mike B was guilty of a shooting or other killings but just couldn't prove it. Now here it was, and major pieces of a puzzle had been dropped into his lap. He intended to put them all together so that justice could be served.

Against his better judgment, he decided to give Mike B an idea of what it was he was exactly up against before he left the room. "Listen kiddo. I respect the way you're choosing to handle this situation. I gotta tell you that the average guy in your shoes would be shitting bricks and sweating bullets, so I give you credit for that. But based on what we have on you, when you go before a judge, he's not going to respect you invoking your rights to remain silent or you trying to be this standup guy. Now I gave you several chances to come clean and give your side of the story because I know how these street situations can be. You stuck to your guns for whatever reason, so now I want you to hear something before I walk up out of here," said Detective Wilson, pulling a miniature hand recorder out of his pocket.

"Yes, I just saw two men running in Greenbrook Park with big dark colored coats on coming from by the pond. I noticed them get into a green Audi SUV and pull off. I went back by the pond and from a distance, it looked like someone was laying back there in the snow."

Detective Wilson stopped the tape. He figured he had let Mike B hear more than what he was privileged to, but nevertheless, he wanted him to know that his reign of terror was officially coming to an end. He didn't even bother to look at Mike B. Instead he put the recorder back into his pocket, picked up the folder that contained the deceased victim's photos, and began walking toward the door.

Mike B continued to maintain his external facade, but on the inside he was totally distraught. He could not believe what his ears had just heard, but he had to believe it. Like the tape recorder it played in, it was real. It was impossible for him to make out who the muffled voice belonged to, whether male or female, but there was no mistaking the words which the anonymous caller spoke. Many different thoughts raced through his mind, but the one that he pondered on the most was the thought of being seen. He was almost positive that the area in which the crime scene was committed was secure, but it was apparent that the, almost part of him being positive had become a detrimental one. He watched Detective Wilson walk toward the door, as mind-boggling thoughts spin cycled inside his head.

Right before Detective Wilson walked out of the room, he turned back around to face Mike B while standing in the doorway. "Just so you know, we're in the process of bringing your boy Jeff in for questioning as well. You might want to think about changing your statement," he suggested, closing the door behind him.

Mike B was not fazed by Detective Wilson's ending remarks. He was 100 percent sure that like himself, Jeff would not cooperate with the authorities no matter what. The two of them had been crime partners for so long, that he could vouch for him. He was absolutely right, there was no way Jeff would cooperate with Detective Wilson or any other detective for that matter, but not for any reason Mike B could have imagined.

The opening of the interrogation room door broke his chain of thought and drew his attention to his left. A tall, thin, African American, well-dressed male in a navy blue two piece entered.

"Detective Wilson?"

He walked over and extended his hand to Detective Wilson. Detective Wilson kindly accepted. "I'm Federal Agent Lewis."

The words, Federal Agent, caused Mike B's stomach to do somersaults.

The feds? he questioned.

He was no genius, but he knew enough about his city to know that when the feds came to town, it was something serious.

"What can I do you for?" Detective Wilson asked.

Chapter Sixteen

"Wait here, I'll be right back," advised Lenore, stepping out of the E350 Benz.

Before Denise could even utter a word, Lenore had already slammed the car door shut and headed toward their intended destination. Denise just watched as butterflies fluttered annoyingly inside of her stomach. She began to feel nauseated, wanting nothing more than for this whole ordeal to be over with, and knew that after this last stop they would be able to put all of this behind them. This was why she was so anxious for Lenore to take care of the affair and get back so they could be on their way. As uncomfortable as the matter was for her, Denise was put in a position and forced to make a decision. One that she'd hoped she would be able to live with for the rest of her life.

Lenore rang the doorbell again for the third time, wondering why no one had answered the door. Especially when she saw that white Denali sitting on the distinguishing twenty-three-inch chrome Giovannis parked outside in the parking lot. Just as she was about to ring the bell for a fourth time, becoming irate and impatient, she heard the locks on the door being released.

"Yo, what's up? What're you doin' here?" she was asked as the door opened.

"I came to see you." Lenore walked up on him and planted a kiss on lips.

"Hmm!" was the sound he made as he embraced the kiss.

He slid his tongue into her slightly opened mouth, then spun her around into his condo and closed the door behind them. “Why you ain’t call before you came?” he asked, breaking their lip lock.

“’Cause I wanted to surprise you,” she seductively answered, rubbing the bulge in his Sean John jeans, causing his semi-erect manhood to stiffen even more.

“Yo, you know you took a chance coming here unannounced right? What if dawg dabbled back or something, how the fuck we gonna explain this shit?” he lectured.

“Don’t worry, I got that covered. I already knew where he was at before I came here, calm down,” replied Lenore.

“All right, I feel you, I’m just sayin’ though, it wouldn’t be a good look on my part. Son wouldn’t understand this right here,” he animated with a hand gesture to indicate them dealing with each other.

Jeff remembered when he first introduced Lenore to his man Mike B after she had just moved from L.A. three months prior. A beautiful three months he recalled. When Denise asked him could a friend of hers come and stay with them for a little while, he was hesitant and reluctant because he didn’t know what type of female Lenore was. He didn’t want someone coming into his home corrupting his wifey. But he agreed to allow her to stay with them only on the strength of the love that he had for Denise, not to mention the overtime persuasion she put in with her lips, tongue, and throat. There was no way that he could resist her fellatio.

When he drove Denise to the airport to pick Lenore up and Denise walked out of the terminal with her, his only thought was, *Damn.*

There was no doubt that his baby Denise was a quarter piece all around the board, from head to toe, but Lenore was definitely a fifty-cent piece. As the two girls were approaching his car, he examined Lenore. *Even her walk is mean like she has on a perfect pair of Seven jeans with that cat-walk strut to the car,* he thought. She reminded him of young version of Pam Grier in her Foxy Brown years in the face, but had the body of Delicious. Her look was more exotic, with her caramel complexion and chinky eyes that made her appear to look as if she were stepping off of the plane from the Fiji Islands or some other Caribbean and not from Los Angeles.

Jeff knew that someone as gorgeous as Lenore had to be trouble, especially if she didn't have a man. He became more skeptical, despite the fact that he was instantly attracted to her. When they were introduced, she sounded just as she looked. He was careful not to stare too long at her out of fear of Denise becoming jealous. He knew how women were, but he had no idea particularly how Denise and Lenore could be. Not until they threw him a surprise birthday party that following month, at the Radisson in Piscataway.

That was a night that he would never forget. It was the first night that he had ever experienced a ménage à trois, with him being the meat while Lenore and Denise played the bread to complete the human sandwich. That night Jeff was told about Denise's and Lenore's past dealings and surprisingly Jeff was cool with it, especially since he was privileged to be a part of the sexual escapade. After all, he was now living out every man's fantasy. That was until Mike B met Lenore at Nell's in Manhattan while out with Denise. Instantly, the two hit it off and began seeing each other. At first, Jeff wondered if he should fill Mike B in on his own behind closed doors activity but then thought better of it.

There was no need to expose his wifey and her friend as being freaky and bisexual. Beside in his book, three was company, four was a crowd and he was not trying to share is wifey with his man, that was out of the question. Initially the threesomes continued, but the more Lenore saw Mike B, the less Denise and Jeff did, in the bedroom that is. It should not have surprised Jeff when Lenore said she was moving in with Mike B but he was.

He could not believe that Mike B had basically wifed Lenore up. He was under the false impression that Lenore was just merely a convenient piece for Mike B, let him tell it whenever he made mention to Mike B about her. He didn't want to seem like a hater, but Mike B was his man and he could not sit back and let him go through with his intent without at least knowing what he was against. He was positive Mike B had no clue, because if he did, he would have never fallen for a chick that Jeff had slept with, knowing the two of them were like brothers. That was against the rules.

Jeff had gotten upset with Denise and approached her, convinced that she had known of the extent and depths of Lenore's and Mike B's dealings. When confronted, Denise admitted to having knowledge, and before the night had ended, she had also deterred Jeff from what she called, interfering with people's happiness. That was years ago, and since then, because he allowed his little head to overpower his big one, around every birthday or whenever they felt the urge, Jeff, Denise, and Lenore still got together and joined in their triangle of sin without Mike B having any inclination.

"Yo, you spoke to Denise? I been trying to reach her all morning at the other crib and on her cell phone but she ain't pickin' up," said Jeff.

"Yeah, I just left her."

"Oh, word, where she at?"

"She taken care of somethin' and then she'll be here."

"That's what's up, we ain't gotta wait on her, right?" he asked with lustful eyes, rubbing his hands together, back and forth.

"You know I been wantin' to get you alone for a minute. You got thick as hell," he said already undressing her with his eyes.

"No, we ain't gotta wait," Lenore paused. "It looks like you were already expectin' me," she said making reference to the print in the front of his jeans, playing along with his greediness.

Jeff smiled. "How long before Denise be here?"

"Probably another forty-five minutes."

"Cool, I need to hop in the tank right quick. I don't want you to have to suck on no salty nuts," he joked, but Lenore found no humor in his words, still she let out a fake laugh.

"Nigga, you crazy, go 'head. I might join you."

"Yeah, no doubt," Jeff replied as he headed toward the bathroom.

Lenore wanted a few minutes until she heard the water to the shower running.

Jeff lathered up his body in soap, and then centered himself up under the shower head, closing his eyes as he rinsed the foam off of him. The thought of having Lenore all to himself in just a few moments excited him, causing him to be fully erect. This would be the first time he and Lenore had ever shared a sexual rendezvous together without Denise being present and he wanted to savor the moment. He began stroking his Johnson rhythmically, with the intent of reaching an orgasm. There was no way he was going to sex Lenore with a starter pistol and prematurely shoot a blank. His intentions were to bed her with a loaded gun and go out in blaze of glory. As he continued to masturbate, he envisioned his hand as being Lenore's mouth that he had the pleasure of experiencing on many occasions but never one on one.

"Yeah, suck it baby, yeah like that," he sighed and moaned, while licking his lips.

Between the steam and heat of the see-through glass doors and the lathered foam of the soap he used as a lubricant, Jeff was caught up in his own rapture. So caught up, that he hadn't even heard Lenore come into the bathroom. As Lenore stepped into the bathroom, she could see Jeff's silhouette through the glass, despite all of the steam. *This was better than I planned,* she thought as she got closer to the shower. She could hear the moans of Jeff coming from inside and automatically caught on to what was taking place. "This freak muthafucka," she uttered under her breath, as she pulled out the silencer equipped weapon. She raised the pistol in the direction of Jeff's silhouette and aimed for his head.

Jeff felt himself reaching his peak and began stroking his manhood harder, increasing his speed, as he became obscener with his words.

"Oh, yeah, suck it bitch. You're the best," he carried on as his body began to jerk. "Drink for daddy, aah! Drink that shit. Drink it all," he moaned and groaned, as the fluid drained from his joint, causing him to hold on to the wall.

Breathing heavily from the intense orgasm he just had, Jeff adjusted the hot water to warm, closed his eyes, and let it run on top of his head in an attempt to cool himself off. While in the process, a strange feeling overcame him. Something inside of him told him that he was no longer alone in the bathroom. This caused him to open his eyes and when he did, he could not believe what he saw. Confusion would have been the best word to describe how he felt. At first, he thought that he was hallucinating as he wiped his face with his hands, but when he removed them, there she was, still standing there with gun a in her hand.

"Y—yo, what the—" was all he had a chance to stutter, never knowing why his life had been taken.

Poom! Poom! Poom! Poom! Poom! Poom!

Lenore dumped six shots into Jeff's body, shattering the glass of the shower. Without hesitation, she turned around and exited the bathroom. *Mission accomplished*, she thought as she headed for the door. Prior to putting on the leather gloves, she was sure that she had wiped down all that she had touched. Reaching the door, before she left out, Lenore dropped the gun on the floor and then she was gone.

Chapter Seventeen

Mike B continued to restlessly sit in the gray walled interrogating room for what seemed like an eternity. Countless minutes had gone by he was sure of, but what seemed like forever had only been a few hours. Determined to stay awake, Mike B tug of warred with the slumber that did it's best to overpower his body, as he tried to gather his thoughts. The anonymous call that Detective Wilson played back to him still had him in a state of disbelief. *How could he have been so careless as to let someone see him leaving the scene of the crime,* he thought. For the first time in his life since being in the game, Mike B did not feel like he was in control of things. He usually was on top of his game and had an answer for everything, but not this time. For the life of him he could not figure out this twisted ordeal.

As he sat there racking his brain with possibilities, the room door opened. When Detective Wilson stepped inside the interrogation room, instantly Mike B could sense that something was wrong. There was a different look about the detective, one that Mike B was not used to seeing on the man's face. Again, he had a folder up under his arm, but judging by the newness, Mike B knew that it was not the same folder as before. Detective Wilson slammed the door behind him shut, causing the sound of wood to ring off throughout the entire precinct.

The murderous look in his eyes nearly startled Mike B, only because he had never seen the detective in such a mood before in all the years that they had their run-ins. He wondered what could have happened between the last time he saw the man and now that would cause him to go from Dr. Jekyll to Mr. Hyde. As he pondered on the question, the only thing that came to mind was his man, Jeff. He remembered that Wilson's last words before leaving the room was that they'd be bringing in Jeff for questioning, so he was sure that played a part in his change of mood. Although he didn't want to believe it and refused to believe it, Mike B wondered what could Jeff had told Detective Wilson. Whatever it was, he would find out just as he would find out the contents of the new folder as well.

As if reading his mind, Detective Wilson again presented Mike B with the folder, only this time he walked up on him and slammed the pictures to reveal themselves from out of the sides, as Wilson leaned over to Mike B and spoke.

"Look, enough is enough," he shouted. "I'm tired of playing games with you Michael," he paused, addressing Mike B by his full first name. He had never done that before, which only indicated to Mike B that he was definitely pissed off about something. As Detective Wilson continued with his ranting, Mike B unsuccessfully tried to figure out who was in the pictures inside the folder as he was only able to see a kneecap and arm.

"I don't know what the hell is going on but if you ever want to see day light again, you better come clean with me. I got enough on you right now to open all of these murders on your behind, you hear me?" he yelled into Mike B's ear.

Murders? All what murders? Mike B thought to himself. Mike B had no clue as to what it was Detective Wilson was talking about. He was convinced that Wilson was barking up the wrong tree when he put the letter *S* on the word murder.

There was a strong possibility that he had enough to indict him on Gee-Live's death but not a guaranteed conviction. Outside of that, Mike B was sure that the detective was bluffing, or so he thought. Curiosity over whelmed him now at the sound of hearing Detective Wilson's words, and he now wanted to know the identity of the batch of photo's before him. Looking down at the folder, before he had the chance to open it, Wilson got back in his ear.

"Go ahead, open it!" he shouted. "As a matter of fact, let me do you the honors," he said, snatching the folder open, revealing Jeff's naked, lifeless body.

Seeing a dead body had never phased Mike B before whether up close or in photos. To see his right hand man lying there with one hole in his forehead, four in his chest, and one in his midsection caused him to react.

"Yo, what the fuck is this shit man," he blurted out as tears began to form in his eyes at the sight of Jeff in the pictures.

Detective Wilson was not impressed by his reaction. "You tell me," Detective Wilson replied nonchalantly.

Mike B was not in the mood for any sarcasm. His first instinct to Detective Wilson's sarcastic remark was to jump up and hook off on him. The fact that he could possibly be insinuating that he had something to do with his man's death had Mike B wanting to kill the detective for disrespecting him. By now, his blood was boiling at an all-time high and he was ready to explode while he inhaled and exhaled repeatedly as if he had just run a hundred-meter dash. All he could think about was who could've violated and done his man like that. He wondered if it was in retaliation for Gee-Live's death? If so, how so? Did someone see them kidnap Gee-Live? Were they followed?

Is that where the anonymous call came from? How did they catch Jeff slipping like that? And was he next? All types of questions raced through his mind as the tears started to fall from his eyes. *How did it come to this?* he thought. As the realization of the matter began to set in. There was no doubt in his mind that he was going down, but there was no way that he was going to wear the weight for the death of his own man. Now he was determined to find out what Detective Wilson knew. As cool as he could, he dried his eyes by wiping his face all in one motion before he spoke.

"Yo, Wilson, I don't know what the fuck is goin' on either man and I don't know who slumped my man. Shit, I don't know who got something to do with it," said Mike B, hoping to get some answers out of the detective or at least some type of indication who was behind Jeff's murder.

Detective Wilson listened as Mike B spoke but didn't hear a word that he said. He thought by showing Mike B the photos of the dead body, seeing that would cause him to tell his side of the story that lead up to all of the chain of events that they had concrete evidence against him. Instead, Mike B insisted on playing the innocent victim role and Detective Wilson was fed up with allowing him to play on his intelligence.

"You know what, Michael?" Detective Wilson paused. "You're a real piece of work. It's funny to me, though, that you don't know anything, but everything thus far leads to you. I mean, what am I to think?" he asked, not intending to receive an answer. "Here we have an anonymous caller that gives a description of two men with big dark coats on running from the area of the crime scene. One coat, which you had on your person, fits the description, and another was found at your boy's crib. Then your SUV was spotted in the area around the time of the call.

"Next, we have another dead body, someone who was supposedly a friend of yours, who you gave us as an alibi, that DNA from saliva found on Gee-Live Young's body matched, not to mention the fact he tested positive for gunpowder residue on his hand. So if the two of you were together, then I can only draw one conclusion, and being that there were two different calibers of bullets in Young's body, you'll be tested as well. However, that may not be necessary seeing as how ballistics came back with your prints on the weapon confiscated, which happens to be an identical match to the weapon used on both Young and your boy.

"Then there's the additional weapon that was found at Jeffrey Smith's apartment that matches one of the murder weapons for Gee-Live Young and for Anthony Twan Roberts, which definitely gives you motive. Seeing as how the deceased was your first cousin. The way I see it, your boy Jeff felt that three was a crowd, seeing how you all were a three-man team, so he got rid of him. Then he tried to pass it off to look like Gee was the one that killed him and convinced you of it, knowing that you'd believe him and seek revenge.

"I suspect during the time you were planning to kill Gee, you had your doubts, but by the time you put the pieces of the puzzle together, it was too late. Young was already a dead man. Just to satisfy your curiosity, you confronted Jeff with your suspicion, not even realizing that he was the actual culprit. He probably answered your questions in an attempt to set your mind at ease, probably even told you that you were bugging out, assuring you that you had killed the right man, and told you to go sleep it off. Agreeing that he was right, you set out to leave, but as you were leaving, something dawned on you, and you realized that your boy Jeff said something out of pocket that only someone involved in your cousin's death would had known.

"In a flash, that realization of the loopholes in Jeff's answers became clear as day to you, and you doubled back into the apartment in a blind rage and total confusion. Your intentions were to confront him, but when you go back in his room, you hear the shower running. You then enter the bathroom, and all types of thoughts are going through your head, without even realizing, you let off six shots, and then you flee. In such a hurry to get up out of there, you accidentally drop your gun at the door when you leave." Detective Wilson concluded with giving his theory of what he thought took place.

"Correct me if I'm wrong," he added but got no response.

Mike B was in such awe behind his words that he hadn't had a chance to even digest or decipher the twisted theory just given to him by Detective Wilson, let alone to correct, add on to, confirm, or comment on the situation. The only two things that Mike B was actually sure he had heard that came out of the detective's mouth was that the murder weapon used to body his cousin was found with his man Jeff's prints on it, and the one used to body both Jeff and Gee-Live possessed his.

This can't be happening, he thought, as he began to pound on his forehead with his fist, trying to make sense of things. Despite his personal feelings, not wanting to believe that his right hand man murdered his cousin, he could not disregard the signs. All evidence pointed to Jeff, but why was what Mike B wanted to know. What happened between the two of them that he overlooked brought it to this? Was it jealousy? Was it over a female, or over money? Or was it just simply a misunderstanding?

These were some of the thoughts and questions that weighed heavy on Mike B's mental. For the life of him, he could not figure out why neither his flesh and blood nor his right hand man could not come to him with whatever problem that they had with the other in hopes of a resolution. What was that serious or so important that it had to end in lives being taken, Furthermore, he wanted to know how did Jeff come to being slumped? Was it in connection to the death of Twan or was it just merely a coincidence and justice was served? And most of all, by whom? Mike B dwelled on their mysterious questions so much until his head began to hurt. He was going through mixed emotions at this point. The ultimate betrayal had been committed and he didn't have a clue as to why. He was so broken up inside behind hearing the fact that Jeff was the cause of losing his cousin, that he didn't even think to ponder on how the authorities obtained a weapon with his prints on it. That is, until Detective Wilson started back up with his conversation.

"So, I guess I hit the nail on the head then, huh?" Detective Wilson asked, breaking Mike B's train of thought.

"What?" asked Mike B, snapping out of his daze.

"Look kiddo, if it happened similar to the way I said it did and you give me a sworn statement that that's how it went down, then it would make a helluva difference in what you're being charged with. It could determine whether you spend the rest of your life in prison or not. I mean, there is a lot of evidence that leads to Jeffery that will stand up in a court of law and possibly prove that you were coerced and manipulated into participating in the murder of Gee-Live Young. And then there's the fact that the plates from the car seen in the area of where your cousin's body was found matched your Mercedes at the DMV. If you could establish your whereabouts on January 11th and prove that he borrowed your vehicle, then it puts him at the scene of the crime. As far as his death is concerned, any prosecutor can see that it was not premeditated. It was done in the heat of the moment, a crime of passion, which is far better than murder in the first. All you have to do is give me your testimony," ended Detective Wilson, now trying to sound empathetic.

As Mike B listened attentively to Detective Wilson, his mind began to back pedal as something the detective said triggered his thoughts. It was a known fact that occasionally he and Jeff switched whips for various reasons. Either the other was creeping or tricking on the side with a next chick and couldn't risk getting caught or seen by wifey or someone who knew wifey. Then there were times when they switched for business purposes. Whether they were paying a visit to their connect or just simply wanted to change it up. The date January 11th floated through Mike B's mind. It was now March 26th, and more than two months had passed. He could barely remember what he did yesterday, thanks to the pounds and pounds of Hydro and Purple Haze weed he had smoked throughout his life time. He knew that two and a half months ago would be somewhat of a task to remember, but still he had to try. It was important because his life depended on it. As he back tracked to the last time he remembered he and Jeff switching whips, it was on Jeff's birthday, which was on March 3rd. He wanted to hold the Range to take Denise to a concert at Radio City Music Hall. Then there were three times in February, once when they switched trucks again because Mike B needed the space that the Denali provided to pick up some materials from Home Depot to fix up his crib. Another time when Mike B borrowed Jeff's Benz because he was creeping with a chick that had a friend that knew Lenore, and then the third time when Mike B gave Jeff his Benz to go to New York to meet the connect.

When he reached the month of January, he came up with a blank. He could not recall a time when the two of them had exchanged vehicles. He thought long and hard, and then just like that, the date popped in his head, January eleventh. That was the day that Jeff kept the Benz overnight because he had consumed too much alcohol at a club out in Philadelphia called Palmers and was unable to drive. Jeff dropped him off at home and took the Benz home with him.

"Ain't that a bitch!" mumbled Mike B under his breath. Now all was confirmed. That night Jeff did have his whip. The same night his cousin was spotted in the area.

That was the very same night they had bumped into Twan down there up in the club. *Could words have transpired that night between the two of them*? he thought. He believed it had to have happened like that.

"Damn!" he cursed to himself. He was thinking that had he not been intoxicated, he would've been more on point and peeped whatever tension was between his friend and family and squashed the beef. Because of his drunkenness, unnecessary blood had been spilled and he had no clue as to why. The only thing that he really could remember was waking up the next morning to a complaining Lenore. *Why was she complaining that day?* he wondered as his mind drifted. There was something about that morning he thought, he just couldn't put his finger on it. There was something that he was supposed to have done that day. No, something he had promised Lenore the night before, he started to remember, but what?

If he was with Jeff on the eleventh then the next day would be the twelft. What did he promise Lenore on the twelth? He questioned himself, racking his brain. *Why am I even trying to remember*? he wondered. What was the importance? Something about his promises meant something, he was sure of. He just didn't know what. *Think, Mike B. Why the fuck I smoke so much weed*?

he thought, continuing to run through his mental file cabinets.

"The twelfth? January twelfth," he kept repeating.

Detective Wilson just stood there watching as Mike B talked to himself. He could see that he was in deep thought trying to remember something. Something that had Detective Wilson curious himself. "What was on the twelfth?"

He began to count the days of January down starting with the first. He was positive that New Years, 2004 was on a Thursday because he, Jeff, Denise, and Lenore spent Wednesday, which was New Year's Eve of 2003, in New York watching the ball drop. From there, he began to tally up the days of the week with the dates. He knew that Club Palmers pumped the hardest on Saturday nights. So he was sure that the eleventh fell on a Saturday, but still he counted any way.

"Monday the fifth, Tuesday the sixth, Wednesday the seventh, Thursday the eight, Friday the ninth, Saturday the tenth, Sunday the eleventh." He stopped when he reached the eleventh. There had to be a mistake he thought. There's no way the 11th fell on a Sunday. There's no way they would've went to Palmers on Sunday, that much he knew. Again, he started from the first and counted again, only this time something clicked.

"Oh, shit!" he said aloud to himself.

It had all come back to him now. Saturday was the tenth, and on the tenth Jeff did have his whip. And on the eleventh, that's what the complaining was about when Lenore woke him up, now remembering what he had promised her.

She had been reminding him all week that her and Denise were going to church on Sunday and she wanted to take the Benz. It was her complaining that caused him to call Jeff and have him give the Benz to Denise to come pick Lenore up for church. What he once was sure of before, he now had doubt, realizing that Jeff was not in possession of his car. *Maybe it was just a coincidence that a Benz that favored mine was in the area,* he thought. But then he realized that couldn't be the case because the DMV traced it back to his Mercedes. Now Mike B was more confused than before. Realizing that Lenore had his car and not Jeff threw him for a loop. Quickly, he began to play back Detective Wilson's words. He remembered him saying that Jeff's prints were found on the weapon used in the killing of Gee. That made no sense to Mike B at first, but then he thought about something else Detective Wilson said. That his prints were found on the weapon retrieved from Jeff's crib that bodied Jeff and was involved in Gee-Live's killing. Mike B cursed himself for being so stupid. He wondered why he couldn't figure out this twisted triangle sooner as evidence appeared and revealed itself. Outside of him and Jeff, there were only two other individuals that had access to and knowledge of the whereabouts of the business, and that was their wifeys, Lenore and Denise. Now it started to make sense to him. Neither Jeff nor Gee-Live played any parts of his cousin Twan's murder, nor did he play any parts in Jeff's. The fact of the matter was, that he and Jeff had been played like puppets and if he had to bet money on it, he would bet that both Lenore and Denise were the puppeteers. How two females could be so devious and deceptive was amazing to Mike B. In all of his years in the game, females or anyone else for that matter, had never played him to this degree.

Now after summing up somewhat of the situation, Mike B was now faced with an uncomfortable dilemma. He now had an idea who was the cause and the mastermind behind such a scheme, and no clue as to what drove these scandalous chicks to concoct such a plan. Whatever the case, Mike B was now put in a position to where as though he had two options. One he could respect what took place and charge it to the game and take all that happened on the chin, or two, he could go against the grain and give the detective the spill in order to help make it easier on himself.

Mike B sat there silently just shaking his head in disgust, fighting with the decision he intended to make.

By now, Detective Wilson's patience had run out. He had given Mike B ample time to get his thoughts together and now he wanted answers.

"So what's it going to be Money? Is it going to be my version or your version?" Detective Wilson asked, waiting for a response.

Mike B took in a deep breath then exhaled. He had come to a decision and made up his mind. He knew what he decided would change his life forever, but nonetheless he was prepared to live with the consequences and repercussions behind his decision.

"All that you just said to me Wilson," Mike B started out with. "I don't know nothin' about," he emphasized.

Detective Wilson was thrown back by Mike B's response. He was confident that Mike B would cooperate being his compromising position but when he refused, the detective no longer felt sorry for him. He made up his mind that Mike B belonged where the rest of the criminals were, in prison, and he was determined to see to it that that's where he wound up at for a long time.

"Okay, tough guy. Have it your way!" were the detective's concluding words before leaving Mike B to himself.

The only thought that crossed Mike B's mind, as the door slammed was, "Grimey hood bitches!"

Chapter Eighteen

"All passengers please take your seats and fasten your seatbelts, flight number sixty-seven, departing from Newark Airport to Miami, Florida," the stewardess voice announced over the PA system.

Both Lenore and Denise complied, along with the other passengers. *It is finally over,* thought Lenore. She couldn't believe it. All of her planning, deception, and conniving these past months had paid off. She had not an ounce of regret or remorse for her actions. To her, when it came to survival, she strongly believed that the only thing in this world that could help you was money. Her motto was to obtain it by any means necessary, which is exactly what she did. She knew both the history as well as the bad blood between Jeff and Gee-Live based on what she learned from Denise. She used the tension between the two rivalries to execute her twisted plan and capitalize off of it. Timing couldn't have been better when Denise introduced her to Mike B. For her, it was never about attraction. Although Mike B was nice to look at and was an all-around good dude, it was strictly business from day one. It took a lot of blunt smoking, Alize Bleu drinking, and not to mention a lot of coochie licking, to convince Denise that it was a good plan. Upon agreeing as fate would have it, Lenore met Gee-Live one night at Deltas in New Brunswick while Mike B was out of town. The two of them instantly hit it off. After several shots of Hennessey, a couple bottles of

Rosé, and a nice blunt of Purple Haze exotic weed, the two of them found themselves in the same bed together in a sex crazed frenzy.

Gee-Live found out later that Lenore was from L.A. but lived in Jersey, in a town near his, Piscataway. But what he didn't know was that she was the wifey of his arch nemesis' right hand man. The more they sexed, the more open Gee-Live became. He had been allowing her to be up under his roof whenever she wanted. In a short period of time, Gee-Live was catching feelings for Lenore and expressed this to her. He started wanting to see more of her than just the two times out of the week he was limited to. He had even offered her to move in with him, but she said it was too soon. He didn't agree. The fact that he didn't know where she lived or who she lived with didn't matter to him. Her past or her present outside of him meant nothing, all he was concerned about was having a future with Lenore.

One particular night when both Jeff and Mike B were down south, Lenore reached out to Gee-Live and asked if she could she come over. She told him she had a surprise for him. More than happy to be seeing her for an additional day outside of the two that he was privileged to, he answered yes without hesitation. Unbeknownst to him, but not the least disappointed or with complaint, the surprise was Denise. That night they smoked, drank, sexed, and partied until Gee-Live passed out. A combination of exhaustion and intoxication had him counting sheep and snoring like a grizzly bear, which couldn't have been any better for Lenore and Denise. They combed through his home with a fine tooth comb in search of some type of safe or stash spot. Finding the location of what they were looking for, the two girls exited the house, leaving Gee-Live laying knocked out in bed.

Two weeks later, again as fate would have it, when she went to pay Gee-Live a visit he was highly upset about an altercation with someone at a bar who had thrown a drink in his face at a strip club. That someone was Twan, her boyfriend's cousin. That gave Lenore the final piece of her masterminded plan she had been working on. For the next few weeks, she made it her business to find out what Twan's days consisted of, trying to figure out the best opportunity to ignite her scheme. On the third week, shortly after she had just been an accomplice to a kid that owed Mike B and Jeff a substantial amount of paper, both Lenore and Denise followed Twan to the Scotchwood Diner. It was where he went every Sunday morning for breakfast. They patiently waited for him to come out. It was like a scene straight out of a West Coast movie. As soon as Twan stepped out of the diner and headed toward his car, the engine of the stolen Honda started. Lenore and Denise were parked a short distance away from where Twan's car was parked. As soon as he reached the parking lot on the side of the diner, Denise flipped on the high beams and threw the car in drive. Had Twan not been high and a tipsy he may have been able to react differently and more efficiently. Instead, he threw up his right hand to block the blinding lights out of his face. He never had a chance. Lenore cut him down with the silenced, semiautomatic weapon that Jeff had used on his and Mike B's last hit, before peeling off. Denise planted the gun in Jeff's house. It seemed like only yesterday that her plan had gotten off the ground, but it had been an entire nine months and things had gone just the way she expected them to. Twan's life was sacrificed. Gee-Live became the fall guy decoy. Mike B and Jeff took him out the equation. Jeff would've been the actual accused for Twan's death but taken out of the equation also. Mike B would become the real fall guy and wear the weight for everything. Lenore and Denise would make tracks to Florida for a better life, to live happily ever after, with no worries. Those were her all her thoughts as she sat next to the woman she loved. She grabbed a hold of Denise's hand and squeezed it. The two of them faced each other.

"I love you," Lenore offered.

"I love you too," Denise returned.

They shared a smile, only Denise's was partial. She turned and looked out of the jet's window. Her mind was somewhere else. As her and Lenore held hands, she couldn't help but to think about the last part of their scheme they had just carried out, or rather Lenore carried out. Unlike Lenore, Denise actually had feelings for her ex-lover, whom she had just agreed to have murdered. Her heart no doubt belonged to Lenore, but a piece of it also belonged to Jeff. He was the first and only man that ever made her feel like a real woman and that meant a lot to her. This was part of the reason why it was so hard for her to come to terms with what she had allowed Lenore to do. With her free hand, she placed it on her stomach as the turbulence began. Tear drops began to trickle down her face. She had hoped that Lenore didn't see them. The other part of the reason that made it so difficult for her to cope with, hurt her the most. She rubbed her stomach. How could she live with herself, knowing that she played a part in the death of her unborn child's father? But furthermore, how could she explain to Lenore that she intended to have this baby?

So many thoughts circled around inside of her head as she gazed out the airplane window into the clouds. She knew that she had to inform Lenore of her condition before the two of them got settled in Florida. She hoped Lenore would understand and accept her decision to keep the baby. The two had talked about kids in the past so she knew Lenore was totally against it, since she herself was unable to conceive. It had been years since the subject had come up, but she was almost certain that Lenore still felt the same way about the matter. No matter the case, her mind was already made up. Seven months from now, God willing, she would be giving birth to a child. Her biggest concern was not how Lenore would react to the news. Her concern was how she would explain the absence of her child's father. With that in mind, Denise sat back and closed her eyes as the 757 Boeing began to lift into the air.

Epilogue

The Courier News
Local News
Union County

A Plainfield man has been arrested in connection to a kidnapping and double homicide, linking him to a third. Police say, the body of Plainfield resident, Gregory Young was found in Greenbrook Park over the weekend after information was given to them. Although cause of death was due to gun inflicted wounds, Mr. Young sustained major body injuries in addition. That same day, an anonymous tip led authorities to the North Plainfield home of Jeffery Mackson. Mr. Mackson was believed to have been one of the alleged perpetrators in the Young murder. According to police, Mackson, who was originally from Plainfield, was found dead in his North Plainfield home. Police arrested, Michael Bennett, of Plainfield. He was apprehended during a stop on Route 22. He has been charged and being held without bail for the kidnapping of Young and the murders of both Young and Mackson. Although it has not been confirmed, police believe that this may have been in retaliation to Mr. Bennett's cousin, Antwan Roberts, who was gunned down at the Scotchwood Diner last week. If you have any information concerning the deaths of Gregory Young, Jeffery Mackson or Antwan Roberts, please contact the Plainfield Police Department or 1-800-CrimeStoppers.

Baby Mamas Club

by

Teeny

Chapter One

Keysha

I paced the floor with a cigarette locked between my fingers. My face was twisted from anger and I could have killed somebody. Tremaine was late picking up Keith again. I'd been with him for three weeks straight, and Tremaine's ass hadn't come over to pick him up like he was supposed to.

Whenever it came to those other bitches' kids, he was always on time. They didn't have to fuss or cuss like I did. They didn't have to wait until his ass decided to show up and be a father, and Tremaine always put the well-being of his other kids before Keith's.

I couldn't understand why he was always trying to make it hard for me and mine. I mean, what the fuck did I do to deserve this? Why didn't he step up his game when it came to us? My son didn't deserve this shit. That's why I would eventually go to court and make Tremaine handle his responsibilities.

For a while, things worked out fine. Now, he was back to being late and slacking on giving me money. I needed all the money I could get. Bills had to paid, clothes had to be bought, and Keith had to have the best of everything. I didn't want him around here looking like no goddamn bum, especially since Tremaine always wore brand name, expensive clothes that made him look like the millions he was worth. If he looked that damn good, we needed to look that good too. But if it was up to Tremaine, Keith and I both would look homeless.

I smashed the cigarette out in the ashtray and picked up my cell phone again. This fool was going to make me late for my hair appointment. My hair was short and layered; therefore, if I didn't get it done at least once every two weeks, it appeared nappy like I have a fro. My hair was real coarse like that, so I had to give it as much attention as I could. Keith's hair was the same way. I couldn't allow him to go more than a week without getting it cut. Tremaine knew that as well, but we always had to wait until he got here to get shit done.

While waiting on him to answer his phone, I looked at my chipped long nails that were polished hot pink. A manicure was calling me; so was my growling stomach. I was hungry and was supposed to meet my girls for lunch. If I don't leave soon, my whole day will be messed up. Yet again, my call went straight to Tremaine's voice mail.

"Listen up, you lame-ass fool. I'm tired of yo' tail not showing up. You almost ten minutes late and I got something to do! Your son over here with nappy-ass hair and he needs to get his hair cut. If you prefer that I take him and that I cancel all of my plans for the weekend, then call me to say that. In case you forgot, this is supposed to be your weekend to keep Keith. Once a month, Tremaine, and you can't even handle that. What a low-life nigga you are!"

I hung up feeling angrier than I was before. Keith was sitting on the couch in the living room watching cartoons. He loved the hell out of his daddy, but truthfully, I didn't know what for. I was the one who did everything for Keith. I couldn't teach him how to be a man, but at the rate we were going, I would have to put on the pants, grow a penis, and see what the fuck I could do to show my son a few things.

I lit another cigarette then went to the kitchen to see what was in the fridge. I haven't been to the grocery store, but there was some bologna and cheese inside. I hurried to make me and Keith sandwiches. I wish I had time to thaw the steak, but I didn't want to start overeating again.

Since I'd known Tremaine, my weight had fluctuated. He stressed me the fuck out. When we met, I was one hundred and forty pounds. Now, I was up to one hundred and sixty pounds. It was a good thing that my curves were in all the right places, and my heart-shaped ass hadn't spread too much. Tremaine claimed he loved every bit of it, but I didn't care what he liked right about now. What I cared about was him bringing his tail over here to get his son, so I could go do me.

After I ate my sandwich, I went to the bathroom. I looked it the mirror at my buttery-soft light skin and loved how well my makeup was on, like a work of art. My stretch jeans were so tight that they looked melted on my curves, and the hot-pink shirt I wore was dipped low to show my healthy cleavage. I considered myself a real sexy chick. Didn't know why I put up with Tremaine and his mess, but after today I was so done with him.

I glanced at my watch, realizing that I would have to cancel my plans and take Keith to the barbershop myself. I turned off the TV and picked up my keys from the table. Knowing that we were getting ready to leave, Keith put his jacket on and grabbed a fistful of Hersey's kisses from the table. That was another thing I often complained about. Tremaine was fit as ever. Body was tight, and he worked out faithfully at the gym. But Keith was only six years old, and he was overweight. I tried my best to get him to eat the right things, but he always fussed about wanting sweets. I asked Tremaine to help him lose weight, but he wasn't even down with that, He said Keith would eventually lose his baby fat and that it made no sense for him to work out with him at the gym. What kind of excuse was that? The only reason he didn't want Keith at the gym with him was because Keith would interfere with Tremaine trying to get on hoes. That's all he did twenty-four/seven, and he had no shame in his game, as he traveled from one bitch to the next.

I truly felt like I was in this mess by myself. Realistically, there was no need for Tremaine to be a part of Keith's life. He was doing more harm than good by showing up when he wanted to. I swear his actions work my nerves, but I had no one to blame but myself for upping the goodies the first week I met him.

Back then, he was so fine to me. When I spotted Tremaine in the club, I was like, *Damn, that's going to be my future husband*. Many of the chicks in the club were riding his nuts, but all I did was stay back and watch. When he approached me, I played him off. That didn't last for long, though. I gave him my phone number, and every time he called, our conversations were cordial. I seriously thought he was on some real shit. I thought he was about handling his business, but I soon found out that he wasn't. By accident, I discovered that he had a seven-year-old son with a chick named Bree. After Keith was born, and several years later, Tremaine had a daughter by a chick I used to go to school with, Monica. Him and Monica just had a son too, and with all these kids, I didn't understand why the nigga didn't just strap the fuck up. He was always complaining about catching heat from child support, but that's what happens when a motherfucker doesn't pay up like he's supposed to. I had no sympathy for him, and you better believe it that Keith and I were going to get what was due to us.

As for them other bitches, none of us got along. I despised Bree and Monica just as much as they despised me. Tremaine was trying to play all of us, but he wasn't doing nothing but playing himself. I still dished out the pussy from time to time, because I had a motive. It was green and he had plenty of it.

The second Keith and I arrived at the barbershop, Tremaine called. "I'm at your apartment. Where are you?"

"Where do you think I'm at, Tremaine? I'm at the barbershop, waiting for Keith to get his hair cut. We've been waiting all day for you to come. I got business that I need to take care of, and I wasn't going to sit around all day waiting on you."

"Calm down, a'ight? I was only fifteen minutes late. You act like it was an hour or something. Traffic was backed up and I got to your apartment as soon as I could."

I was tired of arguing with this fool, so I hung up on him. I don't have time for excuses. Tremaine had too many of them. If he thought I was going to waste my breath going back and forth with him, he was sadly mistaken. I told myself that what he wouldn't do, I would. Where he fell short, I would pick up and do what needed to be done. That's why Keith was now in the barber's chair, getting his hair cut and trimmed to perfection.

"Girl, remove that mean mug from your face," Big Mike said. "You too fine to be coming in here all mad like you do all the time. Every time I see you, you got that same tight look on your face."

I could only laugh. Big Mike was right. Because every time I had to come here was because Tremaine was a no show.

"I hate to be ugly like this, but Tremaine be working me. He needs to step up, so I can step back a little."

"As a mama, you don't ever need to step back. Keith gon' always need you, so get that thought out yo' head. Tremaine just be going through a lot. He got a lot on his plate, but at the end of the day, he tries to be there as much as he can for his kids. You can't knock him for that, and he be doing way more for his kids than some of these other niggas do. Ain't that right, li'l man?"

Big Mike poked Keith in his stomach and he nodded, agreeing with Big Mike's statement.

"Y'all can defend Tremaine all y'all want to. The bottom line is he ain't right. If I have to spend the rest of my life telling him so, I will."

"You're wasting your time. From what he told me, that noise you be spilling goes in one ear and out the other. You need to chill, Keysha. Being that way ain't going to make him change one bit, and talking all that ill shit in front of yo' son like that ain't cool either."

"It's cool to me, because Keith needs to know the truth about his daddy. I'm not going to sugarcoat shit. If he's a deadbeat, so be it. I can't fake it and pretend that everything is all good when it's not. Sorry."

Big Mike didn't have anything else to say. He kept cutting Keith's hair, ignoring me. I got up to go holler at some of the stylists I knew. When Tremaine came through the door, a thirsty trick sitting in a chair damn near broke her neck as she snapped it around so fast. Several of the stylists were eyeing him too, but out of respect for me, they didn't say anything.

I, on the other hand, had to admit that Tremaine had it going on. He rocked a pair of sagging jeans and the compression black T-shirt he had on clung to his muscular frame. His biceps were covered with tattoos, and the cap on his head was cocked slightly to the side. Shades shielded his hazel eyes, and the richness of his chocolate skin was as smooth as his walk. I understood what all of the stares were about, but nobody knew what a headache he was but me.

"I think I just spotted my next baby's daddy," the chick sitting in the chair said. "Damn, he fine. He is definitely knocking at the door to my pussy."

Bitch, please, I thought. Tremaine wouldn't dare give her the time of day. She was not his type. She needed to lose at least a hundred pounds to be considered.

I cut her off quickly and halted her thoughts of bringing another fatherless child into this world. "Don't get your hopes up," I said, exaggerating. "He already got four kids and four more on the way. He broke as fuck, and to be truthful, his dick ain't all that."

Some people laughed, causing Tremaine to look my way. He was trying to ignore me while he stood talking to Big Mike and playing with Keith.

"Well, it must be about something if he's popping out babies like that. Evidently, somebody is enjoying his sex."

I didn't bother to comment. If she wanted to take her chances that was on her. But just to let her know that I was speaking from experience, and that I knew what I was talking about, I walked over to Tremaine to confront him about his tardiness. Like always, he blew me off.

"Do me a favor. Let's step outside and then you can talk yo' shit. I'm not gon' let everybody up in here know my business."

I took Tremaine up on his offer and went outside to get into his Lexus with him. He thought he was going to tune me out by turning up the radio, but I turned it down.

"I know you get tired of me griping all the time, but here's the deal. If you can't be on time, for one damn week out of the month, then don't come. I made plans to have some me time, Tremaine. It is so unfair when I have to sit around waiting for you to show up. Then you never answer your phone when I call you. I have no idea when you're coming, and you always make excuses about being late."

"Like it or not, those excuses be my reality. I know I be late sometimes, but you know damn well that there has never been a time when I simply didn't show up. I do my best, Keysha, and you know it. For once, just one damn time, I would like to hear something positive from you, instead of all of this negativity."

"You want to hear something positive? Here you go. Nice shoes. Nice haircut. Nice clothes and nice car. Your son needs shoes, his hair was fucked up, his clothes are too little, and his mother is riding around in a 2007 car, when it's 2013."

Tremaine laughed and flipped his cap on backward. "No offense, but Keith's mother needs to stop working these part-time jobs and get a full-time position. That way she can buy her own car. As for all of that other stuff you mentioned, the problem is you be spending too much money on name-brand shit that Keith don't even need. He quickly outgrows that stuff and you be throwing money out of the window. Then you expect for me to keep dishing out money when you ain't even spending it right. Truthfully, you need to be shopping at flea markets, discount stores or Walmart. Figure out how to budget the money I give you and get off my damn back."

I could have punched Tremaine in his face. At first the conversation was going cool, but this nigga tripped when he started talking about my son wearing clothes from flea markets and shit, especially when his ass wore the best of the best.

"Do your other kids wear clothes from flea markets? Do you encourage that bitch Monica to buy shit from Walmart? The last time I saw her, her and those other two crumb snatchers you got were rocking the best of the best. That purse she was carrying did not come from Canal Street in New York. The bottom line is you're playing favoritism when it comes to your kids. I will not stand by and let you treat Keith any kind of way. As he gets older, he's going to recognize that shit, and that's gon' be a real big problem for you."

"There you go trying to make me feel guilty. You really need to go sit yo' ass down somewhere because I treat all of my kids the same and you know it. Monica may have more because she holding things down for me, Keysha. She makes it where everything ain't on me. How many times do I have to tell you that, before you get it through that thick-ass head of yours?"

I threw my hand back at him and rolled my eyes. "You can say whatever you want to, but I know the real deal. Keith is treated like your stepchild, and it's very unfair to him."

I knew how to get underneath Tremaine's skin. I also knew how to get him to give me some extra money—money that he definitely had to give, and his full-time job was truly enough to support us all.

His father, Papa James, was one of the biggest drug dealers around. Tremaine was reaping the benefits of his father's empire and money was not hard to come by. He proved that to me when he reached into his pocket and pulled out a wad of cash that he could barely grip with his hand. He flipped backed four hundred-dollar bills and gave them to me. I refused to take them.

"See how you do," I said. "You got all that money in yo' hand and all you can dish out is four hundred dollars. That's a shame, Tremaine, and real, real low. Don't you feel bad?"

"Not hardly. You'd better take this shit or else I'm gon' put it back in my pocket and pretend that an offer was never made. One, two . . ."

Before he reached three, I snatched the money from his hand. I wasn't no fool, and anything he offered, I for damn sure was taking it.

"Yeah, that's what I thought," he said. "Now, are you done griping for the day?"

"Only for the next four minutes. After that, I'm sure I can think of something else you failed to do."

We got out of the car on a good note, but after we went back inside and Tremaine started conversing with that hoochie who was getting her hair done, I was pissed. He had the nerve to give the bitch his phone number right in front of me. Like always when he dished out his disrespect, I pretended that it didn't bother me. I never said one word when he got his ho on, but deep down I was fuming. Fuming so badly that when his cell phone rang and he walked off to use the bathroom, I paid Big Mike for cutting Keith's hair and we left. I expected to hear from Tremaine real soon, and when he called my cell phone, I pretended as if everything was all good.

"Where the fuck did you go?" he yelled into the phone.

"Keith was ready to leave. I looked for you, but I wasn't sure where you went. I thought you left with that hooker you gave your phone number to."

"You know damn well that I didn't go anywhere, Keysha. Stop playing games and bring my son back here."

"No can do. He's on his way to my mama's house for the weekend. He asked me if he could stay with her, instead of with you."

I could hear how upset Tremaine was getting over the phone. His voice went up several notches. "Don't fucking lie like that. If he told you that shit, let me speak to him so he can tell me."

"No can do. If you wanted to speak to him, you should have done so while he was at the barbershop. Instead, you were too busy chasing ass."

"Listen, I ain't got time for your jealous-ass games, Keysha. Let me speak to my son right now."

"No can do. We'll holla later, and don't bother to call back because I'm blocking your number."

Tremaine knew I wasn't playing with him. I was so sure that he would call back, I blocked his number. I took

Keith over to my mama's house, and I was so glad that she had just moved and Tremaine didn't know how to get here. Keith fussed a little, but two of his best friends lived two houses down from my mother. When he saw them outside playing, Keith was fine. My mama invited the boys to come inside, and before I left, they were in Keith's room playing video games.

"I'll bring Keith back on Friday," my mama said, standing behind the screen door with her nightgown on. Her hair was in rollers and she had a joint squeezed in between her fingers. "Tremaine needs to be ashamed of himself for not showing up. I'm really starting not to like him. He hasn't been much good to Keith since the day he was born."

"I know it and you know it too. But it is what it is. If you need to reach me, I'll have my cell phone on. Going shopping and I'll get you those tennis shoes you wanted for keeping Keith. Size ten, right?"

"Ten or ten and a half. My ankles have been swelling up on me from walking so much, and I want my shoes to be comfortable."

"Okay, Mama. See you Friday. And if Keith starts talking back to you like he did the last time, be sure to let me know."

"I will. Have a good time, and keep Tremaine's number blocked so he doesn't interrupt your time with your friends. He reminds me so much of that foolish father of yours, and in the long run, he's only hurting himself. Tell Porsha and Angel I said hi too."

"I will," I said, getting into my car and pulling out of the driveway.

I couldn't agree more with my mama. While Tremaine had stepped up way more than my father had, he was still slacking. My father and I barely got along. I hadn't spoken to or seen him in years. When my mother told me how he played her and left us behind, I didn't want to have nothing to do with him for real. The times I did see him, all I did was cope. Deep down, I despised the man. The only thing I appreciated was the hundred bucks he gave me, and the two hundred dollars he gave me for Keith. To me, he didn't exist and I got tired of fronting to please him.

The four hundred dollars Tremaine gave me wasn't enough for me to get my shop on, but every now and then I'd put money aside that he kicked out to me. Today, it was enough to get me the handbag I wanted from Nordstrom, and I also bought two pair of shoes. I got Keith some more tennis shoes, and I went to GameStop to pick up him a few more video games. After that, Angel, Porsha, and me went to the nail shop to get the works. Like always, Porsha tried to convince me that I was wrong for not letting Keith spend time with Tremaine.

"Girl, you better have your fighting gloves on tonight, because Tremaine is going to be pissed about what you did. I know you be messing with his head a lot, but don't you think you went too far this time? I don't think you should have taken him over to your mama's house, and how does Keith feel about all of this?"

"First of all, Tremaine was late, and I'm the mother here. Keith has no say about anything, I do. Second of all, Tremaine insulted me by only giving me four hundred dollars and telling me to shop at the flea market and Walmart. Lastly, he shouldn't have disrespected me by hoochie searching around me, and that was the last straw."

"I know how you feel, but you do be kind of hard on him, Keysha," Angel said. "Either way, Porsha don't know what she talking about because she doesn't have any kids. You have to take what she says with a grain of salt."

I didn't bother to comment on Angel saying I was too hard on Tremaine. Everything I dished out, he deserved it.

"Trust me when I say I don't pay Porsha no mind. I don't care how anybody feels about how I conduct myself. Everything I do is for a reason, and my son will be better off if he knows the truth about his father."

"I don't have to have any kids to know that y'all be playing too many games, especially you Keysha. Y'all kids are going to be the ones hurt, and I don't get why y'all don't seem to understand that."

Porsha was pissing me off. I hated for a bitch who didn't have the same worries as me to comment on something she had no experience with. She was on the outside looking in and didn't know the half of it. All she knew was what I had told her. That in itself should have been enough for her to realize that while Tremaine claimed he was doing the best he could, he really wasn't.

"Can we please change the subject?" I asked. "Until you have kids and have to deal with these messy niggas out here, anything you say will fall on deaf ears. You're wasting your time with me. Maybe Angel is listening, but I'm not."

"I don't care if you're listening or not. I'm just telling you how I feel. You're the one who is messy, and anytime a bitch does what you did today, I consider that reckless."

I cocked my head back, and as I nearly jumped out of my chair to get at Porsha, I almost kicked the Asian lady who was working on my feet in her face. She said something to the other Asian lady that I didn't understand.

"Come again?" I said, standing next to Porsha who had jumped up from her seat as well. "So now I'm a bitch because I don't listen to you? Really?"

The Asian ladies kept talking to each other. Their voices were loud, so I assumed they were going off on us. I didn't care because Porsha's ass was out of line.

"Maybe I did go too far with the bitch thing, but since you jumped out of your chair like you gon' do something, then I may let what I said about you being a bitch stick."

It took everything that I had not to hurt Porsha. She already looked like she'd been beat in the face already, so I didn't think that my punches would do much more harm. What I did was politely put my shoes back on, and I paid the Asian lady for the half job she'd done. After that, I headed toward the door.

"Girl, call me later," Angel said. "Y'all need to quit tripping and make up."

I rolled my eyes and didn't think twice about making up with Porsha. She was running out of friend passes. She had already used up two of them. She had one more left, before I cut that bitch out of my life for good. The same thing went for my baby's daddy.

Chapter Two

Keysha

I was glad to be home and away from who was starting to become one of my haters—Porsha. I parked my car and opened the trunk to remove my shopping bags. As I was getting ready to close it, I felt something sharp against the side of my neck, pricking my skin. A hand slipped over my mouth, and I was so afraid that I dropped my bags on the ground.

"One question. Where is my son?"

I sighed from relief, but I could tell in his voice that he wasn't in the best mood. He released his hand from my mouth, but held me around my neck. The sharp object remained there as well.

"I told you he was at my mama's house, didn't I? Now, let me go and move that blade away from my neck."

Tremaine added more pressure to the blade and threatened to cut me. "Game over. Go inside, call your mama and tell her I'm coming to get my son. If you don't, I swear the police gon' find this sexy-ass body of yours in a bag somewhere stankin'."

I'd be the first to admit that there were plenty of times when Tremaine and me went to blows with each other. He didn't hesitate to put his hands on me, and I never hesitated to fight back.

"I'll call her in the morning. I promise. It's late and I don't want you dragging him out of her house. Now would you please get that blade away from my damn neck?"

Tremaine removed the blade, but his chokehold got tighter. I was getting angrier by the minute. I didn't appreciate him out here tripping like this. As he started to speak again, I used my elbow to punch him in the gut. I hit him hard enough for him to loosen his grip and back away. My next move was to kick him between his legs. I knew how to bring him down, and when I karate kicked him in the nuts, he fell to his knees. I made my escape by sprinting to the door. I was hoping to unlock the door and get inside before he regrouped, but that didn't happen. The moment I tried to close the door, he pushed it open and rushed inside with my bags. After he dropped them on the floor, he picked me up and body slammed me on the couch. As he held me down, I swung wildly at him.

"Get off me, punk! And if you put your hands on me, I'ma burn yo' shit up like I did the last time!"

Tremaine pressed his knee into my stomach and pulled my hair so tight that my head felt like it was bleeding and I could barely move it. "I'm not here to fight you, you stupid bitch! All I want to do is spend some fucking time with my son! Why do yo' ass keep denying me? What the hell is going on with you, where you think it's okay for you to keep my son from me? I don't know what else you want, Keysha. All you're going to do is push me away for good!"

I squeezed my watered down eyes, hoping that he would have some sympathy for me and loosen his grip. "I want you to do right by me and do right by our son. I'm sick of your disrespect, and I hate that you spend more time with Monica and your other three kids, than you spend with us. I don't even care about Bree as much, but you gotta know that this shit hurts, Tremaine. It hurts that we don't get any of your time!"

Okay, I said it and I meant it. Maybe some of this anger inside of me was because Tremaine and me didn't have the kind of relationship I wanted. I wanted more, but I knew that he couldn't give me more. He was too caught up and occupied with the other chicks, and his kids, that he couldn't give me the time I wanted. All we did was fuck every now and then, but to me, having his dick on occasion wasn't enough.

Tremaine removed himself from on top and sat next to me. He cracked his knuckles then removed the cap on his head.

"We've been over this too many times before." His voice was much calmer. "I told you this ain't about me and you, and I wish you would stop putting Keith in the middle of this. I'm not trying to hurt you, but you already know I don't do right when it comes to relationships. It ain't no disrespect to you when I tell you what's up. As far as Monica is concerned, again, Keysha, we tight like that because she understands me better than you do."

"You mean y'all tight because that bitch let you run her ass over, and I won't allow you to do it. While she sits back quiet as a mouse, you hear about my concerns and issues that I have with you. I get that you don't like confrontation, but what else do you want me to do? I have feelings, you know, and I wish that I could throw yo' ass away and be done with you for real."

"Nah, you don't want to do that. And the reason that you don't want to do that is because you know damn well that I'm good to you. I'm also good to my son. You were the one who set the rules about him spending one week of the month with me, but if it were left up to me, he'd spend more time with me. But you don't want him at me and Monica's house, so I'm going with your flow. Or should I say I was going with your flow. Since you've been tripping with me lately, I may have to change some things, just to make sure I'm allowed to see my son when I want to."

I rolled my eyes at Tremaine. He was so right. I hated for my son to be at his house with Monica. I didn't trust that bitch with my son. If she ever said anything out of line to him, I was going to have to hurt her.

"Tomorrow. You can go get Keith tomorrow. I'll call my mama and she'll meet you somewhere. She doesn't want you to know where she lives, because she doesn't like you like that."

"She don't like me because you've been telling lies and spilling ill shit about me. Through the eyes of many, I'm a deadbeat, a no good muthafucka who don't do shit. That couldn't be further from the truth and you know it. And then you be putting my business and your lies out there on Facebook and Twitter. I get tired of people telling me about what you be saying, but I chalk it up as attention. You seeking attention, but you're going about it the wrong way."

"I do it to vent. And whoever telling you what I write shouldn't be stalking my page to see what I be saying. I know Bree be the one telling you what I say, but she doesn't tell you that she be liking my comments too. As soon as I get a chance, I'ma delete that heifer from my page."

"Do whatever you gotta do, but please stop putting me on blast to the whole world. That shit ain't cool at all."

"I'll think about it, but you need to get your tricks in check. Why do Bree be up in my business like that? I know you're still fucking around with her, but she doesn't need to be worried about what I'm over here doing."

"I'm not doing nothing with Bree. She got a man in her life, so we don't get down like that anymore. Who I want to get down with a little more often be tripping. She be sweating me and making things real difficult for me."

I pointed to my chest. "Uh, would that person just happen to be me?"

Tremaine stood in front of me and unbuckled his belt. "Yeah, that would be you. But I'ma do my best to fix your problems and help you take care of mine. You don't mind taking care of this little problem with my dick being hard, do you?"

By now, Tremaine had his hard dick hanging out of his zipper and swinging his steel from left to right near my face. I wanted to reject him, but it had been at least a month since we'd last had sex. The truth was, I missed him. I missed his touch and I loved the way he handled me during sex. I reached out to touch his muscle that had grown over ten inches. It was thick and smooth just like he was. He held it in his hand and I inched forward to take him all in. I got a thrill out of sucking his dick, and as it rubbed against the back of my throat, I closed my eyes.

"See, I knew we could get along," Tremaine said in a whisper. "All it takes is a little of your cooperation."

I couldn't respond because my mouth was full. Tremaine held my head steady and tightened his ass every time he went in. I gripped his butt—ready for him to spark a fire between my legs.

Minutes later, Tremaine released his fluids in my mouth. I stood, and he helped me remove my clothes. A small pile formed on the floor next to us, and as we both stood naked, we searched into each other's eyes.

"What am I going to do with you?" he asked.

"If you don't know, maybe I need to fall back on the couch and let you decide."

I sat back on the couch, opened my legs, and invited him to come inside of my hairless slit that was already dripping wet. Tremaine dropped to his knees, but before he could dip his tongue into me, I stopped him.

"Not now," I said eager for his dick instead. "I want that. That with a condom on it. Please."

Tremaine always tried to go there without condoms. That's why he found himself with so many damn kids. Claimed he didn't like the way condoms felt, but that was too bad. We had to roll with it.

After putting on a condom, Tremaine kneeled on the couch and poured both of my legs over his broad shoulders. He beat his dick against my pussy then used his thick head to part my slit. As he pushed inside of me, all we could hear was the sounds of my gushy juices. There was no doubt that I was overly excited, and so was Tremaine as I started to move with him. My breasts wobbled around, but not so much that he couldn't suck them. I held on to his ass, and every time he pushed, I pushed harder. When he rotated his hips, I grinded mine. My heavy cream was all over him, and as I felt my first orgasm coming, I tightened my fist and beat it on the couch.

"Damn, nigga, you just don't know how I feel about you. I love this shit, Tremaine. Why you always gotta make this feel so good?"

Tremaine responded by sucking my lips into his. He whispered for me to turn on my stomach, just so he could tackle my pussy from the back. I turned around, hiked my pretty ass in the air and let him have at it. I knew how to make him cum too, so I threw myself back and listened to the loud sound of his thighs slapping against my ass.

We worked so hard together that by the time we were finished the condom was off. I accused Tremaine of purposely removing it because he kept changing positions.

"Don't blame me," he said, laughing and making his way to the bathroom to wash up. "That was your wild ass."

He had a point, but I still blamed it on him.

Minutes later, Tremaine and I were in the shower fucking again. I could never get enough of him, and since I didn't know when we'd be able to indulge ourselves again, I tried to get all that I could from him. Once we were done, I thought he was going to leave. I was surprised when he said he was spending the night. I called and told my mama to meet Tremaine in the morning at a gas station down the street from her house so he could spend the rest of the week with Keith. She wasn't happy about it, and I was shocked that she didn't put up a fuss.

After I ended the call with her, I went back into my bedroom and saw Tremaine lying across my bed. He hadn't spent the night over here in months. Maybe things weren't going well with him and Monica. I was so sure she would be ringing his phone tonight, and around one in the morning, somebody kept calling. Tremaine was sound asleep. I removed his cell phone from the nightstand and tiptoed into the living room to see who it was. Monica had called twice, but the one o'clock caller was Bree. I sat on the couch, reading her text messages. One after the other, she cursed him for not coming over like he said he would, she told him she was lying in bed naked waiting for him, and she threatened to call someone else if he didn't show. She kept referring to their "relationship" as whack, but then said she loved him.

I figured Tremaine had lied about his involvement with Bree, but he really had me convinced that she had another man. It didn't appear that way, especially when I looked through his pictures and saw trifling pictures of Bree with a little of nothing on. She was such a tramp, and as a so-called professional stripper, I guess she assumed the way to Tremaine's heart was through her pussy.

After looking at her pictures, I was sick to my stomach and had seen enough of them. Or at least that's what I thought, until I saw a text message from Tremaine telling her that he loved her. That really had my blood boiling, especially when I thought about our conversation from earlier when he hesitated to say the love word to me. I mean, I couldn't make his ass fall in love with me, but after all that I'd done for him, how could he not?

My initial thought was to go back there and wake his ass up to confront him. But I quickly changed my mind. I wanted him to rest well. By morning I had something for his ass.

I was so upset that I didn't dare go back into the bedroom to where he was. I remained on the couch, but as I started to fade, his phone rang again. This time it was Monica. I didn't hesitate to answer. She recognized my voice and paused before she said anything.

"Hello," I repeated.

"Keysha, where is Tremaine?"

"Busy."

"Busy doing what?"

"It's after one o'clock in the morning. What do you think he's been busy doing, or are you too stupid to figure it out?"

"It sounds like you're implying that y'all are having sex. If that's the case, why are you answering his phone?"

"I don't answer your questions, little girl. You called here, so you can answer mine."

"Keysha, I'm not doing this with you again. Wherever Tremaine is, tell him to call me back soon. It's very important."

"Don't expect to hear from him soon, because he'll be busy for the rest of the night. You can deal with him in the morning, which may turn out to be late morning or early afternoon because me, him, and Keith have things to do. You and your crumb snatchers over there can manage without him for a few hours, can't y'all."

"Watch yourself, trick. I didn't say anything about Keith, so don't go throwing my kids up in this. When you get done talking, you need to go sit down somewhere because Tremaine knows where home is. It's definitely not there in that shack with you."

"Well, it is tonight and it may be home for plenty of more nights too. Then again, I'm sure you won't say anything to him about him sucking my goodies all night, making me cum four times and fucking me like sex is going out of style. All you'll do is throw your arms around him and embrace him. Just know that when you kiss him, you'll also be tasting my pussy from his mouth. I know you don't mind, I just thought I'd let you know."

I hung up on Monica's ole weak self to take another call from Bree. She called twice, obviously waiting for Tremaine to come fill her hot pocket tonight.

"Go take a cold shower, bitch. He ain't coming tonight. His dick is too tired, and while you were over there waiting for it, I was over here occupying it."

"Is that so," Bree said. She laughed, knowing damn well that her feelings were hurt. Unlike Monica, Bree always spoke up and tried her best to let me have it. "Poor baby must've been desperate tonight because I wasn't home. Either way, put that bastard on the phone so I can talk to him about being with sluts with flat butts. What a waste of his time."

Bree also knew how to get underneath my skin more than Monica did. And the only reason she was calling my butt flat was because I didn't get butt injections to make my ass bigger.

"Bitch, please. Trust me when I say he seemed more than satisfied about having the real deal over here, instead of that fake ass, fake hair, fake breasts, all of that shit you got going on to make yourself look decent. Yo' ass got so many dents in it that an auto body shop can't even fix it. Tremaine already told me that you're so used up that he barely wants to go there with you. And the only reason that he does is because you be paying him."

Bree laughed again. "Ho, you wish that's how it was. If anything, Tremaine be paying me and he loves every inch of my body. I doubt that he said anything like that to you about me and you're just saying that to piss me off. The truth is, you're the one who he talks badly about. You don't have a high school diploma, your apartment is junky as fuck, your breath smells horribly bad, your mama is a psychotic bitch, and your son is a fat ass. Tremaine doesn't spend much time with either of you because he's embarrassed. I don't blame him one bit. I wouldn't want to be around a slow bitch who barely can read either."

Ouch. I was so mad that I couldn't even respond to Bree. First of all, Tremaine had to tell her that my apartment was junky because he always complained about it when he came over here. Secondly, how did Bree know I didn't have a high school diploma? Unfortunately, my mama was going through some things at the time, and as we moved from one place to the next, I had a hard time staying in school. I missed so many days that I wound up dropping out.

As for me not being able to read, I told Tremaine that as a kid, I was always behind. Things got much better for me over the years, and now everything was good. But for him to mention that to Bree, and for her to call my son a fat ass, there was no doubt that somebody was about to get hurt.

"Bree, all I'm going to say is I betta not see you anytime soon. If I do, that fake, droopy, dented-up ass you got over there is mine!"

"It's Tremaine's too. He bought it, so tell him to hit me up when he can. Bye, bitch. I look forward to seeing you."

Bree hung up, leaving me feeling some kind of way about the things she had said. Whenever Tremaine got up, he was going to catch hell.

Chapter Three

Keysha

I was in the kitchen cooking breakfast with the music turned up loudly. Tremaine was still asleep, but I expected him to wake up shortly, especially with the smell of bacon and maple sausages oozing through the air. I cooked some pancakes, grits, and cheese eggs for him too. Even threw in a bowl of frosted cornflakes and poured him a tall glass of orange juice.

By the time Tremaine got up, everything was set on the kitchen table. A smile was plastered on my face, as he stood next to the table and stretched.

"Dang, girl, you done hooked me up. I knew my dick was good to you, but I didn't know it was that good."

"Spectacular," I said. "So great that I'm on cloud nine right now. Didn't want you to walk out of here upset about nothing, and I thought this was a good way for you to start the day off right."

Tremaine looked at the food and licked across his lips. "Thanks. I appreciate that and the food looks really good. Need to go drain the vein, wash my face, and brush my teeth. You still got my toothbrush in there?"

"Yep. Look in the right drawer. You'll see it."

Tremaine walked away. I sat at the table and picked up a piece of toast. Before I bit into it, I spread jelly on top and sipped from my orange juice. My orange juice was just fine. Unfortunately, Tremaine's orange juice had a half cup of my piss in it. His eggs were scrambled with floor wax, and his grits were loaded with salt. I wasn't trying to kill his ass, but I did want to make a statement.

Tremaine came into the kitchen with a towel wrapped around his waist. His chest was covered with tattoos and his six pack was stacked just right. It was good to see him look so sexy in the morning, but the sight of him did nothing for me. I couldn't help but to think about what Bree had said, and I realized the reason why she knew so much of my business was because his ass was telling her shit.

"Have you seen my phone?" Tremaine said. "I thought I left it on the nightstand in the bedroom."

I pointed to the table next to the couch. "I saw it over there. Is that it?"

Tremaine walked over to the table and picked up his phone. It looked like he was trying to turn it on, but he wouldn't have much luck. I put that sucker in the sink this morning and let it stay in the water for a while.

"Damn," he said. "I need more juice. My battery must have died."

All I did was shrug, as if I hadn't a clue. I was sure he wanted to know if Monica had called, or if Bree was still hoping for him to show up last night too. I thought that he was going to ask if he could use my phone, but then again he knew better.

Tremaine sat at the table with me, as if everything was all good. My blood was boiling inside, but the outer me appeared happy go lucky.

"Smells good, ma," Tremaine said. "I was back there lying down and when I got a whiff of this shit, I had to get up."

"You already know I can cook, so don't act all surprised. And if my cleaning skills were much better, I'd be perfect, wouldn't I?"

That bastard had the nerve to nod his head. "I won't say perfect, but it would help. You definitely need to clean up around here. Keith's room is a mess. Yours is too, by the way."

"It's not that bad and you know it. Why you always got something negative to say about me? I rarely ever hear you say anything positive. You say I'm guilty of the same thing, so speak up and let me hear you."

Tremaine picked up a piece of bacon and put it into his mouth. He chewed and looked at me from across the table. "I always say good shit about you. I just told you that it smelled good in here, didn't I?"

I didn't bother to reply. After all, I wanted him to hurry up and eat his food. Right after he bit into the bacon, he washed it down with orange juice. Almost immediately, he cocked his head back and frowned.

"This shit taste spoiled. You got some milk instead?"

Tremaine wiped across his mouth. I figured he would opt for milk, so I had a glass of that with my piss in it ready for him too.

"I don't know what's wrong with the orange juice. Mine taste fine. I'll get you some milk in a minute. Meanwhile, finish up eating and stop complaining."

"I'm not complaining. Here, you drink this shit and tell me what you think."

"I already have my own. Like I said, there's nothing wrong with it."

Tremaine ignored me. He started to cut into his pancakes. I hoped he got a taste of some of my toenails that were mixed in with the pancake batter.

"Did you call your mother yet?" he said, chewing.

"I tried calling her, but she didn't answer her phone. I'll call her again when we get done with breakfast."

Tremaine was getting ready to respond, but he picked something out of his mouth. He looked at it with a twisted face then flicked it away. After that, he laid his fork on his plate.

"Something ain't right," he said. "There's an odd odor coming from my plate, not to mention the spoiled taste from my orange juice. Did you do something to my food?"

I laid my fork on the table and wiped my mouth. "Now, why would a nasty, slow bitch who didn't graduate from high school do anything to your food? I'm so fucking stupid that I wouldn't dare be smart enough to think about getting payback to a fool who has purposely hurt me time and time again. One who doesn't think I'm good enough to love, and who thinks his son is too fat to be with him. So, no. I didn't do a damn thing to your food, but I did, however, add a little more flavor to your orange juice."

Tremaine jumped up from the table. "I don't have time for your bullshit this morning, Keysha. I knew something was wrong, especially since yo' ass up in the kitchen cooking for me like you Paula damn Deen or somebody."

"Nigga, if I was Paula Deen, I'd be calling yo' black ass out for talking that dumb shit to Bree. She told me how you really feel about me, and since you're so ashamed of me and Keith, why don't you get the fuck out of here and never come back. We really don't need you, Tremaine. So stop being fake and acting like yo' ass care when you don't."

Tremaine walked up to me and stood over me. I didn't appreciate how close he was, so I stood up to be face to face with him. "If you believe any bullshit that Bree said to you, that's on you. I'm sick and tired of trying to convince you how much I do care, and like I said before, all you're doing is pushing me away. I would appreciate it if you would call your mama to tell her to meet me so I can get my son. That way, I can get the fuck out of here and get out of your damn way."

"You gon' do that regardless. And I'm not calling my mama to tell her anything. Keith is staying with her for the rest of the week, not with you."

I could see Tremaine tighten his fist. But before he tried anything stupid, I reached for the knife on the table that I used to cut my pancakes.

"Think before you act, fool. If you want to make it home to Monica in one piece, or over to that bitch's Bree's house, who you say you love so much, then you'd better back away from me."

Tremaine knew that he could wrestle the knife from my hand, and that's what he did. We tussled and when all was said and done, he had the knife in his hand. My head was being pressed against the table while I was bending over. He stood behind me, holding the knife close to my face.

"I hate you sometimes," he said. "You always gotta make shit so difficult, and all you fucking do is gripe about shit! When I leave here, Keysha, I'm done. Tell my son that you were the one who fucked up and refused to let me be with him! I'm sick of arguing with you, and this is the last goddamn time that I'm gonna do it!"

Tremaine stabbed the knife into the table, right by my face. He then smacked me with the back of his hand and backed away. When I reached for the knife, that's when he pushed me. Pushed me so hard that I fell against the wall and hit my back.

"You dirty son of a bitch!" I said, rushing up to charge at him with gritted teeth.

This time, I was met with Tremaine's fist that went right into my midsection. I doubled over and fell back again. He almost knocked the breath out of me and my stomach was aching so badly.

"If you get up again, my fist will crack your face and split it. Let this shit go, Keysha. I'm warning you."

Tremaine walked off and came back with his jeans on and his shirt thrown over his shoulder. I was in the kitchen dialing 911.

"Could you please send—"

He snatched the cordless phone from my hand and threw it against the wall. We mean mugged each other with our chests heaving in and out. Without saying another word to me, he walked toward the door, snatched up my shopping bags that were still by the door and slammed it on his way out. No words could express how angry I was right now. I had to make his ass pay for this.

Later that day, I was at Angel's house telling her about what happened, when my mama called. She spoke in a panic and sounded as if she was out of breath.

"That nigga Tremaine is crazy," she said tearfully. "Me and Keith were outside and Tremaine pulled up in a car with two of his friends. He threatened to hurt me, and made Keith leave with him. When I tried to take Keith away from him, Tremaine pulled a gun on me. I ran inside to call the police. I didn't know what else to do, Keysha, and I'm afraid for Keith."

I was so mad at my mama for allowing Tremaine to take Keith with him. "Damn, Mama, why couldn't you just go back into the house? I didn't want Keith with Tremaine, and I definitely don't want him at his house."

"I didn't have a choice. And what did you want me to do, other than catch a bullet in my back for trying to keep him? I called the police, but if you have legal papers that say Tremaine is allowed to keep him, there ain't much we can do."

"There's plenty that I can do. I'ma go talk to a lawyer to see if I can get sole custody of my son. Tremaine don't deserve to have any rights to Keith. I'ma make sure that he doesn't!"

I told my mama that I would call her back. How she let something like this happen I didn't know. With Tremaine being upset with me, there was no telling how he was going to treat Keith. Monica wasn't in one of the best moods either, so I suspected that Keith would walk into a house of hell.

"What's going on?" Angel asked. "Why are you so upset?"

"Because Tremaine found out where my mama lives and he went to go get Keith."

Angel shrugged. "What's wrong with that? I mean, just because the two of y'all have differences, it shouldn't affect his relationship with his son."

I pursed my lips and had to put Angel in her place. "Who are you to talk to me about differences, especially from the way you and Jay carry on about Lela? If I'm not mistaken, he's only seen her like three or four times since she's been born. And every time he calls here to come get her, you make excuses."

"That's because Jay is fake and he wants Lela with him on his time. As for Tremaine, you gotta give him credit, Keysha. He is a good father to Keith. He may not be a good man to you, but—"

"I don't know why y'all keep on saying that he's a good father when it's simply not true. I guess y'all think the money he gives us is supposed to make up for him not being there, but it doesn't. The truth is, Tremaine has never been to Keith's school, he's never taught him one single thing, and he's never been on vacation with him either. I asked Tremaine to help Keith lose weight, take him to run with him or put him on a football team. He hasn't done anything. So I'm to the point where I believe what Bree said. He's embarrassed of my son and that shit bothers me."

fall for the foolishness, okay? If he was em-
, Keysha, he wouldn't have just gone over to
...ama's house and threatened her to get his son. You'd better wake up and smell the coffee before it's too late. Plenty of us would die to have a baby daddy like Tremaine. I gotta give him props on being a father."

"Well, I'm not going to give him shit but a hard time. And as for the relationship thing goes, you couldn't be more right. I don't know why I keep telling myself that he's the one I want to be with, when in reality we will never be able to get along. There's been too much damage done, and besides that, I hate his ass for sleeping around so much. I mean, how much pussy does one nigga need?"

Angel shrugged her shoulders. "I guess as much as he can get. With all of these bitches throwing that shit at him, all he gotta do is reach out and catch it. You have to admit, Keysha, the nigga is fine as hell."

I rolled my eyes, silently admitting to myself that he was. Still, it didn't matter because he would always be a deadbeat in my book.

Chapter Four

Tremaine

Keysha had me hot. I was on edge and could have hurt somebody this morning. First, the bitch tried to poison my ass. There was no telling what she had put in my food. I was glad I didn't finish it. If I had, my ass would be laid up somewhere right now with a body bag covering me. Then, she turned around and did something to my phone. I could see moisture through the camera lens, and when I broke my phone apart, there was water inside of it. I took it to Sprint so they could see what was up. The salesperson confirmed that it had been in water. I spent a substantial amount of change on a new phone then I called a good friend of mine to find out where Keysha's mama lived. She gave me the address, so I rushed out to go get my son.

When I got to Keysha's mama's house, I figured she was going to start clowning, just like her fucking daughter. My boys, however, were there to help me handle things, just in case her stupid-ass boyfriend was there. Thankfully he wasn't so I didn't have to blow anybody's brains out. I was so upset that I didn't care if my boys knocked that bitch off or not. The only thing that saved her was Keith. He was the only one who saved me from not beating the fuck out of Keysha too, and she'd better be thankful that I was looking out for what was in her best interest, not so much mine.

The good thing was Keith was glad to see me. I don't claim to be the best father to my kids, but I couldn't accept no title as a deadbeat. I was active in all of my kids' lives, they knew who daddy was and they all loved to be around me. The only reason that Keith and me didn't spend as much time together was because of Keysha. Being around her gave me headaches, and the only time we didn't argue with each other was during sex. During that time, she was all good. I was the best nigga ever and she loved my black ass to death.

Well, I needed more than what Keysha was offering. I needed somebody who appreciated me. Somebody who praised my efforts and who wasn't all about getting fucked all the time. While I definitely loved me some pussy, I also had business to see about. That occupied an enormous amount of my time, and Papa James wasn't too keen on niggas slacking. If I didn't step up, I didn't get paid. And with four kids, it was imperative that I kept my pockets fat with paper.

Keith and I walked into the house, only to find Monica sitting on the couch with her lips poked out. Her eyes narrowed as she looked at me, and her arms were folded across her chest.

"Nice of you to finally show up," she said then looked at Keith. "Hi, Keith. Do you mind if I talk to your daddy for a few minutes? I made some cookies and they're on the kitchen table. Help yourself to them, okay?"

Keith nodded and headed toward the kitchen. Monica stood up with our son in her arms.

"What's going on with you and Keysha? I wasn't aware that you were still having sex with her, and who do you think you are showing up the next day without calling me?"

"I don't think, I know. I know that I'm the man of this house who doesn't have to answer to anyone, unless I want to. I know that I pay every single bill here, and that my woman and children are well taken care of. So much so, that she has no right to bitch about my late hours, especially when she knows I spend way more time doing business than I do so finding pleasure. She also knows that I love no one but her, but if that ever becomes a problem, she knows where the front door is. I promise you that I will never stop you from walking out of here, if you ever come to the conclusion to do so."

I walked away from Monica, expecting not to hear anymore. She, however, came after me, refusing to let things go.

"Did you have sex with Keysha last night or not? That's all I want to know."

"Let me repeat. I don't have to answer any questions, unless I want to."

"So, that means you did. She didn't lie to me when I called then, did she?"

I went into the kitchen to where Keith was. He was sitting on a stool, eating cookies, and watching TV.

"Tremaine, do you hear me talking to you? I asked you a question and I expect for you to answer me, damn it."

Keith looked at me and I looked at him. I didn't bother to turn Monica's way, because she was about to catch hell if she didn't end this right now. "We're done, Monica. Quit while you're ahead. Please."

She walked away, but before she got too far, I spoke out again. "And if you ever talk to me like that in front of my son again, you won't have to walk out because I will open the door for you to leave with a foot stuck in your ass."

"That may not be such a bad idea because I'm sick of this shit. All of it."

I let Monica speak that noise, but the truth was she wasn't sick of it when she rode around in a brand new

Mercedes I purchased for her a month ago. She wasn't sick of it when she was out buying expensive clothes, getting her hair and nails done, or when she gave money to her family. When she invited them over here to brag about how lavishly we lived, she wasn't sick about it either. So, her words went in one ear and out the other. She was just upset because she had no control over my dick. She knew damn well that she was wasting her time and mine, trying to argue about where I'd been all night. She just hated the fact that I was with Keysha, because the two of them never got along.

After I cooked dinner for me and Keith, and we went for a swim in the backyard, my boy Rico and his son, Lamar, came over. He was one of Keith's friends and while they played video games, me and Rico sat by the poolside talking business. My daughter was asleep on my chest and Monica was inside with our son. She hadn't said more than a few words to me all day, but I didn't trip.

"We need to make that move by next week. Let me know when you're ready so I can rent that van," Rico said.

"Will do. Who's all going with us?"

"Just me, you, and Carmelo. You know Papa James don't want a bunch of niggas traveling with us."

"Yeah, I know. By next Friday I should be good. I need to work out a few kinks in my personal life before then, but other than that, it's time to shake some things up and do what we gotta do."

Rico slapped his hand against mine, before leaving without his son who stayed to play with Keith. After I closed the door, I carried my daughter upstairs. When I opened the double doors to my master suite, Monica was lying across the bed with our son in front of her asleep. Her long, wavy hair was spread out on the pillow, and with her skin being so light, I could see the puffiness in her eyes. At times, it bothered me to see her so upset. The last thing she needed to do was worry about tedious shit, like Keysha, who didn't even matter.

I laid my daughter on the California king bed and sat on it. Monica looked past me to look at the TV.

"I'm sorry about earlier. I hate to get at you like that, but I wasn't in the mood. I had to deal with some shit with Keysha and her mama, and the last thing I wanted to do was come here and start arguing with you."

"I don't care what you've been through with Keysha and her mama. All I wanted was for you to answer my question. I still want to know the truth. Did you or did you not have sex with Keysha last night?"

I didn't want to answer Monica's question, because I would never hear the last of this. Months ago, I told her I was done fucking with Keysha because the bitch was crazy. She'd done some foul shit over the years and said some harsh things to Monica that neither of us appreciated. For me to go have sex with her wasn't good, but the way she looked in those tight jeans, gave me a rise that needed immediate attention.

"What difference does it make, Monica? As long as I don't bring no shit here, you shouldn't even care about what I'm doing out there?"

"I do care, and don't you think for one minute that what you do out there doesn't come here. It does. I want to know what's up because it will make a difference."

Now, she had my attention. "What might that be? I'm eager to hear it."

"Yes or no, Tremaine? Did you or didn't you?"

"Yes. Now tell me about this difference." I stood up.

Monica stared at me without a blink. I could see that she despised me in her own little way, but I knew that I had this entire situation on lock. She wasn't going anywhere. She wasn't going to do anything but be mad at me for a few days then shit would get back to normal. The one thing that I knew about Monica was that she loved money. She wanted the best of everything, and she also wanted our kids to have everything they needed. She knew that walking out on me would tremendously change her financial status. And there was no other nigga out there who would give her all that I had given.

For now, all she could do was go into the bathroom and shut the door. I knocked to tell her I was getting ready to jet.

"I'll be back in an hour or so. Lamar and Keith are in his room playing video games. They already ate, so no need to fix them anything else. They also got some movies in there to watch, so when you get time, ask if they want to watch them. Other than that, if you need anything hit me up. I love you, ma, whether you realize that shit or not."

Monica didn't respond. I kissed my sleeping babies, said good-bye to Keith and Lamar then left.

Within the hour, I was at Bree's apartment. Bree was the kind of chick who didn't give a fuck. She got in my shit from time to time, but for the most part we were all good. She accepted my situation with Monica, but she hated Keysha with a passion. I think Bree didn't trip off of me as much because, with her being a stripper, she had plenty of niggas trying to pay up for the pussy. She was only upping it, though, to a specific few, so she said. But when all was said and done, I could have her the way I wanted her with the snap of my finger.

Bree stood in the doorway with her yellow bra and panties on. Her chocolate body looked as if it were dipped in baby oil, and her long braids flowed all the way down her back to the tip of her apple bottom ass.

"Before you enter, do you mind telling me what happened to you last night?"

"Questions, questions, questions. This is what my life consists of, but the answer is I was busy and couldn't make it. Sorry."

Bree stepped away from the door to let me inside.

"Apology not accepted, but it is what it is. I was hot and bothered last night, but another nigga came over to take care of that little problem for me. He's still here, so you need to make this really quick."

"I just dropped by to see my son. Where is he?"

"He's at his friend's house. I'm not picking him up until later. If you want to stop by then, call ahead of time and let me know."

"A'ight. I'ma let you get back to your company. Whatever you do, don't hurt that fool. I know what you're capable of, especially when you're so hot and bothered."

"I know what you're capable of too, that's why I preferred you over him. But there are times when I don't mind settling for less. A sista gotta do what she must, especially when she's trying to get hers. With that being said, before you go, can you do me a favor?"

"What's that? Or should I say, let me guess. Money, right?"

Bree put her praying hands together and nodded. "Just a little. Niggas at the club ain't making it rain like they used to, so I've been short on cash for a while. I've been looking for another job too, 'cause you know this stripping shit getting played out."

"Yeah, I know. I wish you would do something else, but that's like you telling me that I need to do something else. So do you, ma, but also do whatever to make some changes, especially for the sake of our son."

"I feel you. Same to you, though. Now, go. Call me later and be good, punk."

Bree leaned in for a kiss. I had no problem reciprocating. I left so she could get back to her business, and then made another quick detour before going back home.

Porsha lived about twenty minutes away from Bree. Yeah, Porsha was one of Keysha's good friends, but they never really got along. Why? Because of me. Porsha and me had been hooking up for the past two years, off and on. I didn't intend for anything like this to happen, but I always noticed her watching and checking me out whenever I was at Keysha's place. Then, one night we were at a club together and I pulled Porsha aside and asked her what was up. That's when she expressed how much she'd been feeling me. We didn't say much to each other at the club that night because Keysha was there. But later on that night, Porsha called me and I went to her house. I was tipsy, but when she threw that good pussy on me, I woke the fuck up. Ever since, we'd been sneaking around doing our thing. Porsha was the one who told me all the foul shit Keysha had been doing and saying behind my back. She kept me tuned in to everything, and that's how I was able to find out where Keysha's mama had moved to.

I rang the doorbell, and within a few seconds, Porsha answered with a huge smile on her face. She threw her arms around my neck, pulling me into the house.

"I miss you," she said. "Why haven't you been answering your phone?"

Mo' questions, mo' questions, mo' questions, I thought. "I've been a little busy today. But either way, I missed you too. I can't stay long, because Keith is at my house and I need to get back to him. I just stopped by to see what was up with you."

Porsha backed away and pouted. "Aww, I wish you could stay. I'm bored to death, and I thought we could maybe go get a pizza and drinks or something. You sure you don't have time?"

"Not tonight. Maybe when I get back from out of town I will."

Porsha appeared disappointed. I followed her into her bedroom where she had been sitting on the bed playing cards. They were spread all over her bed, a glass of juice was on her nightstand, along with a bag of weed. A fat joint was next to it, so we sat on her bed and started to get high.

"You know you ain't supposed to be messing around like this, and when you gon' stop," I asked.

"Soon. Now on another note, Angel called and told me what had happened between you and Keysha. I can't believe that she pissed in your orange juice and put floor wax in your eggs."

I pulled the joint away from my mouth. "She did what!" I yelled. "Did you say she peed in my orange juice!"

"Yes," Porsha giggled, but I didn't see shit funny. "I thought you knew what she had done to your food. That's why you fucked her up."

"I fucked her up because she was tripping. I can't believe that nasty bitch went out like that. I'm glad I didn't eat those eggs and I only took one swallow of the orange juice."

"What about the pancakes? She clipped her toenails and put them in there."

I thought back to when I ate the pancakes earlier. I remembered something being in my mouth and I had to spit it out. I held back on kicking Keysha's ass earlier. Now, I wish I would have torn her ass up.

"I knew something was in those pancakes, but I wasn't sure what it was. All I can say is that's fucked up. I bet I won't eat shit else from nobody's house. That's it for me."

"Aww, boo, don't be like that. I wouldn't do nothing like

that to you, but you already know how Keysha is. That bitch coo-coo, like her mama. I don't know why you keep fucking with her, and from what Angel said, y'all had sex last night too. What's up with that?"

"She raped me, like I'm about to rape you, before I get out of here."

I removed the joint from Porsha's hand and lay on top of her. She released the smoke from the joint directly in my face then placed her hand over my mouth.

"If you got Keysha's piss in your mouth, don't kiss me because I don't want to taste it."

"Fine," I said, lowering myself down between her legs. "If you don't want me to use my mouth to kiss you, maybe I can use my mouth for other things like this."

I lifted Porsha's long T-shirt and saw her peach silk panties. While she remained on her back, I moved the crotch section of her panties aside and lightly licked my tongue between her moist folds. Not only was her pussy nice to look at, but it also tasted like a juicy, sweet cherry. Her clit was swollen, and as I turned my tongue in circles around it, Porsha spread her shaking legs wider.

"I think I'm falling in love with you, Tremaine. I hate that shit too, because the last thing I want to do is be a member of your baby mama's club."

"At the rate we're going, you may as well prepare yourself to join the party."

All Porsha did was laugh. I did too, but we both already knew that she was three months pregnant.

Chapter Five

Keysha

I stood on the porch, ringing Tremaine's doorbell. It was late, but I wanted my son to come home with me. I didn't appreciate the way Tremaine had gone over to my mama's house and showed his ass; therefore, Keith was going to spend the week with me instead.

Since no one came to the door, I banged on it. Minutes later, I could see Monica walking toward the glass door with a frown on her face. She yanked the door open and lashed out at me.

"What do you want? My kids are trying to sleep, and that also includes your son."

I cocked my head back. "So, in other words, it sounds like you're trying to say my son is your son? I think not, Monica, and you're going a little bit too far with this motherly thing."

"Whatever, Keysha. Like I said, what do you want?"

"Is Tremaine here?"

"No."

"Where is he?"

"I don't know, and quite frankly, I don't care right about now."

"Sounds like you're trying to get some balls. I guess things are a bit shaky over here, huh? And for you not to know where Tremaine is that seems kind of odd. Especially since you're always chasing after him and you can sniff him out anywhere he goes."

Monica's frown turned into a smirk. "You got that right, Keysha, I sure can sniff him out. I don't necessarily chase after him, but I usually know where he is. As in right now, at this minute, you may want to call your girlfriend, Porsha. I'm sure she can direct you from there."

Monica attempted to shut the door, but I stuck my foot in it so she wouldn't. Wrinkles lined my forehead because I was curious about why Porsha's name came up.

"Porsha?" I questioned. "What do you know about Porsha, and how can she direct me on anything that has something to do with Tremaine?"

The smirk on Monica's face was locked there. "Why don't you do both of us a favor and go ask her. You're wasting your time at my house, especially when Porsha has all the answers you need."

If Monica knew something, she needed to tell me. I pushed on the door, and that's when she let go of it so I could come inside. There was a huge part of me that was so jealous because she was over here living with Tremaine like this. The foyer was lit up with a hanging, crystal chandelier and the floors were marble. A winding staircase was to the left, and a beautiful dining room was to the right.

"Monica, don't play games with me, all right? Why are you bringing up Porsha's name, and what does this have to do with Tremaine?"

Monica crossed her arms and tapped her foot on the floor. "You asked where he was so I told you. Now, if you don't mind, I have children to tend to. I'm sure with your loud voice down here, my babies will be waking up soon. I really don't have anything else to say to you, other than what a complete fool you've been."

I was almost speechless. I didn't know if Monica was fucking with my head or not.

"Are you here to get Keith? If so, I can go wake him up for you."

I was still in shock about what Monica had said. I hated for Keith to stay here with her, but things could get real ugly when I got to Porsha's house.

"I'll come get him in the morning. I need to go handle a few things right now. If Tremaine comes home soon, tell that bastard to call me. I need to speak to him right away." I turned to walk toward the door.

"I don't tell Tremaine anything, so good luck at Porsha's house and be sure to tell her I said congrats."

I quickly swung around and opened my mouth wide. "Congrats for what?"

Monica shrugged her shoulders. Her lips we sealed tight. Wondering what in the hell was going on, I bolted out of the front door and hopped in my car. Within the hour, I was parked in front of Porsha's house with rattled nerves. Something inside told me that this bitch had backstabbed me. I had known that something wasn't right all along, but I ignored the way those two always looked at each other. I pretended that nothing was there, even though I knew this thing between me and Porsha was deep. There was a reason why we always stayed at each other's throats. We could never get along. No matter where we went, we always found a way to start arguing with each other. When it came to Tremaine, she defended him. She stood by his bullshit and always made me look like the villain. This explained all of it. I felt like such a fool, and for Monica to be the one to tell me was gut wrenching.

I hurried out of my car and rushed to the door. As I was ringing the doorbell, I could hear Porsha's footsteps.

"Who is it?" she asked.

"Me. I know it's late, but we need to talk."

I could her Porsha sigh. She opened the door and stood there gazing at me. She saw the frown on my face, but her frown was deeper than mine.

"Can't we talk tomorrow," she said. "Or call me later. I was trying to get some rest, after all it is after midnight, you know."

"I know very well what time it is, but what I need to talk to you about can't wait until tomorrow."

Porsha unlocked the screen door to let me inside. At least one thing I could say was, that if she was fucking with Tremaine, he definitely wasn't paying her. Her place was crappy as fuck. She lived here for three years and barely had any furniture. The furniture she had was outdated and looked like it came from the Goodwill. I didn't appreciate the smell inside either. And the more I got a whiff of it, it smelled like Tremaine's cologne.

Porsha tightened the belt on her robe, and I followed her into the living room where she sat on the couch, tucking her feet underneath her. I sat in a chair that felt as if it had no cushion. While sucking my teeth, I gave her an evil stare. She was real fidgety and could barely look at me.

"Somebody told me something real interesting today," I said. "All I want is the truth, Porsha. This all needs to come out in the open, and when it does, it'll explain why I've been having all of these weird feelings inside of me."

"Weird feelings about what?"

"About you and Tremaine. Are you fucking with him?"

Porsha laughed and threw her hand back at me. "You can't be serious. Is this a joke or what? I barely like Tremaine, and even though I always take up for him, that doesn't mean that I want to hook up with his ass."

"I wouldn't joke around with nothing like this. A reliable source told me that you were messing with him, and she also told me to congratulate you on something pertaining to him."

Porsha started to catch an attitude. "To hell with your reliable source. I'm offended that you're over here asking me some bullshit like this. We're supposed to be friends, Keysha. I thought we were better than this. I would never fuck with Tremaine, and he ain't even my type. You over here talking real crazy. I know you and him been through some crazy shit, but how dare you come over here and talk this madness to me?"

Porsha seemed like she was telling the truth. I regretted coming over here with this crazy talk. She must have thought I was a damn fool. Then for me to believe that trick Monica. I had to be out of my mind.

"I— I apologize for coming to you like this, but why does it smell like Tremaine in here? I'm serious too, Porsha. As soon as I walked through that door, I could smell him."

Porsha pursed her lips and shook her head. "You ain't smelling him up in here. He has no reason to be over here, and if he ever came over here I would slam the door right in his face. It seems to me that you got it real bad for that nigga. Anytime you can smell him everywhere you go, something is really wrong with that."

I was too embarrassed. My face had cracked and this was not a good look for me. I had a headache and needed to go home to rest my damn mind. This whole thing with Tremaine had me tripping.

"I get what you're saying, Porsha, and maybe I do need to go chill out for a while. Go ahead and get some sleep. I must say that you over there looking real tired."

"I am. Definitely need my beauty rest, so my dear friend, we'll talk tomorrow. I'm sorry about what happened between us at the nail shop, and you know I don't mean half of the stuff I say."

"Well, I do," I said, laughing. "But it's all good. I apologize too."

We hugged each other and Porsha walked me to the door.

"If you don't mind me asking you this, who was the so-called reliable source that told you me and Tremaine were fucking? I want to know so I can cuss that mofo out."

"I'm too ashamed to say it, only because I know how the trick is and I shouldn't have listened to her."

"Who? Tell me."

"Monica. I stopped by their house tonight, looking for Tremaine. Monica told me he was here with you. She also told me to tell you congrats, and the heifer tried to imply that you were pregnant by Tremaine."

Porsha shook her head. "I could slap you for believing that bullshit, but I love you too much and won't go there. I'm glad you stopped by so we could clear this shit up, and the next time I see Monica, she gon' get it. I wonder why she chose me of all people. She could have said anybody else, but me. I guess she wanted us to start fighting each other, and that would have been right up her alley."

"Right. But it's over and done with. I'll deal with Tremaine tomorrow. As for her, I'll deal with her another time."

Porsha nodded and watch me as I headed toward my car, feeling some kind of way about our little discussion. As I got in my car, I realized that I didn't have my keys. I searched my pockets and looked around inside of my car. Then it hit me. I had forgotten my keys on the living room table. Porsha had closed the door, but when I stepped up to it, I noticed it was cracked. I went ahead and let myself in. I was getting ready to say something, but I could hear Porsha talking on the telephone. As I moved toward the kitchen to where she was, I eavesdropped on her conversation that sounded real interesting.

"Can you believe that shit," she said with her back turned. "You need to find out how Monica knows about us and kick her ass for spreading our business. She be all up in your business, boo, and she probably got a private detective watching you." Porsha paused then laughed. "Yeah, I know. It is what it is, and I miss you already. Your baby misses you too, but we gon' try to get some sleep, now that your idiotic baby's mama is gone. I can't believe she came over here, and the look on her face was so funny. She actually smelled yo' ass in here, and I was like really? You really smell that nigga up in here? I thought I was busted, but next time don't wear that cologne, okay?"

Porsha laughed again. I stood in the kitchen's doorway in shock. My eyes were bugged and I could barely move. None of this felt good to me, simply because all of these idiotic, stupid, dumb, slow titles I had heard about myself were starting to apply. I trusted way too many people and how stupid could I have been not to see through Porsha's lies.

"Okay, handsome. See you soon and be sure to check that bitch Monica when you get home. Also, be careful out there tonight. Keysha is on the loose, and ain't no telling what she may do to you. You need to tell her to go sit her ass down. She knows she be working me."

Porsha chuckled and turned around. That's when she saw me standing in the doorway. Her face fell flat and she barely got out the word "good-bye" before I charged into the kitchen and slammed my fist into her stomach. The phone dropped from her hand and she grabbed her belly while bending over.

"Oh my God!" she shouted. "It hurts. My stomach hurts!"

"Good, 'cause I'm on the loose and I want that shit to hurt more!"

I felt as if my punches weren't hurting enough. And to me, the bitch was faking. Knowing so, I picked up a black skillet that was on the stove and started wearing that hooker out. She crouched down and tried to block my hard blows. I pounded her ass everywhere I could, especially in her stomach as she now laid sideways on the floor.

"You trifling, skank bitch!" I shouted. "This is what you get for betraying me! How could you, Porsha? How could you fuck with Tremaine, knowing damn well how I feel about him!"

"I didn't know!" she screamed. "I swear. I didn't know you still loved him!"

"But you knew he was my baby's daddy, didn't you! Don't lie, bitch! You knew it! And before I go sit the fuck down, I'ma lay yo' ass down!"

When she opened her mouth to lie again, I hit her in the face with the skillet. Her teeth cracked and her head jerked back. Blood gushed from her mouth and all she could do was cover her head with her arms. That left her stomach open. I punted her midsection like I was kicking a football. When she lowered her hand to secure her stomach, that's when I hit her with the skillet again. I tore her ass up, until she dropped her limp arms by her side and could barely move.

"I hope his dick was worth it to you," I said then dropped the bloody skillet on the floor as I stood over her. "Let this shit be a lesson to you. Never ever fuck with a nigga who done had his dick up in me. If you want to be somebody's friend, be that friend, not a motherfucking foe."

Before I left, I punted that heifer one last time. I was so sure that she would reach out to Tremaine, but hopefully I would get to him before she did.

Chapter Six

Tremaine

I had been gone all day. I knew when I left that I wasn't coming back within the hour because I didn't want to see Monica moping around all day long, crying and fussing about the things I'd done. I'd be the first to admit that when it came to relationships, I wasn't shit. I was a dog. I didn't always treat women the way in which they wanted or needed to be treated, and I definitely had some work to do. Thing is, I didn't have the time to give no bitch what she really needed in her life. I made that clear to everybody, that's why I didn't understand why I kept catching hell all of the time. All they said they ever wanted was the truth. But when a nigga told them the truth, they weren't trying to hearing it.

For a long time, Monica kept her mouth shut. But things were starting to change and I didn't like it. That's what made me stay at Keysha's house the other night. That was a big mistake. All that did was make her think there was hope between us. Truthfully, there wasn't. All I wanted to do was take care of Keith and be done with it. But Keysha acted as if the two of them came as a package. Just because I didn't want her, that didn't mean I didn't want him. Sometimes, I felt like taking my kids and running away from all of these bitches. If I didn't have to deal with my kids' mamas, I would run in a heartbeat. But someway or somehow, I did have to deal with them. There was no getting around it.

After I left Porsha's house, I stopped by to chat with Papa James about how to handle everything on our trip. He had been planning this for months so I wanted everything to go smoothly. I was more than ready to do whatever I needed to do to add more paper to our stack. The moment I left Papa James' crib, that's when Porsha had called me. I was in shock that Keysha had been to see her, but even more in shock when I called home and Monica told me Keysha had stopped by there too. When Monica told me she was the one who sent Keysha to Porsha's crib, I was outdone.

"You shouldn't have done that," I said. "Is it hard for you to mind your own business?"

"You are my business, Tremaine, and that's my problem. I can't do this anymore. You think it's totally okay for you to be out there in the streets doing whatever the hell you want, while I stay here with the kids all day doing nothing. And now that Porsha is pregnant, all you're going to do is tell me to accept it and flaunt your new baby around over here. You must think I'm some type of damn fool, and why don't you respect me enough to know that this is wrong? You say you love me, but love shouldn't feel like this. This material shit is not enough for me to turn a blind eye and pretend that none of this is happening."

"I know you're upset, but you already know the deal with me. If you're at your breaking point, I can't do anything about that. If you feel as though it's time for you to walk, then do it. Like I said earlier, I'm not going to stop you or hold you back. All I want you to do is make time for me to see my kids. That's all I want you to do, because, truthfully, nothing else really matters."

I could hear Monica sniffling over the phone. "How can you say this? How can you be so cold and act like you don't care? I've given you years and years of my life,

Tremaine. And now you're talking like you don't care about us anymore."

"I do care, ma, but I'm not going to cry about your decision to walk away from me. I'm not going to change who I am, and I'm not going to accommodate nobody's situation but my own. You want to speak on our years together, but over the years, Monica, I've given you everything. Anything you ever wanted, all you've had to do was ask for it. I tried to show you that I love you more than anyone, and even though I may do my thing in the streets, I always come home to you. The bitches who I fuck with know who I love. They know that when I do settle down, I'll eventually be with you. Unfortunately, my clock is different than yours. What you want right now, I can't give it to you. I'm sorry, but if the love I'm offering ain't enough, what else can I do?"

"It's not enough. Good-bye, Tremaine. I called Vivica to come over here and watch Keith and Lamar. By the time you get here, I'll be gone. I'll call you in a few days to let you know where I'll be. I promise not to keep your kids from you, but understand that I need time to sort things out."

I was hurt that Monica was leaving, but I wasn't about to plead and beg her to stay. As I sat silent over the phone, a call beeped in. When I looked to see who it was, it was Keysha calling. I ignored her calls, but she kept calling back.

"Hold on," I said to Monica. "Don't hang up and don't go anywhere, all right?"

I clicked over. "Let me hit you back later."

"No need," she snapped. "Why didn't you tell me you were fucking with Porsha and that she was having your baby?"

My face twisted from hearing her loud voice. "Man, I don't have time for this. I said let me hit you back."

"And I said you're a low down, dirty-ass nigga! You ain't shit Tremaine, I swear yo' ass ain't nothing!"

"I agree. Now, good-bye."

I clicked back over, but Monica had hung up. When I tried to call her back, she wouldn't answer. Then I couldn't dial out at all because Keysha's calls kept coming through, back to back.

"What!" I shouted into the phone. "We both agreed that I'm not shit, so what else do you want!"

"Why?" she said. "Why in the hell would you go behind my back and screw my friend? Then to get her pregnant was foul! Didn't you know I would find out? What were you going to say to me then, Tremaine?"

"Honestly, I really didn't care. I don't care about none of this, Keysha, and now that you know Porsha is pregnant, maybe you'll be gone and you'll stop fucking harassing me all the goddamn time."

"Nigga please. I'm never going to stop harassing you, and as long as you're Keith's daddy, I intend to make your life a living hell. As for you and Porsha's baby, you can forget about that shit. There won't be no baby because I just went to her house and beat that muthafucka out of her. By now, she may need your help, so I suggest you get back over there and go see about that bloody bitch."

I couldn't believe this was happening right now. I had just gotten off the phone with Porsha and everything sounded all good. No matter what was going on, everything had to wait. I had to go home and see what was up with Monica before I did anything else. I didn't want her to leave with my kids. I had a feeling that if she jetted, it would be a long time before I saw them again.

"I hope to God that you're lying. If you did anything like that to Porsha and her baby, you know you're going to jail don't you? If you do, what is Keith going to do? You need to calm the fuck down, Keysha, and think about shit before you act."

"Don't worry about Keith. I got him all taken care of, me and his daddy both. And surprise, surprise, Tremaine. His daddy is not you. All I ever wanted was your damn paper, along with some of your dick. Now that I've gotten enough of that, feel free to bring my son back home. We're done with you now. With all these kids you got, yo' ass gon' be too broke to support us."

I didn't know if Keysha was bullshitting or not. But by now, sweat beads dotted my forehead, my palms were sweating as I gripped the steering wheel, and my heart was racing. There were plenty of times when I felt as if Keith didn't look like me. Plenty of times when Papa James questioned me about him, and my boys insisted that he wasn't my son. But I didn't want to believe it. I had made a real connection with Keith that I didn't want to let go of.

"Keysha, you're playing with fire. If you've lied to me out of spite and for money, I swear I'm going to kill you. Why in the fuck would you put Keith in the middle of this, huh?"

"He's not in the middle of anything. And if he is, he won't be for long, daddy. You can threaten to kill me all you want to, but come morning, there will be a restraining order against you. Don't come near me, and what you can do is drop my son back off at my mama's house where you got him. After that, our little deed is done. Good riddance to you, and thanks for playing the fool for years! Sucker!"

Keysha hung up, causing a rage of fury to lock in my eyes. I wanted to turn around and go beat her motherfucking ass. I also wanted to go see about Porsha too, but Monica first. I had to get to Monica then I would see what was up with this situation with Keith then Porsha.

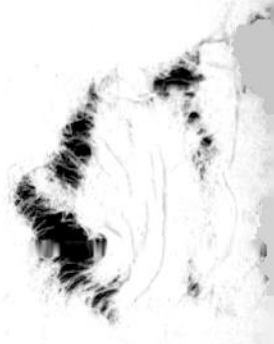

With my mind racing a mile a minute, I slammed on the accelerator, causing my sports car to go faster.

By the time I hit the highway, I was going way over a hundred miles an hour. My car whipped through traffic, but all of a sudden a slow pickup truck jumped right in front of me. I slammed on my brakes, but by then it was too late. The impact was so powerful that my car flipped over and my body went straight through the windshield. My eyes fluttered and all I remembered seeing was a cloud of thick white smoke. The smell of burnt rubber filled my nostrils and my entire body was numb. After that, darkness hit me.

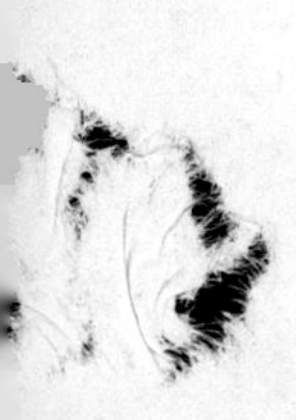

Chapter Seven

Tremaine

All day, every day. The loud beeping sounds was all I could hear. I couldn't move, couldn't talk, and couldn't even open my eyes. Then again, if I strained hard enough, I could open them. My vision was blurred and my mouth was so dry that I could taste blood in the cracks of my lips. I tried to wiggle my fingers, but nothing happened. Attempted to turn my head, but it stayed still. Above me was a squeaking ceiling fan and a bunch of white lights. I heard several people mumbling, but my eyes couldn't shift in their direction. I had no idea how long I'd been lying there, but to me it seemed like a very long time. There was no smell, no nothing. Not even any pain. My thoughts of lying there like this caused tears to rush to my eyes. I could feel those tears running down the corners of my eyes. I tried to blink, but my eyes remained focused on the bright, blinding lights.

After lying there for a while, a pretty face appeared before me. I had no idea who it was, and her voice was so soft that I could barely make out her words. I tried to tell her to speak up, but my mouth wouldn't move. It wasn't until I saw a baby in her arms that I realized that the chick speaking to me had to be Monica.

"Home," she said in a whisper. "Come home now Tremaine. I want you back. We need you to come back."

I tried to lift my hand to wipe her tears, but no go. I wanted to hold my child, especially when I heard him crying. Monica rocked him in her arms, trying to quiet him. But as time went on, the cries got louder and louder. Those cries turned into laughter and another chick appeared. Monica stepped away so she could have her say. Her voice was sassy, so I could tell it was Bree.

"What happened to you, Tremaine? I thought you were going to stop by later? Every time you tell me that shit, I get my hopes up. But it is what it is because you know I'ma get mine."

Bree smiled at me and held my hand with hers. I couldn't even feel her touch. I tried to smile but couldn't. Wanted to tell her to wait for me tonight, but I suspected that I wasn't going to make it.

As I was able to shift my eyes to the left, I saw Porsha with tears streaming down her face. She was holding her belly and kept shaking her head. "What am I going to do?" she cried. "I don't know how I got myself in this predicament, but you gotta get up and help me figure this shit out. I can't do this all by myself, Tremaine. I need you and I'm so afraid right now."

Afraid of who or what? I tried to ask. *And what about the baby? How is the baby?*

Porsha kept sobbing. Unable to hear me she walked away.

Minutes later, everybody had cleared out. I was alone again. I laid there for what seemed like more hours and hours had gone by. My tears kept on flowing. The beeping sound was driving me nuts and those bright lights were killing me. I wanted to close my eyes and go to sleep but this time they wouldn't even close. So many thoughts were swarming around in my head. My mind traveled back to the accident. I saw myself driving fast. I could actually see the crash and my whole body jerked when I witnessed the deadly crash. The man inside of the truck was thrown from his vehicle too. I saw him flip in the air and land hard on the concrete. After that, another car came and ran over his body. There was no doubt in my mind that he was dead, but what about me?

While in thought, I heard the weeping sound of her voice. It was so loud that it made the beeping sounds fade away. Appearing in front of me was Keysha. A black veil covered her face and black, silk gloves were over her hands. She leaned over me, screaming and hollering, "Why?" at the top of her lungs.

"Why, Tremaine? Why did you do this? I need for you to come back to us and handle your damn business. Keith needs you. I need you too! Come back, baby, come back!"

Keysha started pounding my chest real hard. I could feel my body moving and it was as if I was jumping up from the bed. As her fists slammed into my chest, the beeping sounds came back. The frown on her face turned into a smile, and I figured that her pounding so hard on my chest was bringing me back to life. Even I had to smile about that.

"Come on, baby," she said. "I see you fighting. Fight harder! Harder than that!"

"I'm trying," I said to myself.

I didn't think she heard me, until she moved in closer and whispered something in my ear. "You'd better try harder than that, nigga! That way, when you get back here, you can welcome your new baby into this world. I'm eight months pregnant and I expect for daddy to step it the fuck up. This now makes me an official member of your baby mama's club, and I intend to drive yo' ass crazy! So get your lazy ass out of this bed, bring me my money, and don't forget the goddamn Pampers and milk! I need that shit too!"

Keysha backed away from me and laughed. Right then, I didn't care if I were dead or alive. I didn't know if I was in my casket or in a hospital bed. All I knew was the beeping sound went flat and I could feel my body being jerked around. The sound of my heartbeat was now thumping in my ears. I was starting to feel more pain. The room was spinning, and when I opened my eyes, I was dizzy as fuck but still alive. Thing is, I wasn't sure if that was a good thing or not, especially if Keysha's ass was really pregnant. *Fuck*!

The Side-Hoes Club

by

Teeny

Chapter One

MIAH

Many people have it twisted about who or what a side-ho really is. The weirdest thing of all is that almost every chick in her lifetime has played the side-ho role, but she may not have classified herself that way. And for anyone to assume that a side-ho's life is miserable, I would only ask for those individuals to rethink that assumption because, for many of us, that is not the case.

A sidekick, side-ho, side-chick—whatever anyone wants to call it is fine with me. All I consider myself as being is the other woman. A woman who doesn't have to deal with the daily headaches of trying to be locked in a committed relationship. A woman who doesn't have to argue or worry about who or what the player in her life is doing. A woman who is free to fuck with whomever she wishes, who doesn't mind sharing, and a woman who is perfectly fine with being alone sometimes.

Call me crazy or not, but that's the kind of chick I am. If that makes me a ho, so be it. If it makes me a home-wrecker, I'll wear that badge of honor too. At the end of the day, as long as I'm happy, why should anyone give a fuck?

The bottom line is to have your man in check. Hold his ass accountable, not me. While I'm sometimes a willing participant, so is he. Instead of creating titles for bitches like me, why not come up with a title that is fitting for the brothers who continue to juggle more than one chick and play games? Like side-dog-ass-nigga-who-needs-to-quit! I mean, put the blame back where it belongs, because the only thing I've been guilty of is making sure my needs are met before anyone else's is. It's all about taking care of me first.

Like always, Moses was late. He was supposed to be at my apartment for dinner around six, but it was almost seven o'clock. There was no more steam coming from the catfish nuggets I'd fried that had gotten cold. The wine that was chilling in the ice bucket wasn't on point because the ice had melted. The soothing music in the background came to a halt, and I switched from my red negligee to a plain, white long T-shirt that fell above my knees. My hair was sleeked back into a ponytail, and every single drop of makeup that I had on had been washed off. Not that I needed much makeup, because my smooth, brown skin still shone without it. Even the T-shirt I wore made me look sexy. There was no question that I could give Gabrielle Union a serious run for her money.

As I sat on the couch with my feet propped on the coffee table and eating popcorn while watching TV, I heard a knock at the door. The three light knocks let me know that it was Moses. I took my time moving to the door, and when I opened it, all I could do was roll my eyes.

It wasn't that I was upset with Moses about being late, and the truth was, I had gotten used to his tardiness. What bothered me was the way he looked. His droopy eyes implied that he'd been into another argument with his so-called significant other. The sleeve on his shirt was torn, and there was a small scratch on the side of his face. This nigga was definitely killing my vibe, but I opened the door wider to invite him in. He walked in with his head hanging low, hands in pockets.

"Sorry I'm late," he said in a soft tone. "But you already know that bitch was tripping tonight."

"Don't be sorry. No need to be."

I closed the door and stood in front of it as Moses plopped down on the couch, shaking his head. He cracked his knuckles and bit down on his bottom lip

"I get so tired of the bullshit. Every time I come home from work, all I listen to is a bunch of bitching. There ain't ever any food on the table, and she's been there all damn day. The house a mess and the dishes been piled in the sink for two damn days."

He was the one who had proposed to this trifling bitch. Now he wanted to complain.

"Stop complaining, Moses. After all, this is the woman you say you love and who you're going to marry. Calling her a bitch is unnecessary, and even though I don't mind you coming here to vent, I prefer that we not spend the evening talking about your fiancée."

"You're right. I apologize for talking about that bitch, but she really works my nerves. I just wish I didn't love her like I do. It would be so much easier for me to walk away from this. I'm not even sure if I want to get married anymore, and that's for real."

Moses was talking shit. As always, I was there to listen to these sorry-ass niggas I considered cowards. They talked all this crap to the other woman but didn't have the guts to tell the loves of their lives how they really felt. No matter how many times I stressed that I didn't want to hear it, Moses just kept on running his mouth. I didn't dare repeat myself about not wanting to hear it; after all being with Moses was beneficial to me. Not only was his sex on point, but he also kept my pockets thick with paper. There was never a time when I asked him for something and he didn't provide it. He never complained; therefore, he didn't get many complaints from me. This relationship worked well for the both of us. If he needed me to be there for him after the marriage took place, I would be. Then again, that depended on who else was occupying my time too.

I walked over to the couch and stood behind Moses. I unbuttoned his shirt and pealed it away from his bulging muscles. No words could describe how sexy Moses was, and as I began to press my hands against his carved chest, he dropped his head back on the couch and looked at me.

"That feels so good," he said. "I don't know what I would do without you in my life right now."

Like always, I smiled and remained silent. I rubbed the flowing waves on his head and then moved my hands to his broad shoulders that were stacked like a linebacker. Moses cocked his neck from side to side and closed his eyes.

"I thought you were hungry," I said. "If you fall asleep, you'll do so on an empty stomach."

"Nah, I'm not falling asleep. I'm just thinking. Thinking about how great your hands feel. Thinking about how many positions I'm going to put you in tonight, and I'm thinking about what I need to do with my life."

His position statement got my attention, but that other stuff didn't matter. At thirty-two years old, Moses already knew what he was going to do with his life. He was going to marry the lazy trick he'd fallen in love with in college, and do his best to go live happily ever after. He was wasting his time trying to convince me or himself otherwise.

"I don't know what you're going to do," I said. "But whatever it is, I got your back. I got something else for you too, but that'll have to wait until later."

Moses smiled and his mood was starting to change. He got up and went to the bathroom. By the time he got done, I had already gone to the kitchen to warm his food.

I poured both of us a glass of wine, gave him a beer, and we sat in the living room, watching the football game.

"These fish nuggets are off the chain," Moses said, dipping them in tartar sauce. "Girl, you know you can cook."

I always appreciated the nice things Moses said about me. I doubted that he referred to me as a bitch, and when it came to respect, he always delivered.

Moses picked up his bottle of beer; I lifted my glass of wine. As we were about to toast, there was a knock on my door. I wasn't expecting anyone. The other men in my life, Carl and Juan, knew better than to show up at my apartment without calling. And if it was either of them, they would be turned away.

Moses had the audacity to speak up first. Jealousy was in his eyes, and how dare he try to catch an attitude because somebody was at my door.

"I hope I didn't come at a bad time. And whoever it is, you better tell that nigga you're busy."

If I opened my mouth, I'd have to go off on Moses' ass. It was his way of thinking he was in control of the situation. The truth was, there was no need for me to argue with a man like him who was only good for sex and dishing out cash. Cash that wasn't much to brag about, but was helpful to my financial situation.

"Who is it?" I said while standing by the door.

"Karla. Is Moses here? I know he is, so don't lie for him."

I turned to Moses and he damn near choked on the beer he was drinking. For the first time ever, his bitch had shown up at my place. She must have followed him tonight, and whatever they'd been arguing about must've brought her to my doorstep.

Moses got up from the couch and walked over to the door. He was waiting on me to say something but I kept quiet. The one thing I wasn't going to do was lie for him. He needed to man up and handle this shit, especially since he was the one who led his woman over here.

"See what she wants," he said in a whisper. "Either way, tell her I'm not here."

Like I said, this fool was a coward. Now was the perfect time for him to express what a non-cooking, lazy bitch Karla was, but I was sure he wouldn't go there with her.

"I'm going to open the door, but you need to say something to her. It's obvious that she already knows you're here."

I didn't dare wait for another response from Moses. I pulled on the door, and Karla stood on the other side with a mean mug on her face. The sad thing was she was a cute chick. Had a tight body, short layered hair, and blemish free light skin. She probably could have had any dude she wanted, but there she was tripping with a fool like Moses. I guess when you know better, you do better.

Karla folded her arms and stood with much attitude. Her eyes shifted from me to Moses who stood with a blank expression on his face.

"I figured you would be here, and I guess this is the same Miah sending you text messages. I'm sure you won't tell me the truth, so let me introduce myself." Karla extended her hand to mine. I didn't have anything against her, so I reached out my hand.

"Miah, I'm Karla, Moses' fiancée. Do you mind if I come in?"

Surely, Moses didn't want her to come inside, but I widened the door. She walked her snooty self inside, and looked around with a frown on her face. My apartment wasn't what you would necessarily see in *Better Homes & Gardens* magazine, but it was decorated with unique contemporary furniture that satisfied me. Obviously, my colorful taste wasn't suitable to her.

"So, what's it going to be, Moses? Since you have your shirt off and everything, I assume you intended to stay the night here."

"Your assumption may be correct. And it's better than staying at home and arguing with you all the time."

Karla looked me up and down then rolled her eyes. "I don't like to argue with you at all, but what else am I supposed to do when you I see all of these hoochies calling you. Do you not want me to fuss when I smell another woman's perfume on you? I followed you because I knew you weren't going out with the boys like you said you were. I mean, come on, Moses. You bring a lot of this shit on yourself. How dare you talk this marriage bullshit to me, and then turn around and do the things that you do? It doesn't make sense."

Moses wanted to play hard, but as Karla's eyes watered, his tune changed. "I do want to get married, but I'm just so tired of so many things that are going on with us."

"Things like what? You are the reason things aren't working out, so don't go blaming me for our relationship not going smoothly."

By now, I had walked over to the couch to take a seat. I got an opportunity to see Moses be the real wimp that he was, and from the way he acted, he had to be embarrassed.

"I know I haven't been one hundred with you, but like I said to you before, Miah and me are just friends. I come here sometimes to talk to her about what I be going through. Unlike you, she listens to me and doesn't nag or gripe about nothing."

If Karla believed that friend shit she was a damn fool. We were more than friends, but it was up to her to elaborate on what he'd said. Truthfully, I was ready to throw both of them the fuck out of my apartment. But I was too interested in how all of this dumb shit was going to play out.

Karla folded her arms across her chest. "Friends don't cook dinner for you, and they don't send you text messages that tell you how much they miss you. They also don't allow you to walk around their apartment with no shirt on, and they don't wear T-shirts with no damn underclothes on underneath them while you're here."

Well, she had a point. I wondered how Moses was going to counter that.

"What she wears in her apartment is her business, not mine. And friends do cook for friends, especially when some other people fail to do it. I don't ever recall her sending me a text message saying that she missed me. The truth is, the only person I ever miss when I'm away from them is you."

No this nigga didn't just throw me under the bus. That shit was so weak, and I hoped like hell that she didn't fall for it.

"When it comes to cooking, you could cook for me too. And if you give me your phone, I'll be happy to point out the text messages from Miah. Better yet, I will ask Miah for myself."

Karla looked over Moses' shoulder at me. I looked straight ahead, as if I were indulged in the football game.

"Have you ever sent Moses a message telling him that you missed him?"

Moses had a pleading look in his eyes—one that told me to lie.

"Please don't come in here asking me any questions. Maybe I did, maybe I didn't—you be the judge. Besides, if you claim you saw something with your own eyes, why ask me to clear that up for you?"

Karla rolled her eyes then turned them back to Moses. Truthfully, I'd heard enough. It was time for them to wrap this mess up and get out of here.

"I'm not going to stand here and argue with you," Moses said. "Are we leaving together or not?"

Karla smacked away her tears. “No. You stay right here with your bitch tonight. I don’t know what kind of idiot you think I am, Moses, but I’ve had it with you.”

Karla removed the engagement ring from her finger and put it into his pocket. “Keep that shit,” she said. “When you’re ready to be the man I need you to be, holler at me. Until then, Moses, please make arrangements to come get your things and move out. Better yet, it looks like Miah has an extra bedroom in here. I’m sure she won’t mind you living here with her, that way she won’t be missing you so much.”

Moses for damn sure wasn’t moving up in here with me. That’s when I stood and made my first effort to get them to exit—together.

“Before either of you start to make drastic decisions, why don’t y’all go home to talk this out? Doing this in front of me is tacky. I have nothing to add to this conversation, and since Karla seems to think that I’m so into you, maybe you need to put forth a little more effort to clear that up.”

Realizing that he might not have a place to stay, Moses looked at Karla with pleading eyes. “I don’t want to leave, and I’m not going to ever leave. Miah is right. Let’s go home and talk this out without all the arguing. I have so much that I need to say to you, but I don’t want to say it right here, in front of Miah.”

Here or not, his words wouldn’t hurt my feelings. I already knew where this was going. It was going right to the altar, where the two of these idiots would stand and profess their undying love for each other, even though they had serious problems that needed to be addressed.

Karla’s stupid self just stood there as if she had nothing else to say. She knew damn well that she wanted Moses to leave with her, and it didn’t even matter that he was full of lies and games. I mean, what was her purpose for following him here? If anything, she should have been up in here kicking his ass all over the place. The fact that she wasn't was why Moses would do this crap time and time again. Karla kept giving him passes, and raising her voice or crying didn't mean a damn thing to him.

"No," she said, struggling to stand her ground. "You stay here. Enjoy yourself tonight, and I hope you're better to her than you are to me. I'm done."

She turned to open the door, but Moses grabbed her arm to stop her. I was caught off guard when she swung around and punched the shit out of him. She punched his chest so hard that it caused the nigga to stagger backward. Maybe I had this bitch pegged out the wrong way. There was a little toughness about her after all. Still, I was hoping that she knocked him on the floor and started stomping him.

"Don't fucking touch me," Karla hissed. "I said what I had to say and I will say no more."

Moses stood there like he wanted to cry, but somehow he managed to hold back his fake tears. He allowed Karla to walk out, but when he turned around, the look of embarrassment covered his face.

"I'm so sorry about this, but I need to check out of here to go see what's up. I'll give you a holla tomorrow, okay?"

I nodded and walked up to him. With his ripped shirt in my hand, I put it back on him and pecked his lips.

"Go handle your business, baby," I said. "Don't hurt nobody and call me when you have time."

Moses leaned in and we indulged ourselves in a lengthy kiss before he left. I closed the door, knowing that I wouldn't hear from him for, at least, a few days. It would probably take that long for Karla to forgive him, maybe even sooner than that. One thing was for sure, though. I wouldn't be the one to lose any sleep tonight, I wouldn't be the one to shed any tears, nor would I be the one feeling lost and confused. Side-ho or not, the path I was on seemed to work out fine. Like it or not, I was only trying to keep it real.

Chapter Two

Two days later, my other love interest, Juan, and I sat outside of The Blueberry Café having lunch. I was dressed in a strapless sundress and sandals. Juan was almost ten years older than I was, and the only reason I included him in my life was because I liked his style. Unlike Moses, Juan never talked about the woman in his life, which happened to be his wife. I knew nothing about her, nor had I ever seen her. Everything that I knew was about her husband. He had money, he dressed spectacular, and he was sexier than any older man I had ever dated before. He was another one I could always get money from, but Juan and I only saw each other about two or three times a month. He wasn't as needy as Moses was, but whenever Juan called, I knew exactly what he wanted. That was passionate sex that usually went on for hours.

"When we leave here," he said, sitting across from me and stroking his beard with a hint of gray in it. "Are we going to our usual place or somewhere else?"

"That's up to you. But why would you want to go somewhere else? I love the penthouse."

Juan shrugged his shoulders. "Because I don't want you to get bored with me, baby. I know how spontaneous and creative you are. Doing the same ole thing and having the same routine all the time may be disappointing to you. The last thing I want to do is disappoint you."

"I understand what you're saying, but trust me when I say I'm good. Actually, I'm more than good, and the penthouse you take me to is more than enough. I wish it were mine, though, and I can't stress enough how exciting it would be to live there one day."

"I'm sure it would be, and we'll have to talk about that more, somewhere down the road. For now, let's eat up and check out of here."

Damn right I was going to eat up. Juan thought he was so slick. There wasn't a chance in hell that I would move into a penthouse that had his name on it. How stupid is that? Every now and then, I tossed shit like that out to him, just to see what he would say. And every time, I got the same lame-ass response—we'll talk about that later on down the road. Yeah, right. Later on down the road my ass.

Horny as ever, I hurried to finish my pasta. Since Moses left me high and dry the other night, I was ready to get into something good, or to let something good get into me. Juan's phone call, telling me to meet him here was right on time. And while he thought I was doing him a favor, he was definitely doing me a favor too.

Juan cleared his throat and damn near choked on his water. "We need to hurry up," he said with shifting eyes.

I wondered why he was acting so strange, but when I looked up, I saw several young girls coming our way. I guess I couldn't say young girls, because the three chicks looked to be in their late twenties or in their early thirties like me. Juan was real fidgety as they got closer to us. He turned his head and pretended to look elsewhere. I figured he must've been fucking one of the bitches, but when the chicks approached the table, I discovered who one of them was.

"Hi, Dad," the young girl bent over to give Juan a hug. "What are you doing here?"

Her eyes shifted from him to me, then back to him. Juan was tongue tied.

"I'm here with a potential client of mine. Miah this is my daughter, Stacie."

We quickly spoke to each other. Stacie and her friends looked suspiciously at me, but I continued to eat my food and ignored them.

"What are you doing hanging out around here?" Juan asked. "You're a long way from home, aren't you?"

"I'm surprised Mom didn't tell you I was coming home this weekend. I came to hang out with one of my friends who is getting married. We were out looking for dresses, and decided to stop by here to get something to eat."

Juan nodded and looked past Stacie to speak to her friends. The two white chicks spoke back but didn't say much else.

Stacie looked at me again then cleared her throat. "Where's Mom?" she asked. "I haven't spoken to her since this morning. Have you?"

"Of course," Juan said after a chuckle. "I talk to her every morning and it's not like we don't live in the same house."

Stacie shrugged her shoulders. "Well, I'm not going to keep you much longer. Enjoy your lunch and I'll probably see you later when I stop by the house."

"I'll be there," Juan said.

This time, he stood to give his daughter another hug and said good-bye to her friends. After they walked off, Juan sipped from his glass of ice water. I was sure that he would use the napkin to wipe the beads of sweat from his forehead. It was pretty obvious that seeing his daughter made him nervous.

"I'm getting ready to go," he said. "I don't want her to see us leaving together, and I'll meet you at the penthouse in about thirty minutes."

I nodded and continued to eat my food. Juan dropped forty dollars on the table and left. Minutes later, I finished up and downed my diet soda. Trying to waste a little more time, I dolled up my face a bit and replied to a text message from Nadine about our meeting. She was a member of the club too, and like me, she viewed herself as the other woman.

Once I paid the waiter, I then went to the bathroom before meeting up with Juan at the penthouse. As I was in a stall, I heard the door to the restroom open, but I didn't hear anything else. When I exited the stall, Juan's daughter was standing by one of the sinks with her arms crossed. A blank expression was on her face and she searched me from head to toe.

"So, what's the deal with you and my father?" she asked in a snippy tone.

I was a little shocked by her approach, and it was the first time I found myself in a confrontation with one of my lovers' children.

"I'm not sure what you mean," I said, washing my hands. "Last time I checked, your father and I hadn't made any deals."

"You know exactly what I mean. The question is, are you fucking him or what?"

This chick was out of line. I didn't appreciate her aggressiveness, and who was she to question me about what was going on between me and her father.

"If you have any further questions, I suggest that you go and direct them to your father. With that attitude you got, I don't have anything else to say."

I walked off, but was stopped dead in my tracks when Stacie yanked on my ponytail to pull me back. Anger washed over me. I was stunned and didn't know if I should beat this bitch's ass or not. It had been a very long time since I was forced to get down like this, but I wasn't about to let anyone put their hands on me.

I quickly turned around and pushed Stacie in her chest. Pushed her so hard that she slipped on the tile floor and fell. The hard fall angered her more, so she rushed up and charged at me with swinging fists. I was so unprepared for this. But with slippery sandals on or not, I managed to stay on my feet and fight back. I had a tight hold on Stacie's long hair and pounded the back of her head with my fist.

"If you gon' run up in here being tough," I shouted. "You'd better know how to back that shit up! Come on, girl. You can do much better than this, can't you?"

Stacie's punches weren't about nothing. She was swinging wildly, but most of her punches landed on air. I made sure that mine landed somewhere on her body. That way, she would never attempt to try anything this stupid again and she would learn to mind her own damn business.

"You fucking home-wrecking whore!" she shouted. "I can't wait to tell my mother about you, tramp! And if you think I'm kicking your ass now, wait until you have to deal with her!"

Did this heifer really think she was winning? Just to be sure there was no confusion, I lifted my leg and kneed her hard in the stomach. She doubled over and grabbed her stomach. My hand was still tightened in her hair, so I drug her ass across the floor while she was on her knees.

"I guess you're still winning, right?" I said. "Not!"

Stacie didn't have shit to say, especially when I slammed my fist into her big, fat mouth. All she did was continue to swing and scream like that was really doing something.

"You bitch!" she shouted.

Right then, the restroom's door opened and with my back turned, I quickly turned around to see both of her friends.

"Oh my God, Stacie, what's going on?" one friend shouted.

The other friend didn't say anything. All she did was rush up to us with tightened fists and a beet-red face.

"You leave her alone!" she screamed. "Let her go, now!"

Stacie twisted and turned her body, trying to get away from my grip. She now had backup, and it wasn't long before all three of the bitches started to throw punches at me. I had to admit that it was kind of difficult to keep all three of them off of me, and in less than one minute, I was on the ground, shielding my face from their weak blows.

"Who's winning now?" Stacie asked as she kicked me in the back. "Leave my father alone slut or else!"

I tried to get up, but every time I lifted my head, I was hit. The punches weren't as hard as they could have been, and I was thankful that these tricks didn't have much experience with fighting. I was also thankful for the two older ladies who came into the bathroom and intervened.

"Stop this," the woman said, pushing one of the white girls away from me. "Stop or else I'll call the police."

The fight came to a halt, and the other lady helped me off the floor. "Are you okay?" she asked.

I straightened my dress and wiped blood that was coming from the corner of my mouth. "I'm fine. Just fine."

Stacie and her friends mean mugged me, before leaving the bathroom. I looked in the mirror at my wild hair and at a small bruise that was underneath my eye.

"Are you sure you're okay?" the lady asked again.

"Yes. Thank you. Thank you for asking and for stopping the fight."

"What was that all about?" The other lady said, being nosy.

"I exchanged some harsh words with them and a fight ensued. That's all."

"You need to call the police and have them arrested. There was no reason for all three of them to jump on you like that."

I shrugged and wiped my mouth with a wet napkin. "There's no need for me to call the police. I'm okay, trust me."

One of the ladies wrote her phone number on a piece of paper. "Well, if you decide to call the police and press charges against them, and you need a witness to tell what happened here, let me know."

I took the woman's phone number and thanked her again. After I splashed water on my face and put my hair into a ponytail, I left the bathroom. I wasn't sure if Stacie and her friends were still around, but I watched my back as I made my way to my car. Once inside, I drove off and called Juan to let him know I was on my way.

"What's taking you so long?" he griped. "I thought you would be here by now."

"I'm on my way. I saw a few friends of mine in the bathroom and we kept running our mouths. Sorry to make you wait so long."

"No need to apologize. I should be the one to apologize for leaving so abruptly. But you can be sure that I'm going to make it up to you."

"I hope so. Can't wait."

I hung up, thinking about how I was going to fuck the shit out of Juan today. I was so mad at how his daughter conducted herself. If she thought I was going to back away from him out of fear, she was sadly mistaken. I wasn't going to say one word to him about what had happened. But later on tonight, I expected for him to call and give me an earful. Then again, it was possible that she would get in touch with him before I got to the penthouse. I didn't want that to happen, so I pressed hard on the pedal, hurrying to my destination.

I was a little nervous when I got out of the car, but the moment Juan opened the door, I could tell everything was okay by the smile on his face. He wrapped his arm around my waist and pulled me inside.

"My dick is about to explode," he said. "Assume the position and I hope you got plenty of time on your hands today, because we gon' be here for a while."

Juan pressed his lips against mine, and as our tongues danced together, his hands crept up my sundress and he gave my ass cheeks a light squeeze. My pussy was so moist, and the crotch section of my thong was soaking wet. Juan moved my thong aside and slipped his finger far into my wetness. My heavy glaze covered his finger, and as he poked it in and out of me, I was on fire.

"Can we at least get to the bed, couch, floor or something? Please," I moaned.

Juan was so good at teasing me and his foreplay was always on point. He inched his finger out of my insides and licked his fingers with a smile on his face. Our eyes were locked together as I removed my sundress, but the trance was broken when his phone rang. He started to walk away to see who was calling, but I quickly grabbed his hand and pulled him to me.

"Not right now," I said. "If you answer that phone, like always, your conversation is going to prolong this. We've waited long enough."

"You got that shit right. Too long."

My dress was on the floor and after I stepped out of my shoes, Juan hiked me up around his waist. While I straddled him, he carried me over to the couch, bent me over it and positioned me on my stomach. He squatted behind me and pulled my ass cheeks far apart, exposing my pussy lips right at his face. I felt his tongue go deep inside. So deep that I gasped. My body was limp and I took deep breaths to calm the intensity of his fierce pussy sucking skills.

"Relax," he said as my legs began to shake all over. "I love this sweet pussy, baby. You just don't know."

I couldn't say a word because Juan was showing me just how much he loved it. Within minutes, I was on the verge of cumming. Unfortunately, though, his phone rang again. He ignored it, but the person called back one more time. In the midst of me getting mine, he placed delicate kisses on my inner thighs and stood up.

"Hold your juices," he said. "It seems like something important."

With a dripping wet pussy, I stood and watched Juan pick up his cell phone. He looked to see who the caller was. With a frown on his face, he laid the phone back down.

"Who is it?" I asked as if I didn't already know.

"My wife. I'll call her later. Right now, I need to go get a few condoms from the bedroom, so we can finish what we started."

Juan left the living room area to go get condoms. I hurried over to his phone and turned it off. By the time he came back, I was sitting on the couch with my legs wide open. One of my legs was on the floor and the other was bent on the couch, exposing my goodies. I twirled my finger around my swollen pearl then jabbed my finger inside of me as if it were a dick. Juan stood and watched with narrowed eyes. He licked across his lips as I toyed with myself and massaged my chocolate breasts.

"You look like you need some help with that," he said, moving forward. He stretched the condom over his eleven-inch dick that made me hungry and thirsty every time I saw it. I couldn't wait much longer to feel him, so I scooted down on the couch as he positioned himself on top of me. He poured one of my legs over his shoulder, and with my legs stretched wide, Juan inched his hard, thick meat into my folds.

His lips touched my ear. "I crave this pussy and I love the way it feels. Tell me this, how many times are you going to cum for me today?"

"The last time we were together I came three times. Today, let's shoot for four or five. There's something about today that has me feeling energized."

I didn't want to tell Juan that his daughter was the reason. And as a gift to that bitch, when it was all said and done, I delivered five strong orgasms to her father, and kept him there until midnight. He damn sure didn't want to leave, and as we stood at the door, I had to beg him to go.

"You know I don't want you to get in trouble," I said. "Your wife called earlier and you still haven't returned her phone call. I'm sure she's wondering where you're at."

Juan stood with his arms secured around my waist. "I'm sure she is too, but in the meantime, you be good for me. I'll call you in a few days, and don't forget to lock up when you leave." He pecked my nose and squeezed my ass one last time. "Take care, sweetheart. You know I'll be thinking about you."

After that long sex session, I was sure he would be. In addition to that, I suspected that I would be hearing from him sooner than a few days from now. I watched as he smoothly walked his way to the elevator and got on it. He waved one last time, before I shut the door and went to go shower. Twenty minutes later, I left the penthouse and headed for home. By the time I entered my apartment and turned on the TV, my phone was ringing. To no surprise, it was Juan.

Chapter Three

I tossed my car keys on the table and plopped down on the couch with the phone up to my ear.

"Why didn't you tell me what had happened between you and Stacie?" Juan whispered.

I played clueless. "I don't know what you're talking about. What do you mean?"

His voice went up a notch. "About the fight, Miah. Did you really have a fight with my daughter?"

"Yes, I did, but I figured it wasn't worth talking about. Besides, I assumed she would tell you about it anyway."

"She did tell me about it. She also told my wife about it, and now all this shit is coming down on me. Why didn't you just leave and ignore her? You didn't have to tell her anything."

I didn't appreciate the tone of his voice, nor did I not appreciate him refusing to take responsibility for his own damn actions. Of course he was looking for someone else to blame for his life falling apart, but it damn sure wasn't on me.

"Just so you know, I didn't tell her anything. But since you think I did, oh well. And since you think I started the fight, that's fine too. I don't have time for this Juan, and my suggestion would be for you to get off this phone and try your best to work things out with your family."

"I could have worked them out earlier, had you not turned off my phone. Why did you turn off my phone,

Miah? You know that shit was foul, and there ain't no other way to look at it."

"I told you earlier that I didn't want any interruptions. If you had a problem with that, then you should have answered your phone when your wife called."

"Maybe I should have. As for now, I'm done with this. I'm done with us, and I don't like how you handled this. Good-bye, Miah. Have a nice life."

Juan hung up on me. Now, there were plenty of bitches who would start crying right about now. Plenty who would call his ass back, begging and pleading with him to give her another chance. Me? I laughed at the shit. I was so sure that Juan was catching hell right now, and for weeks to come. During that time, where in the hell was he going to turn? Just who was he going to call for comfort, and who would he feel a need to apologize to? The answer—me.

I had fallen asleep on the couch and was awakened by my phone ringing. I glanced at the clock on the wall and it was almost four o'clock in the morning. I wasn't sure who would be calling me at this time, and when I looked at the number flashing across my screen, I surely didn't recognize it. Still, I answered in a groggy tone.

"Who is this?" The irate woman said. "Is this Miah?"

I released a deep sigh. I had an idea as to who the woman was. It was apparent that she hadn't gotten much sleep, and I would bet any amount of money that a strong glass of alcohol was clamped tight in her hand.

"Yes, this is Miah. Who is this?"

"This is Rebecca Anderson, Juan's wife. How do you know my husband?"

I sat up on the couch, quickly pondering about which way to go with this. Normally, if the significant other reached out and spoke to me like she had some sense, I remained cordial and did my best to calm the situation. Most of the time, I lied by saying that I had no involvement with the man, other than just being good friends.

But there were also times when some women rubbed me the wrong way. Already, Rebecca was rubbing me the wrong way, and her demanding tone and four o'clock phone call told me that she was about to get an earful.

"Speak up," she demanded. "I can't hear you, little girl. Again, how well do you know my husband?"

"Well enough for him to suck my pussy dry. Well enough for him to give me five orgasms today, and well enough for him to help me pay my bills. Is there anything else you would like to know, old lady?"

Without seeing her, I was so sure her jaw was dropped on the other end. "I don't know who the hell you are, but don't you know that you're involving yourself with a married man? Women like you disgust me, and you will regret this. With all of these single men out there, I don't understand why you're wasting your time with my husband. He is to no benefit to you, and if all you want is a wet ass, you can easily get that from a single man with no ties."

"I could, but I chose not to because your husband carries on like a single man and he's the one who makes himself available to me. In addition to that, I have yet to find a man who can fuck me as well as he does, so until I get tired of him dipping those long, eleven inches into me, you're going to have to share. Get over it, and please don't contact me anymore."

Rebecca gasped and shouted at me through the phone. "You slimy, trashy bitch! I will not share a damn thing with you, and if that's the case, ho, you can have him! He's packing his shit right now, and I hope you feel good about destroying other people's lives. Yo' ass better not ever get married, because I assure you that this shit is going to come back and bite you in yo' ass real hard!"

"Sorry, but marriage ain't for me. It's for dumb tricks like you who need to know that type of man you're dealing with, before you send him out into the world and cross the paths of fine bitches like me. Obviously, he doesn't know how to control himself, so work on that with your husband and maybe he'll change. You'll never work anything out with me, and all this conversation is, is a waste of time."

I yawned and ended the call. I was infuriated with this mess, but I had to admit that it, sometimes, came with the territory.

My whole weekend had been interesting, and even though I hated to say this, I was glad to be back at work. I worked as a secretary for Mr. Carl Wilson, a wealthy white man that was a general contractor with properties all around the city. Carl and I started hooking up when he discovered his wife had been seeing another man. He would come to work so stressed out from the situation, and his lack of enthusiasm started to affect his business. That's where I came in. I reminded him how important the company his father had left him to run was, and I encouraged him to do whatever it took to make his company the priority. There were too many people's jobs at stake, and the last thing we wanted was for this company to go under.

After a while, Carl got his mojo back. He thanked me for my encouraging words, and told me how much he appreciated me for not giving up on him. He invited me to dinner one day, and then one thing just led to another.

Ever since then, we'd been at it. He couldn't get enough of me, but there were times when I seriously got tired of fucking him. He seemed a bit obsessive with me, and I hated that he was in my personal business so much. He always wanted to know what I was doing and who I was with. None of that even mattered, because at the end of the day, he still had a wife and I wasn't interested in being with just one man.

"Miah!" Carl shouted from inside of his office.

I hated when he did that, because that meant I had to hurry out of my seat to go see what he wanted. To me, it was a control thing. Kind of like, he snapped his finger and he knew I'd come running. Why? Because I needed this job. I needed the extra paper that he dished out and it was more than any of my other love interests. Carl was the one who took good, no, great care of me. That didn't necessarily mean that I was satisfied. I mean, sex with him was just okay. He wasn't slanging eleven inches like Juan was, or not even ten like Moses was. Moses and Juan were on hit with their foreplay, but Carl always seemed to be in a rush. He was in and out. Within ten or fifteen minutes we were done. What I did, however, like was the spontaneous sex we'd had. Carl would do it anywhere. He liked to just pick up and go. I traveled a lot with him, and I did appreciate a man who was loose with his cash.

"Yes," I said, standing in the doorway of Carl's office.

He was dressed in a Nike compression shirt that tightened on his washboard abs. A Nike cap was on his head, covering his blond hair that I loved to run my fingers through. I appreciated how preppy he was, and the best thing about him was his olive-green, panty-dropping eyes.

"Come inside and let me show you this. Hurry."

Carl patted his lap, inviting me to sit on it. How we carried on in this office wasn't a big deal, because nearly everyone who worked here knew we were fucking. Hell, even his wife knew. She was the kind of woman who made her smart remarks about the situation, but pretended as if nothing was going on. As long as Carl continued to dump money into her bank account, she was all good. Or, at least, that's what I thought.

"What's so interesting?" I asked as I sat on his lap with my arm around his shoulders.

"My lawyer just sent this to me. Looks like Patricia wants a divorce."

I read the e-mail from his lawyer and shrugged my shoulders. "It's not like you didn't see this coming. She's been threatening to divorce you for a long time. How do you feel about it?"

"I'm elated. After what she did to me, I could never forgive her."

"Do you think she's divorcing you to be with someone else? And what kind of money will you have to pay her?"

"I'm not sure, but it doesn't matter. Anything to get rid of that headache, and I don't care if she's going to be with someone else. All I care about right now is this business, and you, of course."

I smiled, but I also knew that Carl cared about much more than that. We kissed, and as we locked lips for quite some time, the kiss halted when we heard someone knock on the door. Both of our heads snapped toward the door.

"Sorry to interrupt this little love session," Patricia said. "But I came here to deliver something in person to you. While I'm sure you won't shed any tears, I at least hope that you respect my wishes and pay me every dime that I'm due."

With her Michael Kors clutch tucked underneath her arm, Patricia sauntered into Carl's office with a wide smile on her face. While dressed like a million bucks, her long, reddish hair looked like it needed a wash. She couldn't get any skinnier, but to many of the white men around here, she was model-like sexy

Feeling a little uncomfortable sitting on Carl's lap, I stood and licked his wetness from my lips. Patricia rolled her eyes at me, but turned her attention to Carl.

"Here you go," she said, handing him some papers. "The sooner you read this over, get with your lawyer and sign it, the better. That way you can make all the time you want to for your whores. If you'd like to move any of them into our house, at least give me a few more days to be packed and gone."

Carl took the papers from her hand but didn't bother to read them. "Must you be such a fucking bitch," he said to her. "All you've ever wanted was my money, but just so you know, you will get whatever I decide to give you. I don't know what the hell you've proposed here, but all I will say is I'll be in touch. As for moving out, please hurry. I do have someone I'd like to move in and she's going to need every inch of the closet space you have."

Patricia laughed and looked at me. She shook her head and raked her feathered hair back with her fingers.

"I guess you'll be the one moving in. I guess it doesn't bother me one bit because I'm sure a nigger like you can do a much better job of cooking and cleaning for him. You do such a superb job around here, Miah, but be sure to watch your back. You're not the only colored woman my no good husband has his eyes on, and there is something about y'all lips that he can't seem to get enough of."

Yes, I was pissed, but the last thing I ever wanted to do was show a bitch that she had gotten underneath my skin. Carl jumped from his seat and pointed to his door.

"Get out! Get the hell out and you will be hearing from my attorney soon!"

Patricia made her body shiver. "Oooo, I'm so frightened, Carl. And look at you defending your little nigger friend. She must be doing one hell of a number on you. I don't think I've ever seen your face this red and twisted."

Carl rushed around his desk, but I grabbed his arm to stop him from moving any further. Words were simply words, but this bitch was about to strike out if she didn't leave.

"Out, Rebecca!" Carl yelled.

I pulled him toward me and made him face me. As he looked into my eyes, my arms fell on his shoulders. "Sometimes," I said in a soft tone. "You have to ignore bitter-ass people who don't know better and refuse to grow and learn from their mistakes. What you do is move on to bigger, better, and colorful things, like me."

I reached down to grab Carl's dick then leaned in for another juicy kiss. Patricia stood speechless. She then bolted out of the door, yelling profanities and calling Carl every name in the book.

"You're so good at handling those kinds of situations," he said to me. "You must have had a lot of experience."

He didn't know the half of it. I backed away from him and crossed my arms. "While I'm certainly happy about your divorce, you do know that it doesn't matter to me either way, don't you?"

Carl looked shocked. "Why wouldn't it mean anything to you?"

"Because it's not like I plan on marrying you or anything like that."

"I know that, Miah, but it does mean that we'll be able to spend more time together."

"We've always spent a lot of time together. And the truth is, I don't know if I can make more time. I do have my own life, you know?"

"I know, but a huge part of your life involves me. I don't expect for you to run home and start packing your clothes to move in with me, but I'd like to think that that will one day happen. I see you being a big part of my future, don't you?"

"I do, but I also see the other women in your life being part of that future too."

Carl cut his eyes at me and walked back over to his desk. He sat in his chair and faced me. "What other women, Miah? I hope you didn't feed into that bullshit Patricia just said to you."

"What Patricia says or has said doesn't matter. It's what I know that does. I know you well, Carl, so stop putting on this front. Just because I don't say anything, it doesn't mean that I'm not paying attention."

"Paying attention to what?"

"To your desires for black women. I'm not saying that you refuse to date women of other races, but for the past several years, you've definitely had your share of black women. I know about the stripper you've been involved with, I know about the chick who works at the bank where you deposit your money, and I also know about the one who sold you your BMW a few months ago. Then there's me. All of us are still active in your life, and just because they don't know about me, I definitely know about them. While Patricia has been nothing but a thorn in your side, it's not like you've been a saint."

Carl wanted to dispute what I'd said, but he knew I had my facts together. He fumbled with his hands then removed his cap to scratch his head. "I may be involved with those women, but you know I would drop them in a heartbeat to be with you. You know how I feel about you, Miah, so don't stand there and pretend that you don't know."

I moved closer to Carl's desk and leaned against it. "No, I don't know how you feel about me, Carl. Why don't you tell me? Are you saying that you love me? Is that what you're saying?"

Carl lips were muffled for a few seconds. He knew damn well that he didn't love me or anyone else for that matter. Like many of the men I'd dealt with, they wanted to have their cake and eat it too. That was perfectly fine with me, as long as I wasn't foolish enough to think otherwise. I wasn't.

"I wouldn't necessarily say love, but I do care deeply for you. I need you, Miah, and I can't imagine my life without you."

"No, what you can't imagine yourself without is my pussy. You want it when you want it, how you want it, and where you want it. Like I said, just because you're getting a divorce, it doesn't change one single thing. There is no need for us to start confusing ourselves about where we stand in this relationship because we already know. I won't be moving in with you no time soon and our time together won't increase. We shall remain as is, and as long as you understand that, I'm good."

Carl sucked his teeth and locked his eyes with mine. "If we're going to remain as is then you're fired. I can't stand to be around you like this, Miah, and you know I want more."

I was shocked by Carl saying that I was fired. I wasn't sure if he was being truthful with me or not. Either way, it was his way of exemplifying control. But just like my other situations, I was the one in control and sometimes, the men in my life needed to be reminded of that.

"You say you want more," I said, pulling my blouse over my head. Without a bra on, my firm breasts stood at attention, making Carl's mouth water. "If you want more, I'll give you more."

I unzipped my skirt and let it drop to the floor. While standing in my purple lace panties that revealed my goodies, I nudged my head toward the door. "If you're interested, go close the door. If not, I'll clear out my desk and get the fuck out of here."

Carl stood, but slowly made his way to the door to close it. He removed his shirt, and I had to admit that I was a sucker for men whose bodies were cut in all the right places. Carl's workout plan was doing him well.

He walked up to me and eased his arm around my waist. As he pulled me to him, my meaty, chocolate breasts were smashed against his carved chest. "I'll give you more, Hot Chocolate, but you must play by some of my rules too. If not, I'm afraid that what I said still stands. You're fired, because there is no way in hell for me to continue on like this."

I shrugged my shoulders. "Have it your way. After all, you are the boss."

Carl bent me over on his desk and had it his way. It was his way in the chair, and his way on the floor. Even after we were done, he still had it his way. I was fired, and I happily gathered my things to go. His decision didn't upset me one bit. Why? Because I knew that he would come crawling back on his hands and knees, begging me to come back. At that point, I would make it hard for him, and needless to say, I would have it my way.

Chapter Four

I would be lying if I said that there weren't times when I didn't incur setbacks. With Carl firing me, it was apparent that I had to find another job. No matter if we managed to work things out or not, I refuse to work for him again. That would be putting myself in a bad situation—more so, it would make him think that I needed him, more than he needed me.

He called earlier, but I hadn't returned his call yet. I was on the phone with Nadine, listening to the drama she'd been going through with these ridiculous women out there, trying to keep a lock on their men. She also weighed in on my situation as well.

"I don't like the fact that Carl fired you, but as long as you got that situation over there under control that's a good thing."

"Trust me when I say I do. I won't say that he's going to regret firing me, but I will say that I'm going to make it real hard for him to get back on my team."

"What makes you think he wants to be back on it? If he's messing around with those other chicks, he probably could care less about what happens to you. I guess what I'm trying to say is don't fool yourself. We tend to think these men are wrapped around our fingers, but many of them have their own agendas. That's why they do this shit to their wives and girlfriends. Don't you think for one minute that they got strong-ass feelings for us. Most of the time, it's all about the sex. Sex that they can get anywhere, honey, and not just from women like you and me."

"I get what you're saying, but I know Carl. He's my weakest link."

Nadine laughed and we continued to talk. I was in the kitchen cooking breakfast. I had a job interview at noon, so I told Nadine I would call her back so I could prepare myself.

After I hung up the phone with her, I sat at the kitchen table flipping through a fashion magazine. I always wanted to be a fashion designer, but every time I moved two or three steps in that direction, something or someone would always push me back. Particularly my ex-boyfriend, Maxwell, who changed the entire game for me. I gave up on pursuing my career because of him. I gave up on men period, because he was a dog-ass nigga who didn't deserve me. It was because of him that I would never commit myself to another relationship. I didn't trust men, and everything that I knew about them said that they were no good.

Maxwell and I had dated for seven years. I gave that nigga seven years of my life, only to realize that all of it was one big lie. We were engaged, and the day of our wedding, I found out that Maxwell had been seeing two other chicks. One of them showed up the day of the wedding. She was there to stop it, and when she entered my room to tell me the details of her and Maxwell's relationship, I was floored. I didn't want to believe it. We definitely had the wrong Maxwell because the man I was about to marry had spent every single day with me. The only time he was away from me was while he was at work.

There was no way that he had time for another chick, but boy was I wrong. He had made time. Made time during his lunch breaks, made time when he told me he was going on business trips, or when he often said he was at home with headaches and didn't feel good. My stupid self didn't have a clue. I trusted him, more than I trusted my gut that often times told me something was very wrong.

Then, the other chick approached me that night, when I didn't have much fight left in me. I was all cried out and Maxwell had revealed his true feelings about marriage. The truth was, he didn't want to be married, but he was afraid to say it. The only reason he had proposed was because, after seven years of being together, I kept threatening to leave him and he didn't want to lose me. Well, if you don't want to lose somebody then that was a clear message to do right by them. But Maxwell didn't want to do right. The other chick was pregnant by him, and I couldn't get over it. It was too much for me to swallow. Too much for my heart to muster. Every time I looked at him, I hated him. When I looked at Moses, I saw Maxwell's cowardly ways. When I looked at Juan, I saw Maxwell trying to keep the one he really cared for a secret. When I looked at Carl, I saw the Maxwell who wanted control because of his money, but knew that the money he had could get him any bitch he wanted. Basically, there were no differences in any of them. The goal was for me to learn how to deal with them and to not play the fool ever again.

The one thing that I regretted was some of the other women getting hurt. But to me, they needed to recognize and get a clear picture of the fools they were with. I wanted them to discover the real deal, because had I known, I wouldn't have been running around here with an engagement ring on my finger, bragging about soon being a married woman. I wouldn't have been faithful to Maxwell for seven, long fucking years, and I wouldn't have spent almost ten thousand dollars on a damn wedding that would never be.

It was the most embarrassing time in my life. To tell all of my friends and family that I wouldn't be getting married was devastating. I had to admit that I hadn't done my homework, and I also had to admit that even after seven long years, I still didn't know the man I was with.

As I was in deep thought, sipping on coffee, I heard a knock on my door. I hadn't spoken to Moses in a few days and I was sure it was him. Instead, it was Juan. I certainly didn't have time to argue with him, and I started to pretend that I wasn't at home. However, he kept on knocking. When he called out my name, that's when I decided to open the door. Juan stood in a gray business suit, white crisp shirt, and a maroon and black striped tie. He was clean as ever, but I ignored how handsome he looked.

"First of all," I said, "you know better than to come over here without calling. Secondly, I have a job interview to go to. Whatever you need to say, say it and be done with it."

"Do you mind if I come in?"

Without saying a word, I opened the door. I stood right by the door, just in case he got any ideas about going to the bedroom.

"Listen. I just stopped by to tell you how sorry I was about speaking to you in an ill manner the other day. You didn't deserve that. The truth is, all of this is on me. I take full responsibility for my actions and I never should have put you in the middle. My daughter told me what happened in that bathroom, and all I can say is that she was wrong on so many different levels. I was wrong for giving my wife your phone number, and I promise you that you will never be put in a situation like that again."

"I hope not, Juan, because I don't get down like that. I don't owe your wife or daughter an explanation, you do. I accept your apology right now, but I'm so troubled by the whole situation that I don't know if I want to continue to involve myself in this relationship with you. It's too much, and I can honestly say that my feelings were truly hurt."

I lied my ass off. I wasn't hurt. Disappointed? Yes. But it was times like these where I could get additional things that I wanted from my lovers. After all, like I said, this side-ho thing did come with some benefits. Bottom line, we were all using each other to fill voids and get what we wanted.

Juan stepped forward and held me in his arms. He kissed my forehead and rubbed up and down my back. "The last thing I ever wanted to do was hurt you. You've been so good to me, and you should not have to pay for my fuck ups. If there is anything that I can do to make you feel better, let me know. Baby, I will do it, but you've gotta give me another chance."

I wasn't so sure how I would get Juan back for what he'd done, but his penthouse did cross my mind. I would love to live there, but like I said before, I didn't appreciate his name being on it. Maybe we could do something about that little problem and have his name replaced with mine. Before I brought that to his attention, I had to let him know that all was forgiven.

"We must move on," I said. "But please don't let anything like that happen again. I don't want to fight with your wife, or with your daughter. If she ever confronts me again, it's not going to be good for her. I'm just letting you know."

"If she ever confronts you again, all you have to do is call me. I will deal with her myself."

"Thank you. For now, I prefer to deal with you."

I backed Juan up to the door and slithered down to my knees in front of him. I unzipped his slacks and lowered them to his ankles. His hard dick went right into my mouth, where I sucked and swallowed all that I could. He pumped my mouth like it was a hot pussy, which, by the way, I gave him some of too. While in my bedroom, I put a deep arch in my back and gave him a ride with my ass facing him. He always commented on how pretty it was and what a pleasure it was to watch me in motion. For the first time, though, he compared me to his wife.

"She never gives it to me like this," he said. "I love watching you in action, and I would rather be here watching you all day like this, than being at that house with her doing nothing."

Yeah, yeah, yeah. Whatever, nigga. You made your choice, now deal with it. That's what I wanted to say out loud, but fuck it. Instead, I gave him much pleasure for the next hour or so, then got dressed to go on my interview.

"Good luck on your interview," Juan said, standing by the door. "I hope you get the job. I'm almost positive that you will."

"Thanks for having faith in me. We'll talk later, and maybe I'll see you at the penthouse tonight."

"I'm looking forward to it. I'll be staying there for a while, or at least until things settle down at home."

Great. Tonight would be the perfect time to discuss my needs, so I looked forward to seeing him too.

I sat in the beautiful lobby completing the application for employment and waited to be interviewed for the

Administrative Assistant position that came with a lengthy job description. The pay was good, so I was determined to get the position. The white skirt I wore hugged my hips and displayed my awesome figure. My button-down shirt squeezed my breasts and my gold jewelry matched my high, peep-toe heels. My hair was parted through the middle and it fell inches past my shoulders. I came well prepared, and I was positive that my experience made me the perfect candidate for the position.

After I completed the application, I gave it back to the bubbly receptionist. She asked me to have a seat and told me that Mr. David Wright would be with me in a few minutes.

"Would you like something to drink while you wait?" the receptionist asked. "He shouldn't be long, but over there is some bottled water, coffee, and sodas. Help yourself."

I thanked the receptionist and walked over to where the beverages were. As soon as I popped the cap on the bottled water, I saw a fine-ass black man standing next to the receptionist's desk. He rocked a tan suit that looked dynamite against his deep, dark skin. Had to be in his early forties, and kind of reminded me of Wesley Snipes in his *New Jack City* days. I loved how thick his lips were, and his trimmed hair had a noticeable shine. The receptionist passed him my application. I saw him look it over, and when he lifted his head, I quickly turned away. I pretended to be occupied with a magazine on a table.

"Miah Jefferson," he said.

I put the magazine and bottled water down then headed his way. There was a little swish in my hips—just enough to keep him zoned in. Without him saying a word, I could see him undressing me. I could see a squeaking bed in our future. And whether I got the job or not, we would definitely be fucking. Okay, so maybe I was a ho. But then again, I was just good at what I did.

I extended my hand to Mr. Wright's hand. "Yes, I'm Miah Jefferson. How are you?"

"I'm doing well. Come on back to my office and let's talk."

He didn't have to ask me twice. I followed Mr. Wright to his office. Needless to say, it was spectacular and was decked out with a cherry-wood desk, a leather couch for lounging, and windows that viewed the downtown Chicago area. I sat in a chair in front of his desk and crossed my legs.

Almost immediately, Mr. Wright got down to business, telling me what my responsibilities would be and inquired about my experience. I was very thorough with my answers and made it clear that I knew how to operate all of the computer programs that were a requirement for the position. As a matter of fact, I knew even more. I used Carl as a reference, and I was positive that he wouldn't have no problem throwing in a good word for me.

"I'll give your previous boss a call and see what he has to say. I think you may be a good fit for this company, and I'm delighted to say that my search for a new employee may have just ended."

All I could do was smile. "I hope so. How soon can I expect a call from you, either way?"

"Maybe within a day or two. I'll need to do a background check, check your references, and then we should be good."

Yeah, he was going to do a background check all right. As soon as I stood up and turned around, I was sure he would. I already knew what to expect from Mr. Wright. That was a nice, fat dick that was busting through his slacks as it hardened. The moment we got into his office, the ring on his finger that I had seen while he stood by the receptionist's desk had magically disappeared. Moments after we entered his office, a picture that I spotted on a credenza behind his desk had been turned face down. I even saw when he switched his phone to take messages, and I guess that was because he didn't want any interruptions.

"Thanks so much for your time," I said, standing and extending my hand again. "I'm so excited and I'm so sure that those references will check out for me."

Mr. Wright thanked me too. He walked me back to the lobby, and the whole time I could see that dirty look in his eyes that I had seen plenty of times before. All I could think was—men. How thirsty could some of their asses be?

On the drive home, I checked my messages to see who had called. Moses left me a message to call him back, and so did Juan. Since we had spent time together earlier, I wasn't up to seeing him again. Besides, him and Mr. David Wright appeared to have a lot in common. He would be stiff competition for Juan, especially if everything panned out as I had suspected they would.

I did, however, call Moses back. I wanted to make sure his fiancé hadn't sliced his damn throat yet. Unfortunately, she hadn't. Stupid bitch.

"Did you call me?" I asked.

"Yeah, I did," he said in a gloomy tone. "Where are you?"

"I'm on my way home. Just got done with an interview."

"That's cool."

Moses seemed to be beating around the bush. I could tell something was on his mind.

"If you have something on your mind, why don't you just say it," I said. "You didn't call just to see what I was doing, did you?"

"I was calling because Karla is right here. She wanted me to call and tell you that we can't see each other anymore. I'm going to marry her and there is no reason for me to continue to involve myself with a woman like you."

Before I could respond, his trick snatched the phone. "Right. Because women like you are trash and he doesn't need to surround himself with trashy whores. If you ever come near him again, Miah, I swear I will hurt you myself."

I just shook my head at this idiot. I didn't know who the biggest fool was, Moses or her. As she continued to spew her stupidity, I hung up on her. I blocked Moses' number and was done with it. I hated a nigga who presented himself as a puppet, and I was positive that Moses would somehow reach out to me, singing a new tune. While I accepted Juan's apology, there wasn't a chance in hell that I would accept Moses. Our relationship was done.

Minutes later, the so-called bad news was replaced with good news. And while there were sometimes minor setbacks in my life, there were always better things to come. Mr. Wright had called to discuss my references.

"I wanted to let you know that I spoke to your boss, Carl, at Wilson Contractors. He said some interesting things about you. Things that left me somewhat skeptical about hiring you."

To be honest, I was caught off guard. Carl and I didn't go our separate ways on bad terms, so I suspected that he would come through for me on a reference.

"If you don't mind me asking, what exactly did he say that's causing you to be skeptical about hiring me?"

"I prefer not to go into further details, but, uh, listen. I like you, and I like your style. I called to offer you the position, if you still want it. If so, I would like it if you could start on Monday. Monday at eight, and I'm willing to up your offer a bit, just because of your experience."

I knew that he wasn't upping my offer because of my experience. Mr. Wright wanted to be sure that I accepted the position. Through his eyes, he saw it as very beneficial to him.

"Thank you for the offer, as well as for your understanding of whatever Carl said to you. I'll see you Monday morning, and I look forward to serving you."

There was silence, before Mr. Wright and I said our good-byes and ended the call.

Instead of going home, I took a detour to Carl's office. I was eager to find out what he'd told Mr. Wright, but the last thing I wanted to do was argue with Carl. That would make him think he had the upper hand, and that he had me under his control.

When I arrived at Carl's office, I saw his car parked in the parking garage. What was so alarming was the way it was rocking. Now, I had been in his car before during plenty of lunch breaks, so I kind of knew what all the rocking was about. I started to drive off and try him later, but then I thought, what the hell? I parked my car across from his and made my way up to it. While looking on the backseat, I could see Carl lying on top of a woman whose moans were loud enough for me to hear. Her light brown legs were on both of his shoulders and he was banging her insides like she was the last woman on earth. Carl's sweaty hair was sticking to his forehead. The frown on his twisted face implied that he was all into it. That was until he looked up and saw me. I knocked on the window and smiled.

"Excuse me," I said. "But can I talk to you for a minute?"

Carl looked surprised to see me. His eyes widened and his swift movements came to a halt. The chick's legs slid off his shoulders, and when she lifted her head, I recognized her as the chick at the bank. I'd gone in there several times to deposit money. I knew who she was, but

I doubted that she knew there was something going on between me and Carl.

"Give me a minute," he said.

I thought the grimy bastard would at least finish up. If I was her, I wouldn't dare allow him to pull out of me, until I got mine. But that was her and I was me. It's how I did things, whether anyone liked it or not.

They both got out of the car bringing the smell of sex with them. Their clothes were wrinkled and the chick's hair was a mess. She searched me from head to toe with jealousy in her eyes. Carl had lust in his, but he tried to play it down like my appearance was no bother.

"I gotta go," he said to the chick who was now buttoning her shirt. "See you later, sweetheart, around seven or eight."

She nodded and leaned in to seal his words with a kiss. I assumed that was to make me jealous, but that nappy head bitch didn't come close to making me feel that way. She was the one who was unaware of Carl's behavior. And eventually, she'd be the one with her heart broken, wondering why.

After she walked away, Carl's arrogant self, leaned against his car with his arms folded.

"What do you want, Miah? Your job back?"

"No, thank you. I already have a job, and I'm not interested in working here anymore."

"Why not? Haven't I given you everything you ever wanted? I mean, what more do you want, Hot Chocolate, that I haven't already given you?"

"A good reference. Didn't you get a call today from David Wright?"

Carl stroked his chin as if he were in deep thought. "David who?" he asked.

"Wright. Don't play, Carl. You know who I'm talking about. What did you say to him about me?"

"Look, he asked for business and personal references. I told him you were excellent in the workplace, as well as in the bedroom. The reason why I said those things was because I don't want you working for anyone else. I want you to continue to work for me. I'll even consider giving you a raise."

I rolled my eyes and could have choked the shit out of Carl. If I hadn't been fucking his ass, I would have sued him for telling another employer that bullshit about me. I could only imagine what Mr. Wright was thinking about me. He probably thought I was some kind of slut.

In an effort not to put my foot in Carl's ass, I walked away without responding to his new offer. He rushed after me and tightened his arms around my waist.

"Miah, sweetheart, don't be so uptight about this. Just give some thought to what I said, and if you need me, I'll be right here."

I removed Carl's arms from around my waist and kept it moving. His ignorance didn't even deserve a response. There were many times when I was forced to keep my mouth shut and this was one of them. He kept saying shit to me that worked my nerves, but I silenced his noise when I got in my car and shut the door. As I looked at him, I could see a smirk on his face that let me know how much he enjoyed this. The bottom line was Carl had been hurt badly by his wife. In return, he wanted to hurt others. I knew that was the case, because in a sense, I felt the same way. Maxwell had put me in the same position where I didn't think it was possible for me to ever love anyone again, other than self.

I had been thinking about Maxwell entirely too much today. And the more I thought about him, the more I had desires to see him. It was rare that days like this happened, but whenever I felt like things were getting a little out of hand in my life, that was when the need to see him came about. I'd be lying if I said I was the kind of chick who always had it together. I didn't. Sometimes, I felt as if some of the things I was doing was wrong, and sometimes I didn't want to be the other woman. I wondered if true love would find a way to slip into my heart again, but I was so damn afraid of letting my guards down. This way seemed much easier. I seemed more in control and I protected my feelings. I had to, because for as long as I lived, I never wanted to face the severe pain that Maxwell had delivered.

Every once in a while, I had to remind myself of that pain. I drove to his house that was about forty-five minutes away from where I was. It was after five o'clock, so I suspected that he'd already picked up his son from school and was at home. When I parked my car by his house, his car was in the driveway. His wife's car was parked beside his and everything appeared peaceful and quiet. The garage was up and I could see his motorcycle parked inside, his tools stacked neatly on shelves and a few bicycles hanging on the walls. I couldn't believe that Maxwell had married the other woman, and on the outside looking in, everything appeared to be so perfect.

I couldn't help but to wonder if it was possible that I was the other woman and I just didn't know it at the time. I never got around to asking Maxwell that question, because he spent so much time trying to convince me that he loved me, but he just wasn't ready. If that was the case, then why was he here? Why two months after Amber delivered their baby, why did he marry her? None of it made sense, and I was still in the dark about so much that had happened.

As I was getting ready to drive off, I saw Maxwell come outside. He removed a lawnmower from the garage and shook a gas can that appeared to be empty. I saw him put the can into his car, so I assumed that he was heading to a nearby gas station to get gas. I quickly drove off and made my way to the gas station around the corner. I figured that's where he was headed.

When I arrived at the gas station, I parked my car in front of a pump and hurried inside. The gas station was crowded and there were about ten people waiting in line. I got a cup to get a fountain soda then looked down the chips aisle for Doritos. I walked to the line and could see Maxwell park and make his way inside. Like every time that I saw him, my heart melted. My stomach felt queasy and my palms started to sweat. Maxwell's hair wasn't even trimmed. Looked like it hadn't been cut in weeks, and he didn't appear as fit as he used to be. All he had on was a pair of gray jogging pants and a black T-shirt with holes in it. His tennis shoes were dirty, and I figured he didn't have to go all out to cut the grass.

No matter how he looked, though, there was no secret that there was still a soft spot for him in my heart. After all that dirt he'd done, I don't know why, but some of those feelings were still there. That was unfortunate.

Maxwell came inside, but by then I was already standing in line with my back turned. The two dudes in front of me kept turning around, and one of them was right on time when he cocked his head back and paid me a compliment.

"Damn, ma, you sexy as fuck," he said. "You want to hit me with those sevens before you leave here or what?"

I smiled and spoke kindly to the young thug who was ugly as fuck. "Thanks for the compliment. I wouldn't mind hitting you with my seven digits, but unfortunately I'm already taken."

"Lucky man," he said. "I hope that brotha knows how lucky he is."

I couldn't have planned this any better. I was positive that Maxwell was behind me in line and had heard every single word. I stepped to the cashier to pay for my items, and also paid twenty dollars for gas. When I turned around, I purposely looked in another direction. I heard Maxwell clear his throat then he called my name. That's when I looked at him and smirked.

"Hey, Maxwell, what's up? How are you?"

"I'm good. Real good. How about you?"

"Couldn't be better. Anyway, it was good seeing you. Take care, all right?"

I pretended to be in a rush, but Maxwell didn't want to let me go. "I will, but, uh, hold up a sec. Let me pay for this gas and I'll be outside to holler at you."

"Sure," I said then walked off.

I went to go pump my gas then stood by my car. Maxwell came outside and jogged up to my car, making sure I didn't leave.

"Aye, is there any way I can get your sevens," he teased, trying to sound like the thug who was inside of the gas station. "That fool should have known better. A dope-ass chick like you wouldn't be caught seen with him."

"He didn't know any better, but you can't knock a man for trying."

"I guess not. But I know you'll knock me for trying, won't you?"

"Of course I would. Only because you're happily married and it wouldn't be wise for me to interfere."

Maxwell sucked his teeth and licked his lips. He folded his arms and leaned against my car. "Who says that I'm happy? I never told you that, did I?"

"No, I assumed that you were. But what do I know, Maxwell? I'm clueless because I also thought you loved me. We both know that I was very wrong about that."

"Now, you know you wrong for that. I did love you. Loved you as best as I could, but I just wasn't ready to make moves like you wanted me to. I told you all of that before, so I'm not going to rehash the past. I will, however, bring up the future because somehow or someway, I want you to be a part of it."

I pursed my lips and looked at him like he was crazy. "How? How do you want me to be a part of your future and you're married? Not only that, you have a child and I'm sure you're planning to have more, especially since you always talked about having such a big family."

"It's funny that you said that because my wife is expecting another child. But this ain't about that. It's about me missing you and thinking about us. I miss you, Miah. Really wish I didn't let you go, and that we could have worked on our relationship. At the time, I was trying to do right by the chick who was pregnant with my child. Amber had me in a bind and I didn't know what to do. I couldn't put you before my child, and if I have moved on with the wedding thing, she would have aborted my baby. You never gave me a chance to explain any of this to you, and you were so mad at me that I thought you were going to kill my ass. There is so much more that I want to say, but I'm sure you don't want to hear it. But if you let me take things one day at a time with you, maybe I can somehow figure out a way to turn a wrong into a right."

Hearing that his wife was pregnant with another child was hurtful. I didn't know whether to believe Maxwell or not. He was so damn good at lying, but he was also very good and getting people to believe him.

"One day at a time" I questioned. "I'm not sure what you mean by that, and it's too late to turn your wrongs into a right."

"It's never too late, as long as we're still alive. Just give it some thought, and when I call tomorrow, let me know if it'll be okay for me to stop by. If so, hook me up with some of that good lasagna you used to make for me. I miss that shit, ma, and you know I miss that sweetness between yo' legs too. See what you can do about that as well, all right?"

I sat against the car thinking about how fucked up I would be if I ever opened the door for Maxwell again. What if it were me at home, pregnant with our second child? His ass was still up to no good, and if anything, I should've been thankful that the motherfucking wedding was off. Most of the time, there were major consequences from going backward. And fucking around with him again would be one big, huge mistake.

I moved away from my car and stood in front of Maxwell. His persona was so smooth and he knew it. His eyes were trying to lure me in, and so was the mountain sized hump in his sweatpants.

"I'm seeing somebody who I really care about, Maxwell. I'm as faithful to him, as I was to you. While I will always have a soft spot in my heart for you, there will be no traveling backward for me. I wish you and your wife the best. I'm sure she would like for you to give your marriage your all, and the least you can do is figure out a way, happy or not, to put your family first."

Maxwell ignored everything I said to him. "I don't give a shit about the nigga you're with. I'm stopping by your place tomorrow. The choice is yours, if you decide to open the door or not."

I walked away from in front of him and opened the door to my car. "You'll be wasting your time, Maxwell. I'm telling you that that door will never open again."

I sat in the car, but before I closed the door, I heard Maxwell say, "We'll see. We will definitely see about that."

I guess he thought I was still the weak chick with the broken heart that he had run all over. That was not the case anymore and he should have known better than to think it was that easy to get me back in bed with him.

I drove away, looking in my rearview mirror at Maxwell wink at me. All I could do was pray for strength and hope that I found the courage to stand my ground and slam the door in his face, if he did show up tomorrow.

Chapter Five

I was excited about going to work on Monday, but the thought of my conversation with Maxwell also weighed heavily on my mind. He called twice today, but I ignored his phone calls. I was lying across my bed while polishing my fingernails and talking to Juan over the speakerphone.

"I thought you were going to come see me last night. What happened?" he asked.

"By the time I got home, I was kind of tired. Had a lot on my mind and all I wanted to do was relax. I knew that being with you I would get no rest at all."

"You got that right. None whatsoever. So when you get here this evening, make sure you're well rested and full of energy."

"Wait a minute. Who says that I'm coming your way tonight? I didn't mention anything about seeing you today."

"I know, but I was hoping that you would want to see me. I've been kind of lonely over here. You don't want me to keep on being lonely, do you?"

"I guess not. Besides, we still need to have that little conversation about when you move back home, how you can make that little penthouse over there mine."

"You already know that you're welcome to it anytime."

"I know that, but I want my name on it, not yours. I want to own it, if you know what I mean."

Juan got quiet. Of course he knew what I meant. It meant he had to give a little to get a whole lot in return.

"I know what you mean, but, uh, we'll have to talk about that when you get here."

"Why wait until then when we can talk about it now? Is there a problem with you gifting the penthouse to me?"

Silence again. I had to put Juan on the spot because he was reaping way more of the benefits from this relationship than I was.

"No, it ain't no problem, baby. Like I said, we'll talk about it when you get here. Come around nine o'clock, and like always, the door will be open and I'll be in my favorite spot waiting for you."

I was so sure that he would be. I told Juan I'd see him later and I finished polishing my nails. Afterward, I watched television for a while and read a book by one of my favorite authors. By that time, it was getting late. I was kind of hungry, and as soon as I got off the couch to go cook something to eat, I heard knocks on my door. My breathing halted, because I suspected it was Maxwell. I tiptoed my way up to the door and looked through the peephole. Sure enough, it was him. He had been to the barber, and his hair was now trimmed. The silk sweat suit he wore looked spectacular on him, but he appeared a little nervous too. His hands were in his pockets and he kept biting down on his bottom lip. I stood by the door, thinking about how I'd waited for this moment to come. It was my moment to get revenge, fuck the shit out of him, and give his wife payback for messing with my man. It was my chance to hear him beg and plead for me to give him another chance and ask for forgiveness over and over again. I had Maxwell right where I wanted him, but what I didn't want to do was open the door. If I did, that would be opening the door to the past.

"Miah, open the door. Baby, I know you're in there. Why haven't you been answering my calls? I told you I was coming today, didn't I?"

I remained silent.

"Come on, Miah. What about us, baby? I want to make love to you and show you how much I've been missing you. All I'm asking for is your forgiveness, and for you to give us another chance. We deserve another chance, ma. We can make this shit happen again, and maybe one day all of this will work out for us. It can't work if you won't at least try."

I swallowed and shook my head. My heart was too weak, but my mind was much stronger. I stood with my back against the door, closed my eyes, and rubbed across my aching forehead. I opened my mouth, but nothing came out.

"Are you there, baby? At least tell me if you're there. That way I don't feel like a crazy fool, talking to myself. Your car is on the parking lot, so I assume you're somewhere in there. Are you alone? Just tell me something—anything to give me some hope."

I took a deep breath and opened my mouth again. Like the first time, nothing came out. I knew that if I started talking, he would somehow or someway convince me to open the door. Silence was key.

"Okay, fine," Maxwell said, sounding defeated. "If you don't want to talk, I'm leaving. I can't believe that after spending so many years together that you won't even sit down and talk to me. I had some deep shit to say to you, and I do see a path to you becoming my future wife. Just think about that, baby. Think about us finally being together again. After you've given it some thought, call me."

I couldn't believe that he had the nerve to spill that dumb shit. I mean, how stupid did he think I was? Future wife my ass. That shit was an insult.

He stood for another minute or two, waiting to see if I would make a move. I didn't. I watched him walk away, then I walked over to the window and watched him get into his car. For me, it was good-bye and good riddance. Forever.

Later that day, I put on a fitted black dress with slits on each side. After leaving Maxwell hanging, I felt pretty damn good. I looked spectacular too, and spent a little extra time, preparing myself to go see Juan. He was the last man standing in my life, but that wouldn't be for long because David Wright would somehow fit in eventually. I was thrilled about going to work on Monday too. I already had an entire week of clothing picked out, and I was eager to find out more details about the man I would soon call boss.

I laughed at the thought, as I drove to Juan's penthouse. The penthouse that after today would be mine. If not, some things with us had to change. I wasn't one to hang on to a man for that long, especially one who wasn't willing to cater to some of my requirements. I didn't think that Juan would let me down.

I entered the penthouse and could hear soft music playing in the background. Juan's scent was all over the place, and it hit me the moment I had opened the door. I knew he was in the bedroom waiting for me, so right at the door, I pulled my fitted dress over my head. Wearing nothing underneath, I sauntered down the narrow pathway, switching my hips from side to side. My high heels made a clacking sound as I stepped on the hardwood floors, and I could already feel the lips of my pussy getting moist. Maybe just a little because I thought about Maxwell saying that he wanted to make love to me, but more so because I was eager for Juan's big dick to relieve me from some of the stress I'd been under. I pushed on the bedroom door, and like always, Juan was underneath the covers waiting for me. His wallet was on the nightstand with several hundred dollar bills busting out of it. His clothes were in a pile on the floor and his leather shoes were kicked in the corner. There were plenty of times when he had fallen asleep, so it didn't surprise me that he was getting it in. Work must have done him in today, but I was happy to be there to give him the relaxation he needed.

The room was dim and a melting candle was flickering on the nightstand. I kicked my heels off and crawled on the bed. The silky covers traced his muscular frame, and as I started to pull the sheet away from his body, that's when I got the shock of my life. A Glock 9 landed in the center of my forehead, and the woman holding it had the meanest mug on her face. Sweat dripped down the side of it, and the icy cold look in her eyes told me I had arrived at the wrong place, wrong time.

"You fucking tramp," she said through gritted teeth. "I warned you, didn't I? Didn't you know that this goddamn day was coming!"

Knowing that this woman could only be Juan's wife, I started to slowly back away. My heart was beating fast and I could hear it slamming hard against my chest. My eyes were bugged and my whole body was like a frozen icicle. I didn't know if I should run my ass off, or try to talk this bitch out of what she was about to do.

"I know," she said with a smirk on her face. "You're speechless, right? But what I'm about to do is make an example out of you. Let this be a lesson to all of the side-hoes who believe that fucking with other people's men have no consequences. They do, and I will not tolerate you upping the pussy to my husband any longer."

The look in Rebecca's eyes let me know right away that there could be no reasoning with her. My instincts told me to duck and run. That's exactly what I did, but as I broke out running, I could hear gunfire ring out in my ears. It was a good thing that Rebecca's aim wasn't worth a damn. Many of the bullets hit the wall and tore into the doorway. One bullet did graze my shoulder, but by the time I reached the door, I didn't have time to address my wound, to pick up my dress or grab my purse. All I could do was pull on the doorknob and bolt to the elevator, hoping and praying that it would quickly open. Unfortunately, it didn't. Rebecca stood in the doorway with the gun aiming in my direction.

"You can run tramp, but you can't hide from a scorned woman. Bye, bitch. May you rot in hell!"

I had nowhere else to run to. Rebecca pulled the trigger, but nothing came out. She pulled it again and again—nothing. I wanted to drop to my knees and thank God that the gun was out of bullets. The elevator opened, and I rushed inside and right into Juan's arms. I didn't even see him, and I was so hysterical that I couldn't even tell him what was going on. He shook me in his arms.

"Why are you out here naked?" he shouted. "What's going on?"

His answer came when his wife charged onto the elevator and started hitting him with the butt of her gun. He tried to back away from her, but she was in a rage.

"Is this the kind of bitch you want?" she yelled. "Tell me now, Juan. Just say it!"

He grabbed her waist and did his best to calm her down. That was so hard to do because with smudges of mascara running down her face and staining it, she looked like a madwoman. While Juan held her tight, she was now unable to move. I was backed into the far corner of the elevator, staring her down as she stared at me. All I could say was this was one big, huge mess!

Chapter Six

I was so glad to see another day. The girls in our club couldn't believe what had happened when I told them about it during our meeting. But many others had stories to share about their confrontations with other women too. It surprised us all as to how far some women would go, yet it was also a wake-up call for some of us as well.

For me, I was never in these types of relationships to infuriate the other woman or take her man away. Realistically, I didn't even want him, and more than anything it was about covering up my pain and sex. Surely I had some work to do, and while I continuously pretended that I had it all together, realistically I didn't. I'd like to think that I was making progress.

Today was a new day. I was learning as I moved on. I decided not to see Juan ever again, and we both agreed to go our separate ways. I wasn't sure how things would turn out with him and his wife. Quite frankly, it wasn't none of my business. I knew the kind of man Juan was, so his wife might need to keep that gun handy. From what I figured, she would spend her lifetime shooting at women who her husband fucked with. That was the sad part about it.

On Monday morning, David gave me a tour of the facility and had everything waiting for me in my new cubicle that sat right outside of his office. Being this close to him would be quite interesting and challenging as well. While I wanted to chill out and not get to that dangerous level with him so quickly, it was kind of hard to back off. When I say the man was fine, I really meant he was fine as fuck. I couldn't stop looking into his sexy eyes and his cologne was luring me in rather quickly. I wondered if he knew what I was thinking, and every time he opened his mouth, I had a vision of where I wanted to place it.

"I'm going to leave you here," he said, standing by my cubicle. "If you need anything, all you have to do is come knock or buzz me by phone. I have some important things to take care of this morning. See if you can transfer all messages to my voice-mail, and I'll do my best to return them later."

"No problem. But what if your wife calls?"

I looked at his ring finger that still had no ring. I assumed that he removed his ring again, even though he knew damn well he was married.

"If my wife calls, transfer her calls to voice-mail. Thanks for asking, and I'll see you later."

David walked away and went into his office, closing the door behind him. I got busy on entering data into a spreadsheet, and almost right away, his phone started to ring. As I was told, I transferred every call to his voice-mail. And when his wife called, I chuckled a little as I listened to her prissy, white self over the phone.

"Well, whenever he's done with his meeting, please tell him to call home. It's urgent that I speak to him right away."

"I will, Mrs. Wright. As soon as he returns, I'll have him call you."

She didn't bother to thank me. All she did was hang up. I shrugged my shoulders and got back to work.

Around lunch time, I got up from my desk to go tell David I was heading out to get a bite to eat. I knocked on his door then opened it. He was indulged with some papers on his desk, but looked up as I stood in the doorway.

"I just wanted you to know that I'm on my way to lunch. You have about eleven phone messages waiting for you. Also, your wife called, saying it was urgent that you returned her phone call."

Without responding, he grunted a little. I could tell everything wasn't good at home.

"Thanks, Miah. Enjoy your lunch and don't forget to give me those spreadsheets before you leave."

"Sure. I almost forgot."

I returned to my desk to print the spreadsheets. After they printed, I went back into David's office and shut the door behind me. I gave the spreadsheets to him and he looked them over. He then looked me over, as I stood close by him.

"Like I said, I'm on my way to lunch. Would you like for me to bring you anything back or do you need for me to do anything else before I go?"

David answered my question when he stood up next to me. "I do need for you to do something. Only if you're willing to do it."

The look in his eyes expressed his needs. He didn't have to say no more. "I'm willing and able to do it. As long as you can promise me that you'll make cancelling my lunch plans worth it."

David opened his drawer and dropped a condom on his desk. I responded by hiking up my skirt and sitting on the edge of his desk, watching carefully as he unzipped his pants and revealed his heavy package. I helped him ease the condom on his mouth-watering dick, and the second it entered me, I threw my arms around his neck and silently confessed to myself that I wasn't always the other woman, but a proud member of The Side-Hoes Club instead. If I continued to carry on like this, there was simply no way to deny my status.